GIRL GIANT
AND THE
MONKEY KING

GIRL GIANT
AND THE
MONKEY KING

VAN HOANG

Illustrated by
Nguyen Quang and Kim Lien

ROARING BROOK PRESS
NEW YORK

Text copyright © 2020 by Van Hoang
Illustrations copyright © 2020 by Nguyen Quang and Kim Lien
Published by Roaring Brook Press
Roaring Brook Press is a division of Holtzbrinck Publishing Holdings
Limited Partnership
120 Broadway, New York, NY 10271
mackids.com

Library of Congress Control Number: 2020908621
ISBN: 978-1-250-24041-5

Our books may be purchased in bulk for promotional, educational,
or business use. Please contact your local bookseller or the Macmillan
Corporate and Premium Sales Department at (800) 221-7945 ext. 5442 or
by email at MacmillanSpecialMarkets@macmillan.com.

First edition, 2020
Book design by Aurora Parlagreco
Printed in the United States of America by LSC Communications,
Harrisonburg, Virginia

1   3   5   7   9   10   8   6   4   2

For anyone who's ever been told they were too quiet,
too loud, too dark, too pale, too much, or too little.
This book is for us.

1

"COACH?" THOM SAID. BUT NO one heard her. Everyone was too busy gearing up for the second half of the game.

"Coach?" Thom called, a little louder.

Coach Pendergrass whirled around, looking at the space above Thom's head in confusion before spotting her down below. "Oh, uh. No."

Thom was used to hearing the word *no*. But the problem was, she never knew if people were really telling her no, or if they just didn't know how to say her last name, which was pronounced literally how it was spelled, like ING-O without the I: Nng-O.

So when Coach Pendergrass said no from behind her clipboard, Thom wasn't surprised. She was a nobody. Invisible.

But Thom wanted to be on the field. She didn't want to go back to the Bench of Shame and Decay—so old and worn that you had to make sure not to let your exposed skin touch it or you'd get splinters. She wanted to feel the crunch of grass beneath her cleats, run alongside the other girls, know that she was part of something. She wished her mom was there. Ma would have made sure Thom played in the game, but Ma had to work late again.

"I want to play," Thom said before one of the other girls could grab Coach's attention. The words squeezed out of her like the last bits of an empty toothpaste tube. "I thought you said earlier? That I could play in the second half."

"Oh," Coach said, looking at her clipboard. "Right. Okay." She turned to Bethany Anderson, whose mouth was all tight and pursed. Bethany didn't look at Thom, though. She never looked at Thom—like she might contract some sickness just from the eye contact. "Anderson, center forward. Jones, grab some water for this play. No, you're on left defense."

Thom's stomach did a weird flippy thing. Left defense wasn't even a real position. Okay, it was, but it was a filler spot, the weakest angle. You barely got to play from that position; you were just there to stay low and wave your arms around, hoping the ball accidentally rolled your way.

Still, it was better than sitting on the bench. Thom ran onto the field and joined the rest of the DeMille Middle School soccer team standing in position against Monrovia Middle.

Shelley Jones glared as she took Thom's place on the bench.

The referee blew his whistle, and Bethany kicked the ball. Everyone ran forward, even the other two defense players on Thom's team, even though they weren't supposed to leave the goal. Thom glanced at Coach Pendergrass, but she was too focused on the ball and on DeMille's dynamic trio—Kathy, Bethany, and Sarah—weaving across the field like they were performing a dance routine.

Kathy Joon, Bethany Anderson, and Sarah Mazel were the stars of the team. They *always* got to play. Granted, the team was pretty small, so there was only one person on the bench at a time. That person was usually Thom.

It wasn't that Thom was bad at soccer. She was actually pretty good when she had played for her last school, in West City. Back then, soccer had been fun, an escape, where she and her friends played and hung out and got boba and popcorn chicken after. She was good then. She was still good now, when she played by herself, anyway. But because soccer isn't exactly a play-by-yourself kind of sport, she couldn't prove this to everyone else.

The thing was, Thom couldn't kick the ball. Well, no, she could kick the ball, but she *shouldn't*. The last time she'd tried ended in a small disaster, and she hadn't found the courage to try again since.

Suddenly, Monrovia's offense stepped it up, and the ball was rolling toward Thom. She hesitated.

"No," Coach Pendergrass called from the sidelines. Thom stopped. "No! Go for it, No! Send it flying!"

She *could* send it flying. She could show them all how good she really was.

But what if something went wrong? They'd never give her another chance. It was her first time in a game that season, the first time playing for DeMille, and she had to be perfect.

A flash of white charged toward her, Monrovia's jersey. Too late, Thom ran for the ball, but the other player knocked it out of reach. The ball brushed the tips of the DeMille's goalie's fingers as it hit the net, followed by dead silence.

White uniforms bobbed up and down, their Monrovia's cheers drowning out DeMille's groans.

Girls in striped jerseys glared in Thom's direction.

"Nice job," Linda, the center defense, hissed at Thom.

"I thought you wanted to play!" Shelley shouted from the bench.

Thom didn't meet anyone's eyes as she retook her position and stared straight ahead. She should have gone for the ball. She should have kicked it like they'd said. Who cared if it hit anyone or exploded or something terrible happened? It couldn't be worse than this feeling, like her insides were turning inside out.

Everyone shook their heads. "Should have just stayed on the bench if you're going to choke," Linda said. She sneered as she placed her hands on her knees.

Thom ignored her, but it was difficult to keep her eyes on the ball when heat blossomed behind them, traveling into her nose and throat. She focused on the smell of the wet grass, the breeze cooling the sweat on her skin.

The ball flew back and forth across the field, Monrovia pulling ahead by one goal, and then two. Each time the ball came toward Thom, someone else got to it first. It wasn't like she wasn't trying; she was. But even when she called it, like you were supposed to do when you needed the other players to take different positions to receive a pass, Linda or Madison would knock it out of her way.

It was getting more difficult to breathe. It could have been from running, but Thom knew the lump in her throat was the real culprit, and it only grew bigger each time a team-mate snatched the ball away. She was the worst player. She couldn't even get near the ball, and this time, it wasn't by choice.

She glanced at the sidelines, where Shelley was bouncing next to Coach as they shouted after the players. She wished she could just go for it, could play the way she was supposed to, the way she knew how.

"No!"

She didn't realize someone was calling her until Linda snapped her fingers.

"Hey, No." She rolled her eyes as if Thom's very existence were annoying and saying her name was the most tiring thing anyone could do. "Coach is calling you."

Sure enough, Coach Pendergrass waved Thom over. She

was calling her out of the game. That wasn't fair. She'd only gotten to play for like ten minutes.

"No!" Coach shouted again.

Thom turned to the referee, who hadn't noticed Coach waving and was starting the next play. If she was going to get benched anyway, she should at least do something to earn it.

The play started. She wiped the sweat off her forehead and focused on the ball until she saw nothing else, the shouts around her dying, the coach's voice fading. The ball glowed against the grass, its glossy white surface reflecting sunlight in all directions. She ran past one girl, then another, and another, catching a whiff of Kathy's lavender perfume. Then suddenly the ball was there, right in front of her.

"No," Coach Pendergrass shouted, waving her arms, but as usual, Thom couldn't tell if she was telling her, *No, don't do it*, or if she was shouting her name, cheering her on. For a second, she let herself believe Coach was cheering, that everyone was, that she was back at her old school, that she was playing with her friends.

Her teammates looked at her with wide eyes. Thom had never done anything like this before. She always listened, always obeyed, always stayed away from the ball.

Breaking the stillness, a white, opposing jersey thundered toward her, and she had to act, to do something *now*.

She kicked. The ball connected with the top of her foot

with a pop. It soared . . . past the white shirt across the field, past the midfield line.

The goalie jumped up to catch it, and the ball hit her right in the stomach, forcing an *oomph* out of her mouth that Thom heard from across the field, before knocking her down completely. But the ball didn't stop in the goal. It tore clean through the net and kept going until it was out of sight.

2

ALL HEADS TURNED TO THOM. Kathy's mouth dropped open, eyes wide. Linda took a step back, her hands lifting as if shielding herself. Their expressions filled with horror.

This wasn't how Thom had expected them to react when she scored. They were supposed to cheer, jump, and slap her back, the way they'd done when Kathy scored earlier.

This was a *goal*. And they were looking at her like she'd pushed over a puppy learning to walk.

Then Monrovia's coach knelt over the goalie, still flat on her back.

Thom's hand moved over her mouth. A hush fell over the girls, the coaches, the referees. The wind stilled, the blades of grass crumpling beneath her shoes, the stillness imitating the body that lay unmoving beneath everyone's stares. Was the goalie *dead*? Had Thom killed her?

"Is she okay?" Coach Pendergrass's voice broke through the silence.

Monrovia's coach checked the girl's pulse. "Knocked out cold." Her blue eyes pierced Thom in place. "That was some kick."

Thom couldn't read anything in her flat tone. "Did I kill her?" she whispered.

The coach laughed, but the other girls, even the ones on Monrovia's team, looked at one another with concerned frowns. They eased away from Thom as if she were going to turn and attack them next.

"You can't kill someone like that, sweetie," the coach said. "You'd have to be Superman."

◆ ◆ ◆

The girls remained silent as they trudged back to the lockers. Thom's teammates glanced at her, turning away sharply whenever she looked back. Their expressions were full of wonder—and something else. The way you look at the new lunch option, not sure if it's meat or pudding.

"Well," Coach said as they all twisted the dials on their combination locks. "The good news is, we won the game."

Usually, this would have been followed by applause and high fives. But no one made a sound. They all shot side-eyes at Thom, who stared at the inside of her dark locker. Her clothes hung on the hook—a black graphic T-shirt, dark jeans, and a hoodie, as usual.

"The bad news is," Coach continued, rocking back and forth on the balls of her feet, "the goalie, Cassie Houghton, is in the hospital."

Cassie. The girl had a name now, not just a jersey number, thirteen—unlucky or lucky depending on how you looked at it, but probably unlucky in this case. Unlucky enough to play against Thom, anyway.

She leaned into the locker, hiding behind the door, but she could feel the eyes on her like pinpricks. If only her locker were big enough to crawl all the way inside. She'd killed the goalie; she must have. Her mouth and throat were dry, and yet she started to salivate at the same time, tasting something bitter and rancid. She knew exactly what this feeling was, and knowing what it was only made it worse. Thom was going to vomit.

"A few cracked ribs." If Coach felt the tension in the room, she didn't show it, speaking cheerily as if nothing were wrong. "But nothing that . . ." She cleared her throat.

Thom peeked from behind the door. Coach had her thumbs hitched in the belt loops of her jeans, her head down.

"Nothing that can't be fixed."

"So . . . No didn't kill her?" Bethany asked. She'd already changed out of her uniform and into navy-blue-and-gold sweats. Her sleek ponytail made her eyes look sharper as they flashed at Thom. They didn't linger enough to acknowledge her, just enough to make her know Bethany was watching her, wary of her.

"No. No didn't kill her."

Thom let out a breath. She could have melted right onto the floor, joined the puddles created by the swim team, trailed down the cracks, and dripped into the drain. Instead, she sagged against her locker door.

"And, er . . ." Coach added, still not looking up. "Nice shot, No."

If anyone else agreed, they didn't say so. They barely looked at Thom as they finished getting ready. It wasn't any different from how they usually treated her, but today it was worse. Because she had finally done something right, something that should have made them all like her or, at least, respect her, treat her like she existed. She had scored. Not only that, but it had been the winning goal. They'd won! The first game of the season, and they'd won. Because of her.

But it felt wrong. Of course it did; she had knocked a girl out. She had broken her *ribs*. Who did that? Not anyone normal.

Thom hovered at Coach's office door, the last one to leave the locker room. The drip of a faucet echoed behind her, the lingering traces of chlorine from the swim team stinging her nostrils.

"What's wrong, No?" Coach asked, peeking out behind

an overflowing box of shin guards. The fluorescent lighting above flickered, casting ominous shadows over her face. The others were gone; even the assistant coach, Martha, had left.

"I was just wondering . . . is the Monrovia goalie . . . is Cassie really going to be okay?"

Coach heard the crack in Thom's voice. "Oh yeah, sweetie, she's fine. She's in stable condition. They just called me." She tapped her phone and then paused. Thom knew she was doing that thing grown-ups do, trying to find the stupidest way to say something—like that was the only way kids would understand. "The ball probably hit her at a weird angle and she landed awkwardly, that's all. Come on. Tiny thing like you—couldn't have been all your fault." She had the kind of laugh that involved her whole body, every wiggly bit that could wiggle wiggled. "Don't worry about it, No. You did good today. You scored!"

Thom's smile felt odd on her face, the stiff muscles around her mouth not used to the movement.

"You should have seen yourself. Practically flying across the field! I want to see the same enthusiasm out of you tomorrow." She picked up her clipboard and pretended to slap Thom on the back with it. "Now get out of here before your mom threatens to sue me for keeping you late."

Thom smiled, waved, and left feeling lighter. She wasn't in trouble after all. They hadn't found out. Or, well, they hadn't believed it was really her fault, that she was capable of kicking the ball that hard. And even if it was her fault, it was an accident. She hadn't meant to hurt Cassie.

It was going to be okay. She'd make up for it. Maybe Ma could send Cassie flowers at the hospital.

She spun around to ask, but Coach was busy rummaging through the box of shin guards. Thom thought better of it and slowly turned away.

3

THE THING WAS, THOM WASN'T Superman, but she did have a superpower.

She was incredibly strong. But not in the good way.

Strength was the sort of thing that *seemed* cool, and maybe it would have been if she just didn't have so much of it.

It had started out small last summer. Ma couldn't open a pickle jar, and Thom had twisted it off with no trouble at all. That was kind of nice. If it had stopped there, her strength might have actually been useful.

But then it got worse. She picked up an unopened water bottle and crushed it, water exploding everywhere. Luckily, this had been during soccer practice at her last school and all the girls were splashing themselves to cool down, so they had just laughed it off.

Then one day, she closed her bedroom window too hard and all the windows in the house shattered. Good thing Ma thought it was an earthquake—that was back in Los Angeles, where earthquakes weren't unusual.

For a few months, she'd still been able to kick the ball at soccer without popping it, hurting anyone, or breaking something. She'd managed to get through most of the season without people discovering that she wasn't completely normal.

Then came the very last game she'd played on her old team. When Thom had tried to pass the ball to her teammate Brenda, she kicked too hard. She'd passed the ball to her all right, only it bounced off Brenda's arm and hit Hang, then Quyen, then Anna, and knocked five other girls off their feet. Brenda sprained a wrist and Quyen got a nasty bump on her forehead, but aside from a few bruises, no one else was hurt. They'd all laughed it off, thought it was hilarious, like something out of a Jackie Chan movie.

But Thom knew the truth.

She was a freak.

Something was wrong with her.

Maybe she was like Superman. Maybe they were related. But probably not, because even though he was from another planet, Superman could also shoot lasers out of his eyes and see through walls. She couldn't do any of those things. Thom was just really, unnaturally, dangerously strong.

Which was why she shouldn't have kicked the ball. Because the moment her foot connected with that thing, everyone could see exactly how strange she was.

♦ ♦ ♦

Ma hated to cook, which meant they were having frozen dumplings, scallion pancakes, and broccoli beef, heated in the microwave for dinner. Their dog, Mochi, a white Pomeranian with brown spots, followed her from the dining room to the kitchen, licking his lips and panting each time the smell of a new dish filled the house.

Thom set the table with two pairs of chopsticks, two spoons, and a paper towel torn in half—one half for each of them. Mochi pranced up to her, his fluffy tail wagging, nails clicking on the tiled floor. Thom reached down to pet him. He came close to sniff her hand, started shivering, and then backed away with a whimper.

Ma carried a plate to the table. "Mochi, stop it. It's just Thommy."

Thom straightened, and Mochi stopped shaking. He looked up and wagged his tail, so she reached for him again, but then he started shivering again. Her insides tightened and numbed. Even her own dog didn't like her.

"It's okay, cưng," Ma said.

Thom was usually embarrassed when her mom called her *sweetie* in Vietnamese, but at least they were at home and no one could hear. Funny how back in West City, it had never bothered her—the way Ma talked—but now in Troy, Thom didn't want anyone to hear. Everyone would think it sounded funny. Not haha funny but weirdo funny. And even though she'd never heard anyone make fun of Ma's accent, she was acutely aware of how *Asian* it sounded, here in Troy, where Kathy's family was the only other Asian family they knew.

"He just being weird," Ma added. "Come eat. The food is ready."

They sat down at the glass kitchen table, which was lined with old newspapers instead of a real tablecloth. Ma piled Thom's small bowl with beef and dumplings, topping off the mountain with a scallion pancake that threatened to avalanche onto the table.

"Eat, eat, eat," she said, waving her hand. "You so small. They not feeding you enough at school. Eat, or they think I starve you."

Thom picked up her chopsticks, and they snapped in half, the pieces clattering onto the table. She looked up quickly at Ma to gauge her reaction: Was she mad? Freaked-out? But Ma just tsked, got a different pair from the kitchen, and positioned them correctly in Thom's hand, so that one was balanced on her middle finger and another on her index.

"Thanks," Thom said, reaching for a clump of rice, but her grip must have been too strong again, because this time the chopsticks bent. She was being so gentle, too. She looked at her mother again and caught the widened eyes before Ma fixed her expression into a reassuring smile. "Can I just get a fork?" asked Thom.

"Ayah, you'll never learn to use chopsticks if you never practice. Go get another pair."

"But—"

"You ashamed of your culture?"

"No, I . . . What does that have to do with chopsticks, Ma?"

"Asians use chopsticks."

"Not all of them," Thom mumbled.

"I say go get another pair."

Thom slunk to the kitchen, then sat back down, holding the chopsticks with the lightest touch she could manage without dropping them.

"You talk to Thuy?" Ma asked.

She nodded, even though it was a lie. Thuy was Thom's best friend at her old school. They had done everything and gone everywhere together. People thought they were sisters. Though, thinking about it, that was also probably because they were both Asian and had the same dark hair and were about the same height. Truthfully, Thuy had always been much prettier than Thom—her nose was slim, her hair a thick, dark frame around her small face. Thom, on the other hand, had cheeks so chubby that her aunties pinched them until they turned red, a wide, flat nose, and a ruddy complexion that always made people ask her if she was okay, because she looked flushed.

Now the time difference between Georgia and California and Thuy's strict tutoring schedule made it impossible for the two of them to talk. Texting was easier, but Thuy hadn't responded to her last three messages and Thom had given up on checking her phone every few minutes.

"How she doing?" Ma asked.

"Good."

"You make any new friends at school today?"

Thom tried to take a bite of the pancake, but it was too chewy—Ma had left it in the microwave for too long—so she shoved the whole thing in her mouth, which gave her an excuse not to answer.

Ma tsked. "You never get husband if you eat like that." She shook her head. "Friends?" Ma asked again. She always insisted that this was the true path to happiness. Surround yourself with people, bury yourself in your studies, and keep yourself busy enough that you'll never have time to realize how miserable you are. It didn't explain why she had suddenly taken a new job in Troy at the college library. They'd had to move across the country, away from everyone they'd ever known.

Thom swallowed the lump of pancake. It threatened to lodge halfway down, but then, painfully, it passed. Ma cleared her throat.

Thom shook her head. No friends.

"It's okay. Give it time," Ma said.

"Why can't we move back?" Thom asked. It was the same question she asked almost every day.

"DeMille is a good school. Lots of good teachers—"

"It sucks!" Thom blurted.

"Hey." Ma's chopsticks clattered on the glass table. "No bad words."

Thom cowered under the Asian stare of death, Ma's eyes widening, the whites showing, her pupils hardening to sharp black points.

"'Sucks' is not a bad word," Thom muttered.

"I pay lots of money for you to go to DeMille. You should be grateful you have opportunity. I make lots of sacrifice for you."

Thom stuck her chopsticks into her mound of rice and swirled everything around until the dumpling broke and bits of green veggies and pink-and-white shrimp meat spilled out like guts. She hated it here, hated her school, hated how everyone stared before quickly looking away, hated the way her teachers spoke to her like she was dumb and then were surprised when she spoke English just as well as, if not better than, the other students. She hated how everyone commented on the fact that she had no accent—as if having an accent were a bad thing—hated how everyone laughed behind their hands or how a group of girls stopped talking when she approached.

She missed her old life.

"Are you listening to me?" Ma asked.

Thom nodded.

"Hey," Ma said, trying to sound cheerful. "How 'bout we go get boba, hah?"

Thom's mouth watered at the thought of an ice-blended

lychee frostie with tapioca pearls and jelly, or, no, maybe iced milk tea and popcorn chicken. But then she pictured walking out of the café with her mom, holding her cup with its jumbo-sized straw. It would be just her luck that Bethany or Sarah would see her doing the most Asian thing possible in Troy, as if she weren't enough of an outsider already.

"No," Thom said, and Ma's face fell. "It's too far." Another thing she couldn't get over—the nearest boba place was thirty minutes away. Back in LA, there was one on almost every block.

"That's okay," Ma said, too cheerful. "It's worth it. We can get wontons too!"

Oh God, wontons. Thom missed wontons. But she couldn't risk running into a classmate. So she used the only excuse she knew Ma would understand.

"I have a lot of homework."

Ma went quiet, then let out a breath. She reached out and patted Thom's hand. "I'm sorry, cưng," she said. Thom knew Ma cared about her; she knew that everything Ma did was for her future. It didn't mean she liked it. "I know things are hard, but just give it some time, hmm?"

Thom nodded, and Ma squeezed her wrist—the equivalent of a Vietnamese hug—before picking up her chopsticks again.

But how much time was this going to take? How much longer did Thom have to keep this up?

4

AT SCHOOL THE NEXT DAY, there was an announcement from the administrator's office.

"Good afternoon, Dolphins."

Everyone snickered, and imitated dolphins giggling, which happened every time their mascot was mentioned. The teacher stood up from her desk and shushed them so hard the blood vessel in her forehead threatened to pop.

Thom stared at the speaker at the front of the room, the one part of the wall that hadn't been covered in colorful butcher paper, bright inspirational posters, or examples of other students' art projects.

"Welcome back to another wonderful school year," Peter Jenkens, the student body president, announced over the intercom. "Woo-hoo! Don't forget that the early-bird rate for the fall dance ends September fifteenth. Pay now, or you'll be charged an extra fifteen bucks! Also, DeMille Middle

School's first-ever annual Culture Day is coming up in a few weeks! Students are required to pair up with someone else in their homeroom and present an art project. For extra credit, you can also dress up or join the talent show! Sign up with Mrs. Stevenson if you plan to perform. Slots are open for dancing, singing, and . . . poetry reading?" The sound of papers shuffling came across the intercom. "Uh, okay. Even if you don't perform, participate by dressing up in your culture's best traditional outfit and show us all where you come from!"

As if. Thom looked around the room, but no one was paying attention to her. They were all whispering to one another. One student was busy drawing mustaches on an inspirational poster of a celebrity telling them to read. The teacher was distracted, but it's not like she would notice, since so much motivational artwork covered the walls.

Who was going to want to pair up with Thom? She made a mental note to never tell Ma about Culture Day. If Ma found out about the extra credit, she would probably dress Thom up, from head to toe, in ancient Vietnamese garb, and then Thom could kiss making friends here goodbye.

Maybe she could partner with Kathy Joon. Bethany and Sarah would probably work together, so Kathy would need a partner, and she was Asian, too. Then again, Kathy was different. She was like magic, made of bright, shiny hair and a honey-milk complexion wrapped in the silky sheen of popularity. Was Kathy going to dress up in one of those puffy Korean dresses? A hanbok? *She* would look so cool.

Even among Asians, Thom had always felt like a minority. Everyone usually assumed she was Japanese, Chinese, or Korean before eventually getting to Vietnamese, and probably only because they had heard about the war at some point.

Kathy turned around, and Thom didn't look away fast enough. To Thom's horror, their eyes met for a full second. Kathy's eyebrows lifted slowly before she whispered something to Bethany, who glared at Thom over her shoulder.

Thom lurched upright. She didn't know what to do. She forced her lips into a smile, hoping that would do the trick, but Bethany looked away.

Thom's face grew hot. Why had she stared at Kathy like that? Her mind had been on traditional dresses and Culture Day, but now they were going to think she'd been obsessing over Kathy like some stalker freak.

As soon as the bell rang, she hightailed it out of there. It didn't matter how fast she ran, though; she would still have to face them during soccer practice. *God*, why couldn't she just be normal? No wonder she had no friends.

◆ ◆ ◆

It turned out that she had nothing to worry about, because the dynamic trio treated her the same way they always had: like she didn't exist.

After the nearly lethal kick yesterday, believe it or not, Coach Pendergrass seemed to trust Thom more, sending her after the ball and calling her forward in the drills. But it didn't take Coach long to come to the conclusion that yesterday had just been a fluke. Thom still couldn't kick the ball right—she tried to only tap it with her toe, and even then it flew too fast and too far for her teammates, which made them shoot her dirty looks. Some of them retaliated, kicking the soccer ball straight at Thom. But it didn't hurt—at least, not physically.

By the time practice was over, Thom was ready to burst into tears. Her throat hurt from holding them back, and she didn't even bother changing, just stuffed everything into her gym bag and rushed out of the locker room.

Ma was reading a paperback when she reached the car. Thom yanked the door handle so hard it fell off. Fumbling, she quickly tried to reattach it without Ma noticing. But when she looked up, her mother was staring with her mouth open.

"Thom," Ma said from inside the car.

There was no way for Thom to open the door, now that she clutched the broken handle. Ma looked around, like she was checking to see if anyone else had seen. Then she reached over and let Thom in.

Before Ma could start, Thom apologized profusely. "I'm so sorry. I was just in a hurry. I want to go home. Can we please just go? I'm sorry, I'm so sorry. Will it be expensive to fix?"

Ma regarded Thom carefully. "It's no problem, cưng, we just ask Uncle Kevin to fix it."

Uncle Kevin wasn't really Thom's uncle, just Ma's good friend. He didn't know about Thom's . . . condition, of course. No one did. Ma called him every few months to ask him to fix something—with the car, the house, or whatever Thom had accidentally broken. He never asked any questions, not even after the time she had reached for a light switch and ripped it clean off the wall instead.

"But Uncle Kevin is in California," Thom said.

Ma's face broke for a second, as if she had forgotten they lived in another world now. "Oh, right. No worry. I will take it to different mechanic."

The good thing about Ma was that she could always tell when something was upsetting Thom, but she didn't ask questions, didn't probe. Thankfully, she turned on the radio and began driving.

She hummed a ballad as Thom buckled her seat belt. The car lurched forward as Ma shifted gears to exit the parking lot. No one drove a manual these days, which according to Ma, made it the ultimate antitheft device, since no one knew *how* to drive a manual anymore. To Thom, it only meant lurchy car rides on top of her mom's questionable driving techniques and angry outbursts at other drivers.

"How was your day, cưng?" she said.

"Ma." Thom felt the need to look over her shoulder, even

though the windows were closed and no one could have heard. "I told you not to call me that when we're at school."

"Why? You're my sweetie, aren't you?" At the stoplight, she kissed Thom on the forehead, grabbed her chin, and tilted her face up to look into her eyes. "What's wrong? Something happen? Who you beat up today?"

This was a running joke Ma thought was hilarious because Thom was so small.

"Funny," Thom muttered through the lump in her throat. "Ma..." She looked down at her hands. "Do you think..." She couldn't finish the question.

"What is it, cưng?"

Thom's vision blurred around the edges. "What would happen if I ... quit the ... soccer team?" It had never been an option before, not only because she'd loved soccer too much to consider it, but because Ma never let her quit anything.

Ma was quiet for a long time. "You want to quit?"

"No. Maybe. I don't know."

"But you love soccer."

She *still* loved it. But it wasn't the same here. Not without her friends.

"Why?" Ma asked.

Thom wanted to tell Ma about the bullying, the teasing, the laughing. But Ma wouldn't understand those as reasons to quit. She would just tell Thom to ignore it, and point out that one day Thom would be a doctor while those girls flipped burgers or whatever. Even though Thom was deathly afraid of needles.

"I just don't like it," she said.

"What you mean? You play since you were nine, remember? With Thuy and your friends. I even buy you new shoes! You wanted the ones that go clippety-clop so much."

Thom looked out the window, pressing her lips together.

"Maybe give it a few more months, hah?" Ma said. "Finish the season. And next year if you don't want to play anymore, you don't try out again."

Thom bit the inside of her cheek and nodded.

5

WHEN THEY GOT BACK TO the house, Ma reached for Thom's lunch pack, frowning at its weight.

"You didn't eat the food I make for you?"

Thom reached down to pet Mochi, but he shied away just as her fingers brushed his fur. "Um, no. I bought pizza from the cafeteria instead."

"Why?" Ma took out the bento box full of rice. "I told you not to waste food. You don't like it?"

Thom grabbed Mochi's leash. "It's just . . . no one else brings lunch from home," she lied. Other kids brought food, too, but no one else brought bento boxes with five different side dishes.

Ma frowned as she dumped the food into the trash. "You didn't even eat the meat, cưng. That's precious. In Vietnam, we never get to eat meat like this, you know. Such a waste."

She tsked. "You can't eat greasy American food all day—it's not healthy."

"Can I bring, like, sandwiches and stuff? Or maybe"— Thom gulped—"salad?"

"Salad?" Ma grimaced, looking as horrified as Thom felt. "You don't like rice?"

"I like it," Thom said quickly. "Just not for school." She looked away from Ma's confused expression. "I'll eat extra for dinner."

Ma turned to the sink, so Thom couldn't read her expression. "Okay then," she said, but Thom couldn't tell if it was a good okay or a bad okay.

She left with Mochi on their walk before Ma could ask her any more questions. Thom didn't hate rice, or Asian food in general, but most of the time, the dishes were stinky, and other kids always stared at whatever she'd brought. Maybe someone would sit and eat with her if she brought something less Asian, or if she ate whatever the cafeteria served.

It was four in the afternoon, and the sun was blazing hot. Thom squinted and shielded her eyes with a hand, letting Mochi tug her down the sidewalk. Moisture clung to Thom's skin, making the air feel even hotter. She swatted a mosquito that buzzed and landed on her arm, then almost swallowed a gnat. This place was the worst.

As she walked on the grass beside her next-door neighbor's house, Thom saw something out of the corner of her eye.

Something big and shiny, fluttering in the wind. Or maybe the bright sun was playing tricks on her eyes. But she could have sworn she saw it dart around the bushes that separated the two properties.

A snake maybe?

No way. It was at eye level, and it was too large to be a snake. But it was white and shiny and definitely looked like it had scales.

"Come on, Mochi," she whispered, pulling him toward the fence. She knew she shouldn't walk on private property, but the house had been empty since Thom and her mother had moved in. Except now, the FOR SALE sign was down.

Maybe someone had moved in.

There. Something shimmered again, like off the inside of a mother-of-pearl shell, just above the fence. But that was impossible. Snakes couldn't fly, could they?

She shuddered, but moved deeper into the yard, too

curious to be scared. Mochi whimpered but followed, close to her feet, almost tripping her. Something blue darted behind the house, and Thom rushed forward, with Mochi breaking into a run. When she and Mochi came around the corner, the backyard was empty. She searched the grass, but it had recently been cut, too short to hide much of anything.

She stopped and looked at her dog, who panted, sticking out his tongue. Must have been her imagination after all.

Before she could leave, the door opened. A boy about her age stepped onto the porch and stared at her.

Thom froze, caught standing in his yard, too panicked to run.

The boy didn't stop staring, so she looked directly back at him. He was Asian, but she couldn't pinpoint the exact ethnicity. Great. He probably thought they'd be instant best friends, and even though part of her wanted something like that more than anything, someone to talk to and sit with at lunch, someone who didn't make her feel so lonely, a part of her didn't.

What if Kathy felt the same way—that just because they were both Asian, everyone assumed they would be friends when Kathy didn't even like Thom? Was that why Kathy had never wanted to be her friend? Thom's heart sank with a flood of embarrassment. What if all this time, she'd made a fool of herself by trying so hard when all Kathy wanted to do was be left alone, not bothered by the new Asian kid just because they looked somewhat alike? Thom wouldn't blame her.

The boy tossed his hair back and grinned widely. "Hi."

His skin was pale in the way Ma loved—she was always complaining that Thom was too tan, especially since she'd joined soccer and spent hours every day in the sun. He had longish hair styled to perfection in a way Thom could only dream of, and wore fitted jeans hemmed at his calves.

Say something back. Clever. Not too squeaky.

"Hey?" It came out like she wasn't sure it was the right thing to say.

Mochi lifted his leg and let out a stream of pee on the grass.

"Uh," Thom said, desperately tugging on his leash, but Mochi ignored her, sniffing the air. "I'm so sorry. I didn't know anyone had moved in. I thought I saw a snake or something."

"Really?" The boy's eyes darted back and forth. "Weird." He cleared his throat. "I'm Kha. What's your name?" He was Vietnamese then.

"Thom."

He held out a hand, and she hesitated before moving forward to shake it. His skin was hot, like he had a fever, and she let go quickly, both in shock but also because she was afraid to hurt him. Even when she stepped back, he felt warm, or maybe she was overheated from standing in the sun.

"I have always liked it when girls have boys' names," Kha said.

She blushed. "Well, it's also a girl's name."

"It means 'pungent'?"

"'Sweet-smelling,'" she said, echoing Ma's explanation every time Thom asked why she'd chosen a boy's name. "Like a rose."

"Oh," he said. "Well, my grandma always says it when something smells delicious."

Thom sighed. Every time she told someone her name, she had to defend it somehow, explaining what it meant or giving an excuse for having it. This probably never happened to Bethany. Or Sarah. Or Kathy.

"We just moved in," Kha said.

"Cool."

"You go to DeMille?"

"Yeah," she said. "You?"

"Yeah. I start this week. Seventh grade."

They were in the same grade. They might be in the same classes. Thom had skipped a grade back at her old school, when about half the kids her age were doing the same. It hadn't seemed like such a bad idea then, but here in Troy, everyone was taller, bigger . . . meaner. Even some kids in the fifth grade were a foot taller than her.

"Maybe we'll see each other at school." He smiled.

Kha looked like he could be popular even if he didn't try. You could just tell—some people were like that. Their very existence exclaimed *cool*. He had nice jeans and hair, for one thing, and he just looked comfortable, like nothing could bother him.

It would be nice to have someone to sit with at lunch instead of pretending she wasn't hungry and hiding in the library. But he was probably just being nice, because, one, they were neighbors, and two, Asian. It felt like cheating, somehow, like she was using her culture to gain something she didn't deserve.

And besides, who did he think he was? What if she were popular and too cool for him? How could he charge in and demand they be friends, just like that?

Actually, what she was really annoyed about was why she had never thought she could charge in and demand to have friends, just like that. People weren't supposed to, were they?

"Yeah, maybe." She tugged on Mochi's leash as he moved toward Kha, his nose twitching, his tongue flopping out. He stopped suddenly, then whimpered, easing back and bumping against Thom's leg.

"Um." Kha's wide eyes were fixed on Mochi. Was he afraid of dogs? Of Thom's five-pound Pomeranian? Seriously, Mochi was made of 70 percent fur. "I gotta go," Kha said. He stepped back into his house and grabbed the door.

Mochi growled and barked. She'd never seen him like this. Usually, he loved people and wanted to go home with everyone, as if he owed Thom and Ma absolutely no loyalty for raising and feeding him.

"Mochi," Thom whispered. He whined and pulled toward their house. "What's wrong with you?"

"See ya," Kha said.

As soon as he closed the door, Mochi calmed down, prancing back to Thom and wagging his tail. But when she reached down to pet him, he whimpered and backed away.

"You are such a weird dog," she said before tugging him toward home.

6

THOM KNEW SOMETHING WAS WRONG when she got back from her walk. She walked slowly into the living room to retrieve her backpack, but it was no longer on the couch. The room was spotless like usual, no throw pillows or blankets, just a plain white couch in front of the TV that they rarely watched, and several bookcases organized by genre and then author. Ma hated when Thom left things lying around, but she usually gave her at least until dinnertime to tidy up before scolding her. Why was the backpack already gone?

Ma was leaning against the dinner table, reading a piece of paper, Thom's backpack lying open next to her hip. Thom lurched to a stop in horror.

"Thom, this is great. Why didn't you tell me?" Ma waved the flyer for Culture Day. "You can wear your best áo dài! You'll look cute. Everyone will love it."

Thom opened her mouth to say something, but Ma kept going.

"You can wear the blue one with the pink flowers. Or maybe the white one—that'll look better now that you're dark. You need to stay out of the sun. Maybe if you stay inside until then, you'll be pale enough and won't look orange in the blue áo dài. Okay, that's it, we keep you inside all weekend until Culture Day, and you won't be tan anymore."

Thom glanced at her reflection in the hallway mirror. She was tan even when soccer wasn't in season, but Ma was obsessed with pale skin. She and Thuy's mom had always lectured them to stay out of the sun, shoving hats in their hands and pushing the school to incorporate caps into their soccer uniforms. None of it had mattered, though, since they would never get the milky-white skin their mothers wanted.

But pale skin or not, Thom was never going to wear an áo dài to school.

"You can wear the . . . What you call that in English?" She gestured around her head. "A headdress. Yes, we have a matching one for your blue áo dài. You really need to be careful and stay inside when you not soccer playing, okay? You got it?"

"Ma," Thom started, but Ma, too excited, wasn't listening. Thom never wanted to wear áo dài, not even when they lived in West City, where it wasn't as weird. They were long traditional Vietnamese dresses, like maxi dresses, but slit down the sides and paired with flowy white pants. The neckline went up to your chin, and was made of stiffened silk or chiffon that pressed into your throat and made it hard to breathe. The buttons went across your collarbone and down to your left armpit, and if you so much as raised a finger, they popped open, which meant you always had to be careful and walk around like a robot. Plus áo dài were always too tight and uncomfortable, and she hated them.

But that wasn't the only reason she didn't want to wear them. She would be the only one in her school who would dress up in something so . . . Asian. She really couldn't imagine Kathy wearing a hanbok to school, and even if she did, she would look beautiful and exotic, while Thom could clearly picture how the dynamic trio would laugh if Thom showed up in an áo dài, stiff and dorky. No way.

Ma clapped her hands together. "Shoes! We buy you new shoes. I saw sale at the mall—we go there now, buy two pairs, and then you get to pick which one you wear!"

"Ma."

"I can't wait. You gonna look so cute. Too bad Thuy is not here. Then you girls can both wear like sisters."

"I don't want to wear an áo dài."

Ma's mouth opened and closed. "What you mean you don't want to wear áo dài? I got you some cute ones from Vietnam last year. They cost a lot of money, you know."

"No, they didn't. You go to Vietnam to buy them specifically because they're cheap there."

Ma rolled her eyes. "Okay, fine, but I buy for you, and you never wear. Such a waste. Don't tell me it's because you never get the chance—now the perfect chance." She held out the flyer. "Maybe you can even do a dance, or recite poetry. Or play the đàn bầu. We can get you private tutor until then."

"We don't even own a đàn bầu," Thom pointed out. It was a Vietnamese guitar-piano type of instrument. The ones that made you want to curl into a ball and die, they sounded so depressing. How Ma thought she was going to learn how to play a song on that thing in a few weeks, she had no idea. It was like saying she could learn to play a violin in the same amount of time.

"I special-order."

It was getting hard to breathe. "Ma."

"Why you don't want to dress up for Culture Day? It'll be fun."

There was a strange tightening in Thom's throat. Her nose burned like that time she'd tried wasabi.

"Because they'll laugh at me!"

And then, to both their horror, Thom burst into tears.

Crying wasn't really allowed in their house. Or expressing yourself outside of the two main emotions—serious and happy. Ma always said Thom should never cry unless someone died, because tears were sort of a bad omen, like crying could literally kill someone. Thom tried to stop as soon as she started, but tears squeezed out of her eyes and spilled off her chin.

Ma's expression was furious, her eyes rounded, her fists clenched by her side, as if Thom had told her she was quitting school for good.

"Why you upset? Who hit at you at school? Tell me. I sue them. I sue their parents. I sue everyone."

Thom tried to explain, but nothing came out except more tears. She stomped her foot, feeling like such a brat, but it was the only way she could express how she really felt.

"Okay, okay, stop already. I'm not dead yet. Why you cry?"

This, for some reason, worked. The tears stopped like a dam had sprung up out of nowhere, and inside, Thom felt numb, frozen.

This was why she really didn't want to participate in Culture Day: It was a big fat joke. There were only two nonwhite kids at their school. Everyone else would look so cool in their historical costumes. She could only imagine how uncool she would look if she was the only one who showed up in something like an áo dài.

She sniffled and wiped her eyes.

"Anyone bully you at school, cưng?"

Thom shook her head.

"Good," Ma said. "They bully you, you punch them once and they never bully you again."

Thom choked back a half sob, half laugh. Ma had no idea how close to the truth that was. Because if Thom punched someone, they'd probably never walk again.

"Now tell me, why you don't want to dress up for Culture Day?"

"Because everyone will laugh at me." Thom could already picture Bethany and Sarah snickering behind their hands. She could only imagine what they would think of her and her weird-looking đàn bầu and her Vietnamese áo dài and headdress.

"Why they laugh? Áo dài beautiful. I show you some pictures." Ma grabbed her phone.

"No, Ma, I don't want to see pictures. I know what they look like."

"See this one—so cute." She showed Thom a long white dress with sumi-painted flowers. "And this one—you would look adorable." She made an *aww* face at her phone, then at Thom, and then back at her phone.

Thom shook her head. "I'm not going to wear it. They'll think I'm weird and . . ."

"And what?"

"And fobby," she added in a low voice. The word tasted dirty. It meant FOB, "fresh off the boat," something you called an immigrant who didn't act as American or as cool as they should. It was the worst thing you could call an Asian person, especially when they hadn't just moved and had lived in America for a long time, or in Thom's case, was born here.

Ma crossed her arms. "What wrong with being *fobby*?"

Thom sighed. She regretted saying it, regretted saying

anything. She should have just agreed, pretended to be happy and obedient, like a good, filial daughter.

"What's wrong with being in touch with your culture?" Ma said. "You ashamed to be Vietnamese? Is that it? You don't want kids to know you Asian?"

"Ma, everyone knows I'm Asian. It's not like I can hide it." Thom's voice grew higher. She needed to stop Ma, convince her away from this madness. But once Ma set her mind on something, she saw it through, like the time she sued their old temple for teaching antifeminist ideas. She didn't win, but Thom and her mother had stopped going. If Thom didn't end this now, Ma would get her way and force Thom to dress up for Culture Day, and Thom would die. Emotionally. Psychologically. Literally. It would be the end of her social life.

"Being Vietnamese is cool. Better than being white like everyone else."

"That's not the point."

But Thom couldn't think of what the point was, if it wasn't that. She just knew that no one at school liked her because she was so different. She looked different, she brought strange foods for lunch, and her mom was loud and spoke funny. Thom couldn't change what her face looked like, but if she could hide everything else, if she could be a little less . . . herself . . . maybe they would accept her.

Ma shook her head, clicked her tongue, and pointed her index finger at Thom. "No, I think this exactly it. You think the white girls at your school are so cool you want to be just like them. That's why you don't bring rice to school and why you don't want to use chopsticks and why you don't want to wear áo dài to Culture Day. That's why you hide this from me." She shook the flyer.

"I didn't hide it."

"No, I know *exactly* what going on. Go put on your jacket."

"Why?"

"I show you something. We leave now."

"But—"

"What did I tell you to do?"

It was too late. There was no going back now. No changing her mind. Ma raised her brows at Thom, and Thom slumped up the stairs to get her jacket, even though it was 80 degrees outside and she was already wearing one.

7

MA DIDN'T SAY A WORD on the drive, but she blasted Vietnamese ballads the whole way, which was even worse than any amount of lecturing. The staccato chords of the đàn bầu were painfully sharp, each beat throbbing through Thom's head. She pressed her face against the glass and watched the traffic rush by.

When the car stopped, Thom opened the door, dragged herself outside, and followed Ma across the parking lot. They were at the Thien Than Temple. She hated this place. It was always dimly lit with creepy fake candles and eerily quiet, and it smelled like smoky incense and old prunes. The curving roofs sharpened sinisterly to razor points against the blue and orange sky. The eyes of stone dragons outside followed her, their shadows elongating in the golden light of the setting sun.

"What are we doing here?" For some reason, Thom felt the need to whisper.

Ma didn't look at her. Thom was almost jogging to keep up with her brisk strides.

"To show you that Asian things are just as cool as white people things."

"I believe you. Let's go home." The back of Thom's neck tickled. "Is it even open? It looks closed."

"It's fine. Look, there are people praying."

Inside the temple, candles punctuated the darkness, casting flickering shadows across the three statues. Guarded on either side by goddesses, a huge Buddha grinned at them like he knew a secret, a joke he didn't intend on sharing, his huge earlobes sagging down to his chin. Thom recognized some of the mythical characters, but most of them blended together in her mind. They had once been mortals who had reached enlightenment and gone to the heavens, where they performed duties as fairies until they achieved true immortality and became gods.

"Look," Ma said, pointing at all the statues. "Aren't these cool? Better than your white-people heroes, right?"

Thom rolled her eyes. "Yup. I agree. Let's go."

"I want to light incense while we're here. Come on, I'll buy you a candle."

"I think that's a Catholic thing, Ma." Thuy's family was Catholic, and they were always buying prayers from the priest on behalf of their dead relatives.

"If I want to buy you a candle, I buy you a candle. Here—take this cushion before someone else does."

Thom looked around to see who Ma thought might want to steal cushions. They were the only people there except for an old lady shaking her incense sticks at Buddha. Thom wouldn't have to worry that anyone from school would see her here, or witness how embarrassing Ma was while she tried to prove to Thom how cool the Vietnamese culture really was. She sighed and knelt on the red-and-gold cushion, making sure there was enough space for Ma, and pretended to bow her head. The faster she got through this, the sooner they could go home.

Ma came back a few minutes later and handed Thom a few sticks of incense, which she obediently held up to the golden statues. The gods' expressions were straight-faced and unamused, except Buddha, who, with his wide, dimpled smile, was permanently having a good time. It was silly, worshiping these inanimate objects with their frozen faces. Besides, you would think the gods had better things to do than listen to Thom's petty complaints and silly pleadings.

Ma bowed low, her forehead touching the ground. What was she asking for? She had everything—a nice job, a house, and an obedient daughter. They had moved away from their friends just so Ma could have these things—what more could she want?

Ma tsked sharply, as if she could hear Thom's thoughts, so Thom turned forward and pretended to pray even harder. Buddha would just tell her that suffering was a part of life. She couldn't remember who the statue on his left was, a beautiful fairy goddess with a jade tiara on her head. She turned to the one on the right. Guanyin, the goddess of mercy, seemed like the best candidate to get Thom out of her mess. She aimed the smoke at her.

Please, please, Guanyin.

What exactly did she want?

It wasn't much. Not really. Thom wanted her old life back. To be normal again. To not be superstrong. She wanted to be able to touch something without breaking it. She wanted everyone at school to like her. She wanted to be able to play soccer again—really play it like she had at her old school. She had been good. Soccer had been *fun*. Now, it was something she dreaded, feared. But how else was she supposed to make friends? She wanted Bethany and Sarah and Kathy to smile and talk *to* her, not *about* her. But if she quit soccer now, she would be giving up. Not that Ma would let her quit in the first place.

If only she weren't so strong, she could prove to everyone how good she was. They would like her. She would have a chance.

"Let's look around the temple," Ma said. "You done praying?"

Thom nodded and followed her mother out the main room, half listening as Ma lectured about the temple's history, the fairies and the gods, the sculptures on some of the walls. Most of the stories were ones she'd heard before, like the one about the Jade Emperor, who ruled the heavenly kingdom over the gods, who in turn ruled certain parts of the world.

The fairies had always been portrayed as beautiful, giggly goddesses, playing the đàn bầu and tending to gardens. Her favorites were the ones about the dragons, the immortal warriors who took the form of humans and guarded different areas of the earth, the seas, and the skies.

Ma stopped in front of a mural of what looked like David and a hundred Goliaths. It was a small boy, practically a baby, standing up against an army of huge soldiers.

Ma didn't say anything for a long time, just stood there staring at the image, so Thom wandered away, feeling bored and antsy to leave. She had never liked going to temple, even in West City, but back then all of her friends had also had to go and they didn't like it, either, so they would all just hang out and complain about things together. Here in Troy, *no one* went to temple, and even though there was no way she'd run into anyone from school, it gave her the feeling that if anyone did see her here, they would use it as one more piece of evidence that Thom did not belong.

A noise distracted her, the clink of something dropping. She stopped in front of a shelf built into the wall, displaying a miniature cast-iron sculpture of a temple. As she approached, the door of the sculpture swung back and forth on a half-broken hinge. Thom tried to close the door, but the latch also wasn't working.

Inside the tiny temple was an even tinier gourd, a peanut-shaped bottle carved from dark, polished stone, lying on its side. Thom recognized it from Chinese dramas—monks always used gourds to trap demons and evil spirits, and sometimes she'd seen them sold in Chinatown as souvenirs. That was probably what she'd heard fall. She glanced over her shoulder, but Ma was still staring at the pictures on the wall, so Thom reached in and picked up the gourd to place it upright.

Something fell out of the uncorked opening. It pinged off the base of the metal temple, then bounced onto the floor.

Thom reached for it, pinching it between her thumb and index finger. It was a golden pin, like you'd use for sewing, but it was of a stiff and coarse material, unlike any pin she'd ever held. She turned it over and over, watching light reflect off its surface, mesmerized by the color.

"Cưng, come look at this," Ma called to her.

Thom placed the gourd quickly back inside the miniature temple, stuffed the golden pin-looking thing in her pocket, then went to her mom. Ma was still staring at the mural of the little boy facing an army of giants. They walked down the length of the wall, studying the scenes. In the next panel, the boy had grown taller and bigger. Eventually, he became a giant, larger than any soldier in the army, and defeated them all.

Twin lines formed between Ma's brows. "This is the Boy Giant. Thánh Gióng. You remember his story?"

Thom nodded. "Kind of?"

"He was baby for long time and didn't grow, didn't smile or talk, until the kingdom was invaded. Then he ate lot of rice, became a giant. Superstrong, and defeated the invaders." She stopped and frowned.

"What happened to him?" Thom asked.

"What you mean?"

"After he defeated the invaders. Did he get to go home? Did he stay giant, or did he become a normal boy again?"

"He became an immortal." Ma lightly touched the image of the Boy Giant on the back of a horse, riding into battle. "One of the Four Immortals—they ascended to the heavens and become higher gods. A great honor."

"But what about his ma and ba? Didn't they worry about him?"

Ma turned sharply, and Thom realized she'd accidentally said the bad word you weren't supposed to mention around

her mother, the one that implied fathers existed. Thom swallowed.

"Of course not," Ma said gravely. "He become a god. Nothing to worry about."

"But he was so little. Just a kid, almost a baby." Thom pointed at the Boy Giant in the first panel, where he could hardly stand on his own chubby legs. "His ma and ba *must* have worried about him."

"Maybe he didn't have parents. Maybe he was orphan."

"But even orphans have parents." Thom looked back at Ma, whose scowl set deep folds in her forehead.

"Stop it. I have a headache. Let's go home now."

"But . . ." Thom wanted to argue and point out that Ma always got a headache any time they came close to talking about fathers. Not just Thom's dad, but *any* dad. Like the mention of them would cause Thom's father to just drop out of the sky. Which made Thom want to ask even more questions. Who was her father? Why did Ma never talk about him? Was he dead or alive? Had he abandoned them? But as far as Ma was concerned, he didn't exist.

"I have a headache," Ma repeated. "It's getting late, and I still need to finish some work. Let's go. We can come back tomorrow."

8

THOM WENT UP TO HER room that night, hoping Ma had forgotten all about Culture Day, and dressing her up in a stupid costume and a headdress, and pretty much anything that would ruin her entire social life for the next decade. But there was no such luck. As she was turning off the lights, Ma stopped by, leaning against the doorjamb.

"I think I'm going to order you a new áo dài," she said with a soft smile. She didn't seem as excited as before, her eyes now glazed with a faraway look, but there was still a brightness in her expression, which meant there was no point in arguing. "One with a matching headdress. You look better in pink anyway, since you are so dark."

Thom grew hot and thought about arguing, resisting, being mean. Instead, she just muttered, "Thanks."

Ma smiled, not catching the sarcasm. "Okay, cưng."

Thom crawled into bed after Ma left, and lay there for

an eternity, staring at her ceiling. She kept picturing Bethany's face when Thom showed up in her long Vietnamese dress, how she would ogle and then smirk and then nudge her friends so they could laugh. They had enough reasons to make fun of Thom already. Imagine how much worse it would be if she dressed up as a freak for Culture Day.

She flipped and turned, unable to find a comfortable position. She got out of bed and checked the time. It was one in the morning. How could she stop Ma from buying a new áo dài? Steal her phone? Hide her credit cards? Even if Thom managed to, Ma could always force her to wear one she already owned. If only her growth spurt would kick in so she wouldn't fit them anymore.

There was no way she was going to fall asleep, so she went down to the kitchen to get a glass of water. Mochi's ears perked, and he got up from his bed, clicking after her but never coming close enough so she could pet him.

Their new house was much bigger than the house in West City, and they were still shopping for furniture. The living room looked incomplete, the corners empty, the ceilings high, the fireplace clunky and awkward in what should have been a cozy room.

Everything was different from their old life. Their house had been small and snug, the ceilings low, the furniture arranged like in a *Tetris* game, so that it all just barely fit.

This place still didn't feel like home; it felt like they were staying at an auntie's house. A nice auntie, who let them keep their stuff in the drawers and cupboards.

Ma's door was open—she always kept it open in case Thom called for her or wanted to sneak into her bed, which Thom hadn't done since she was five. Ma's small form was motionless under her blankets. A soft breeze blew in through her window, lifting the gossamer curtains.

Thom tiptoed through her room and quietly pulled the window closed.

Thom was about to get back into her own bed when a glint of gold caught her eye.

It was the pin that she'd found at the temple, peeking out from her jacket pocket. She'd almost forgotten about it, distracted with Culture Day.

She held it up to the light, then laid it on the desk and set it in the slant of moonlight shimmering through the blinds.

It shone like silver, soft at first, and then glowing brighter, as if it were feeding off the moonlight. Suddenly, it grew so bright, Thom had to cover her eyes and take a step back.

And then the glow dimmed.

That was weird.

She blinked, but a blind spot blocked her vision and she could no longer see the pin on her desk.

Then her eyes adjusted. Her mouth opened to let out a scream, but the muscles of her face froze, and nothing came out.

Sitting at the edge of her desk, legs crossed like he belonged there, was a monkey.

A monkey.

Out of nowhere.

Or rather, a part man, part monkey. Like an older boy, maybe fifteen, but covered in reddish-gold hair. His face was mischievous, his long brown eyelashes fluttering as he blinked and surveyed the room. His head tilted back and forth.

"Hello there," he said, his voice high and singsong.

Thom sucked in a breath, but her face remained paralyzed.

The monkey boy looked around the room. "Nice place."

He pushed off the desk and jumped onto the bed, bouncing until his head skimmed the ceiling, and then, on the last jump, he stayed up in the air. Hovering. Flying. His eyes caught on her closet, and he flew headfirst into it. He poked through her clothes, picked up a sweater, sniffed it, and tossed it over his shoulder.

That spurred Thom out of her frozen state.

"Hey," she said in a choked voice, but he ignored her. He went through the rest of the clothes until he found a pair of black cutoff shorts that had once been sweatpants, which he slipped into. The fleece fringe looked too bizarre on his monkey body, on top of his strange robes.

She squeezed her eyes shut. *A dream, that's all it is.* The incense from the temple was making her hallucinate.

But when she opened her eyes, he was still there. He was real.

His brown eyes gleamed in the moonlight, and he batted his lashes as he looked her up and down. Then he moved way too close, his nose almost touching hers.

"Ah," she gasped, and stepped back.

"Who are you?" He sniffed at her. "What is this place? How did you set me free?"

He was speaking words Thom understood, but it was taking a long time for her brain to catch up.

"I'm Thom," she answered out of reflex. Then she shook herself. "What do you mean . . . set you free . . . Who are *you*?" she demanded.

He straightened with an indignant look of disbelief. "You

don't know me?" He puffed out his chest and drew his shoulders back. "I," he proclaimed, hands on his hips, "am the Great Sage of Heaven!"

"The what?"

"Sun Wukong."

She blinked at him.

"Tôn Ngộ Không." He raised his brows.

She shook her head.

"The Monkey King," he said.

No way. She knew who the Monkey King was, of course. Not one Chinese or Vietnamese kid grew up without hearing of him. But he was a myth. This must have been a trick. Some creepy dude dressed in a fur suit had followed her home and snuck into her bedroom.

She touched his face. The fur was rough but fluffy, flattening under her palm. His skin warm and alive, not rubbery like a suit would have been.

But it couldn't be real. He couldn't be real.

There was only one way to find out. She grabbed a handful of fur and yanked. He twitched, then straightened. He narrowed his eyes at Thom, and she took a step back before they both looked down at her open palm. In her hand sat a single strand of hair, stiff and coarse. Just like the golden pin she'd found at the temple.

"The hair." Oh no. It made sense now. "That was you?"

He grabbed the strand she'd plucked and shoved it back

into the side of his head like a pin through a cushion. "You are the one who released me from the temple?"

"I found a golden pin and brought it home. I didn't know . . ." Of course. In the legends, the Monkey King could shrink down to the size of a needle to hide from his enemies. "I didn't know it was you."

"Who else would it be?" He snorted, huffing through his nostrils several times. "They call me the handsome Monkey King. The magnificent, powerful, undefeatable, invincible Monkey King."

"Handsome. Right, okay." Thom *was* dreaming. This wasn't real. The smoke from the incense, the trip to the temple—all of it had gotten to her head.

He straightened to his full height, puffing out his chest. "I have discovered the secret of life and immortality. I have beaten death. I know the Seventy-Two Transformations. I can fly through air. I can become invisible. I can breathe under-water. I can walk through flames. I can clone myself with each hair of my body. I am all-powerful."

"Really?" He looked ridiculous with his chest out and his chin raised, wearing her cutoff sweat shorts. Maybe it was the missing red-and-gold armor she'd always associated with the Monkey King, but there was something off about the way he looked. Something was missing. "Is there anything you can't do?"

He considered this, his shoulders slumping. "I've yet to

learn the secret of resurrecting the dead. But in time, I will perfect that skill and add it to my arsenal."

"Oh . . . kay." It was hitting her how weird this was. There was a monkey in her room. There was a talking monkey in her room. And not just any talking monkey, but the *Monkey King*. She should be having an anxiety attack any moment now.

Except this was a dream, wasn't it?

"But what did you mean," she said, "when you asked if I released you from the temple?" And the way he'd said it— "released"—it was like he'd been some kind of prisoner. "What were you even doing at the temple?"

She'd found the hair inside the gourd, as if someone had put it there for safekeeping and had forgotten about it. But maybe the miniature temple hadn't been decoration; maybe it was a prison, one protected with magic so that the demon trapped inside couldn't escape.

And she had opened it. She had *released* him.

Thom's eyes widened as the realization of what she'd done hit her. She had freed the Monkey King.

Their eyes locked.

He stood very still.

Then he bolted for the window.

Thom acted without thinking and lunged for him. Her arms wrapped around his knees, and they both landed on the floor with a *thump*. She winced. Was that loud enough to wake Ma?

"Be quiet," she whispered.

The Monkey King wiggled, one leg slipping free, his foot slapping against her face. He was strong, stronger than she'd expected. But she was strong, too. She pinned him to the floor.

"This . . . is . . . impossible," he grunted, pushing his foot so hard against her face that her neck bent backward. "How are you . . . ?"

She reached up and pulled his foot away, lifting it high, so he was forced to do the splits, lying down.

This was weird. This was really weird. The weirdest thing she'd ever done, and Thom was in middle school, where weird things happened pretty often.

"Let me go," the Monkey King said, thrashing. For a second, he slipped and lifted into the air like he weighed nothing, but she threw herself on top of him.

"I have to put you back in the temple," she said. "You were a prisoner. If anyone finds out I freed you, I'll be in big trouble." From what she remembered about the Monkey King's story, he'd been a mischievous demon-god who'd caused so much havoc that the other gods in the heavens had to imprison him. Whatever he had done, whatever the reason he had been trapped in that temple, she had to put him back. If someone had locked up the Monkey King, it must have been for a reason.

"I am not going back there."

"You have to."

"I said, let me . . . go!"

He threw a wild punch, connecting with her shoulder, and the force threw her back. She landed on the floor, wheezing as the breath slammed out of her. The room tilted, off balance.

The Monkey King's face loomed over her, blocking out the moonlight. His carefree expression had shifted to something fierce and haunted. "Never going back," he said.

Then suddenly, his dark expression was replaced with a smile. "Never, never. You'll never catch me," he sang, giggling. He stuck out his tongue, wiggled his fingers, and leapt out the window.

9

ON THE DRIVE TO SCHOOL, Ma was in a good mood. She hummed along to the radio, laughed at one of the commercials, and nudged Thom when she didn't laugh back. Thom was too busy freaking out about the fact that she had released a demon-god into the world. Where was he now? How was she going to fix this?

"You okay, cưng?" Ma asked as they pulled up behind the long line of cars at the drop-off. "You so quiet today."

Thom nodded. She rubbed the bruise on her shoulder, where the Monkey King had kicked her last night. Her neck was sore, her arms fatigued. She hadn't felt this much pain since . . . since before she'd developed her superstrength. That meant the Monkey King was also superstrong, not to mention the other powers he was supposed to have.

What did she know about the Monkey King? He wasn't really a god or a demon but somewhere in between, and she didn't think he was truly evil, either. Just mischievous. Enough to get himself into trouble. Enough to be locked in a temple. And she was the one who'd let him out.

"You sleep okay?" Ma asked. But Thom barely heard her.

How could she have been so stupid? That had been the hair of the Monkey King, and that tiny temple he was trapped inside must have been enchanted. In Chinese dramas, those places were warded with spells and magic so demons and evil spirits couldn't come in or escape. And Thom had taken the hair, as if it were a toy. She had released one of the most dangerous creatures in history.

But how could she have known? The Monkey King was supposed to be a myth. Someone should have warned her. There should have been some sort of sign at the temple. WARN-ING: REAL HAIR OF EVIL DEMON-GOD. DO NOT RELEASE. Or *something*.

Whoever had imprisoned him had done it for a reason. And she'd set him free. Freed a powerful mythical being. Who wasn't mythical after all, but real. She had to undo it. She had to find some way to put him back.

"Cưng?" Ma said. She reached across the seat to feel Thom's forehead. Ma wasn't going to let up, not unless Thom gave her an answer. Or an excuse. She ducked away from Ma's hand.

"I didn't sleep well."

"Oh no. My precious cưng. You have bad dream?"

Thom shook her head, then looked at her mom. Her

hair was pulled back into a high bun, bringing out the sharp edges of her high cheekbones. She wore huge glasses, the black frames hip and out of place over her stern expression.

"What do you know about the Monkey King?" Thom asked.

"Ah, Tôn Ngộ Không!" Ma grinned. "That what we call him in Vietnamese. I always love his story when I was a kid."

"Is he . . . a bad guy?"

"Bad? Maybe. A little. Not bad or good, somewhere in the middle. He make a lot of trouble, though. And no one can defeat him. Even immortals and gods can't beat him—only Buddha was able to trick him. Because you have to be smart to succeed, remember?"

Thom turned her face away and rolled her eyes.

"That's why you go to school and have to study hard. Become doctor or lawyer." Ma paused and shrugged. "Or dentist, I guess."

"So Buddha tricked him and defeated him?"

"Yeah, no one else could do it because he outsmart and overpower them all. He's undefeatable! He have lots of power—invisible, strong, he can fly. He's supposed to be a demon-god. He was born from a crystal that fell from the heavens and raised by demons, and then learned a lot of magic from an old master." She glanced at Thom. "Why? You have dream about Monkey King?"

Thom nodded. "Yeah, it was weird. He appeared in my

room last night. He called himself 'the handsome Monkey King.'"

Ma snorted. "Oh, yes, very handsome, with his hairy face. What a weird dream."

"It felt real." Thom wanted to tell her mom the rest of it, but Ma cut her off. They had arrived at the front of the school drop-off line.

"You just have such strong imagination." Ma planted a kiss on the top of her head. "Okay, have good day at school—I pick you up after practice." Then she drove away, leaving Thom conflicted on the sidewalk in front of school.

Ma was right, Thom told herself; it must have been a dream. The Monkey King wasn't real.

The bruises felt real. Thom stretched her neck and felt a slight ache.

But when she tugged on the neckline of her sweater, her shoulder was smooth, the skin tone even. No bruise. No Monkey King. It really had just been a dream.

◆ ◆ ◆

Thom still had fifteen minutes before school started, so she paused by the drinking fountain on her way to class, trying not to look lost and bored as other kids moved around her in groups. Everyone had a friend or a clique to belong to, and she couldn't help feeling alone and isolated, an island in a sea of moving students. She pretended to be busy, studying the walls, which were painted bright yellow, casting a fake cheeriness over the scene. Some teachers had hung examples of good work, mostly posters from art projects or pictures from field trips. Everything here was so clean, so sparkly and gleaming. Even the lockers, painted in the school navy blue, seemed to glitter. And it smelled nice, a pleasant soapy smell.

She checked her phone. Her best friend, Thuy, would know what to do if Thom told her about the Monkey King. She would be able to tell what was real or not. But Thuy still hadn't responded to her last text, from three days ago.

Thuy hadn't answered the texts from last week, either, when Thom had told her about the upcoming Monrovia game, or the one after, telling her at least there was one other Asian girl on the team, or the one after that, which simply read *Everything okay?*—because it was weird that her best friend was not answering.

The boxed READ symbol beneath the last message stabbed her in the gut each time she saw it. Nothing labeled you a loser more than an unanswered read message.

Thom thought about sending another text, but the last thing she wanted was to come off as desperate to the only friend she had—even if that friend was Thuy and Thuy would never think that of her. Or would she?

"Hey, Thom!"

Thom jumped, nearly dropping her phone.

It was Kha, her new neighbor. He waved and grinned like

they were best friends. If Thom had given him any sign of encouragement, he might have thrown his arms around her. Dressed in a long black-and-white-striped tee and tight jeans with Chucks, he was practically bouncing on his toes.

"Uh, hey," she said, and thank goodness the bell rang, because she had no idea what else to say.

"Can you show me to my next class?" he asked. "I don't really know where I'm going."

It wasn't like she could say no. Not without being completely rude, anyway.

Stares followed them down the hallway, kids stopping to look from Thom to Kha, probably wondering if they were related or something. Kha didn't seem to notice, still giving Thom a wide smile, as if they were at Disneyland and not at DeMille Middle School.

"Is that . . . ?" she said. "Are you . . . wearing . . . ?" Something was on Kha's face. His cheeks shimmered like pearl, like the highlighter Kathy used to accentuate her cheekbones, the one Ma refused to let Thom have. "Is that makeup?"

"What?" Kha rubbed at his face, and when he looked at his hands, there was nothing there. His skin wasn't shimmering anymore, either.

That was weird. She could have sworn his skin had been shining. "I thought . . . I saw . . . I don't know . . ." She didn't know what was wrong with her, how sometimes she spat out words like she wasn't sure she was allowed to use them. "Never mind."

The crowd parted to let them through, which never happened at DeMille. Everyone usually shoved one another in the rush between classes, because tardiness was a pretty big deal. Three tardies, and your parents get called. Four, and you get detention.

"Listen," Kha said in a tone like he meant business. "Maybe we can hang out. Later."

Thom's heart stopped completely, and blood roared up her head and into her ears, like she'd reached the top of a roller coaster and dropped. Then her heart gave a sort of leap before she forced herself to calm down.

No one here had ever asked her to hang out. That's why she was excited. And a bit confused. Not because it was Kha.

She was even more confused *because* it was Kha. If any other kid had asked, she would have been happy but not totally shocked. But Kha was a little too cool for her. He looked like he had stepped out of an anime, with his fitted jeans and his fashionable T-shirt, while Thom had thrown on the first thing she'd seen, a comfortable but old hoodie she couldn't remember the last time she'd washed. Even his shoes were cool, the laces tied in a stylish ladder formation. Thom clicked her heels together, trying to hide one of her ratty sneakers behind the other.

And Thom knew Kha was cool from the impressed expressions on people's faces after they looked him up and down. All she'd ever gotten was a raised eyebrow or an unamused quirk of the lips.

Why would Kha want to hang out with her? Whatever he saw in her, she was sure to let him down. This was way too much pressure, especially after the night she'd had.

They reached Pre-Alg, and Kathy was standing at the door talking to her boyfriend, Peter. She looked perfect as always, in a simple black cotton shirt and a pink miniskirt that wasn't too short but wasn't too long, her straight black hair flowing down her back. She glanced over at them, her eyes sliding over Thom with the usual indifferent derision before landing on Kha with sparked interest.

Kha flashed a grin. "Excuse me, can you move?" he said. And even though the words were kind of rude, the way he said them was teasing, like he'd been friends with Kathy long enough to be mean to her. How did he do that? Was it some magical gift? Why couldn't Thom have gotten that power instead of her freakish strength?

Kathy smiled, flipped her hair, and moved out of the way.

Kha turned to make sure Thom was following. Everyone watched them take their seats together. You would think something amazing had happened, like they'd found out Thom and Kha were secret celebrities.

When Mrs. Abbot walked in, she stopped short. "Wow, is

this really my class?" She pretended to double-check the room number. "Why is everyone so quiet?"

"New kid." Oliver Jones pointed at Kha.

"Very astute observation, Oliver. Thank you." Mrs. Abbot was all about that no-nonsense straight-to-business I-don't-care-if-it's-Harry-Potter-sitting-in-the-front-seat type of teaching. She dropped her stack of files on the desk. "I hope everyone did their homework, because you can start passing it to the front."

There was a collective groan.

Mrs. Abbot called Kha up to talk to him privately. Kathy turned in her seat to grab the homework from everyone behind her, and Thom's eyes met hers. Her lips twitched, as if she were about to give Thom a friendly smile but had caught herself in time.

Thom tried to ignore the curious glances people were giving her and Kha when he came back. She was taking notes when Kha tapped her knuckles, then the corner of his notebook. She frowned at him, but he nodded at the paper, and she sighed and leaned down to read the tiny note he'd written in the corner.

Meet after school at library?

What was going on? Why was he trying to be her friend? There was no reasonable explanation. Maybe he was messing with her, like those popular kids had messed with Carrie in that horror movie. Ma hadn't let her see it, but she knew the general idea, and she was not going to fall for it and end up covered in pig's blood. She might not have Carrie's psychic abilities, but she could still hurt a lot of people with her super-strength.

Not that she would ever let that happen, of course, which meant that she wasn't going to fall for Kha's trick from the start. She had no intention of meeting him anywhere.

He was still waiting for an answer, so she shrugged.

When class ended, Mrs. Abbot called Kha again, and they left the classroom together.

Good. Hopefully, Thom could escape to her next class without running into him.

Kathy bumped into her as they both rushed from their seats, knocking her backpack off her right shoulder. "Oh, sorry," Kathy said. She looked at Thom, and Thom froze. Kathy was talking to her. Meeting her eyes.

"That's okay." Thom picked up her backpack and then held it awkwardly, not knowing what else to do.

"Was that your cousin or something?" Kathy asked.

"Who?"

"The new guy."

"No. Just a . . . friend."

"You guys just looked really close, that's all."

"No, I . . . We just met." Thom gave a nervous laugh. "I don't know why he started talking to me . . ."

Kathy smiled slowly, an eyebrow raised. Even though

she didn't say it, Thom suddenly understood the reason why Kha was gravitating toward her. It was this thing Asian kids did: group together, befriend one another, uphold the camaraderie of being minorities. Of course Kha was friendly, but only because he didn't have anyone else, at least not yet. Not because he actually liked Thom or thought she was cool. She was the complete opposite of cool, and everyone knew it.

"See you at soccer practice," Kathy said after what felt like a century, in a tone that seemed to say, *Even though I'd rather die.*

10

THOM DIDN'T MOVE, THE CONVERSATION with Kathy replaying in her mind—the smirk on her face, the knowing sideways glance, like she knew a joke that everyone else was in on except Thom.

"Is this supposed to be a school?" a voice asked out of nowhere.

Thom shrieked, then slapped a hand over her mouth. The Monkey King dropped onto the desk in front of her, cross-legged and poking inside his ear with one hairy finger. He inspected the tip, then licked it.

She was too grossed out to speak. And shocked. She had convinced herself that what had happened last night was a dream or some hallucination. But here he was, still real and talking.

He scrambled to all fours, still on top of the desk, and leaned toward her. "Where are the masters? The fighting sticks, the sparring weapons? The armory? What happened to the fighting? Did I miss it?"

"W-what?" Thom stuttered.

"Do they expect you to go into the world without learning to defend yourself?" he asked, poking her sternum. "I would destroy all these students with one swipe of my cudgel."

He sat back down on the desk, legs swinging. He *was* there. He *was* . . . real. The desk rocked back and forth, creaking, threatening to topple. She rubbed the spot where he'd poked her, feeling another very real bruise forming.

He leapt from the desk and bounded around the room, doing flips in the air as if he weighed nothing.

"They should teach you to fly," he said, "to do something useful. What is this?" He picked up a pencil, chewed on the end, and spat out the shavings. He made a face. "They had better snacks when I was in school." He went to the teacher's desk next and riffled through her papers, sending them flying into the air over his shoulder. "Where are the Taoist teachings? The Seventy-Two Transformations. What is all this?"

"Stop that," she hissed, slipping her backpack on and rushing toward him. "What are you doing here?"

He ignored her, making curious *ooh-ooh* sounds as he picked up Mrs. Abbot's calculator. It was one of those expensive scientific ones that cost almost as much as a smartphone. Thom had wanted one for her birthday, but Ma said she could have it only if she got into the high school geometry course that was offered to some middle schoolers. That was before they'd moved from West City, though. Here in Troy, the highest math level for middle schoolers was algebra.

The Monkey King punched the keys, then tossed the calculator behind him. It clattered against the wall and fell to the floor in pieces.

"Hey!" She ran to pick it up.

She was trying to reassemble the pieces, hoping it wasn't broken, when a large shape hurled toward her. Without thinking, she held up her hands and caught it.

It was a table—one of the large round tables that they used for group work, at least five times her size. She'd grabbed one edge of the surface in her left hand. It should have weighed at least seventy pounds, but it felt like nothing to her, like she was just holding up a book.

The Monkey King was suddenly right in front of her face, crouched beneath the table. His nose twitched. His eyelashes fluttered. "You are *strong*."

Thom looked up. Pieces of dried gum dotted the bottom of the table in globs of blue and green and black. "You threw a table at me." She lowered it to the floor.

"You're strong!" He hopped gleefully around her in circles, clapping his hands and giggling his staccato monkey giggle.

"Hey. Stop that. You could have hurt me."

"How are you so strong?"

"I'm not." Heat spread up her neck.

Footsteps clicked down the hallway. *Oh no, oh no. Someone else might have seen.* She glanced quickly around the room, but they were alone. The door was closed, and Mrs. Abbot still wasn't back. Thom's breath rushed out in a *whoosh*, leaving her deflated.

"Have you fed off the meat of a magical boar?" The Monkey King was still there. The Monkey King who had just tried to kill her. Kind of.

"What? No," Thom said.

"Have the fairies bestowed upon you a magical cloak or

ornament that has given you such great strength because they felt sorry for someone so feeble?" he asked.

"Feeble?" Thom repeated, offended.

"Where is it?" The Monkey King bounced over to her, floating in circles around her, making her dizzy.

"What?" she asked, pulling away.

"Show me the magical object," he said.

"I'm not—I don't have a magical object."

"A ring, a necklace, shoes. It could be anything." He peered closely at her from his spot in the air.

"I don't have any of those things. I mean, nothing magical. I don't even like earrings." They always made her ears itchy and red.

"Then how are you so strong?" He lifted her left arm, then her right, as if checking her armpits. "You are the size of a pea. Where does your power come from?"

"I don't have powers!" She dropped her voice. "And be quiet. People will hear you."

"Someone has bestowed magical powers upon you. I must know the source." He loomed closer, his eyes threatening, focused.

"Stop it." But he didn't stop, moving way too close too fast. She panicked, and before she knew what she was doing, her fist flew out and slammed into his jaw.

The Monkey King jerked back, his eyes rounding in shock. He rubbed the sore spot in consternation and sniffed, studying her from every angle. "No mere mortal can be this strong. You struck me, and I am stronger than ten thousand oxen, I can lift mountains. I have defeated dragon-kings. I am the only person who can lift my iron staff, which weighs seventeen thousand pounds."

It was a nightmare, the recurring one she always had, about people finding out what she was, what she could do. Only this time, like the myth of the Monkey King, who was supposed to be fictional, it was coming true. She had kept the secret for so long. Now that someone knew, it was only a matter of time before the world found out. She was eleven; she knew how these things worked. She'd be taken away, tested, everyone believing her to be some sort of alien.

And yet . . . he wasn't looking at her like she was a freak. He was looking at her like this was a good thing. Like he was planning something. His lips stretched over surprisingly straight teeth and sharp extended canines. She took a step back.

"Why are you looking at me like that?" she asked.

"How strong are you?" he asked, excited.

"I just said—"

"Imagine the things we can do!" he said, talking over her. "With my cunning and your strength—"

"Shh, someone will hear," Thom said, looking toward the closed door. She could see through the small window that most of the students had moved on to their next class. It was only a matter of time before Mrs. Abbot came back. She had to get rid of the Monkey King before then.

"We must discover the extent of your powers!" he crowed.

Thom clapped a hand over his mouth. He jerked away, but she grabbed his ear to keep him in place and stop him from blurting out anything else. He lifted into the air, but with her hand over his mouth and one clamped onto his ear, only his legs lifted. His arms flailed. He giggled into her palm, and she realized why he was so amused when her feet lifted off the floor, too.

"Hey!" She tried to take a few steps back as he dragged her, grabbing his other ear as she lost balance.

He giggled louder. "Ready for your first lesson?"

But before Thom could learn what he had in mind, something crunched under her feet. Looking down, she saw the calculator. She let go of the Monkey King and picked it up. "Oh no." It was completely broken now, the plastic shattered, the screen demolished.

And then, of course, Mrs. Abbot walked back into the classroom.

She and Thom froze. Papers were all over the floor, desks had been shoved against one another, chairs turned over on their backs. "Thom . . . ?"

The Monkey King was gone.

Which was good. Right? Mrs. Abbot would have *freaked out* if she saw a humanlike monkey in her classroom.

But how was Thom supposed to explain this mess?

"What in the . . . ?" Mrs. Abbot's gaze fell on Thom, and the smashed pieces of plastic in her hands. "Is that my calculator?"

All Thom could think of was the trouble she'd be in, Ma's heartbroken expression, the inevitable lecture about family and honor and respect. Mrs. Abbot's eyebrows drew together, and harsh lines appeared around her mouth.

"How did this happen, Thom?" she asked.

"There was a . . ." Thom hated the softness of her voice. Nothing she could say would make this look good.

Mrs. Abbot sucked in a breath. "What happened?" she said through clenched teeth.

"It wasn't me, I swear. I didn't—"

"Who was it then? One of the other students?"

Thom shook her head.

"You can tell me their names," the teacher said, speaking softly now and keeping her eyes locked on Thom's with a careful, kind expression.

She must have thought Thom was afraid of being a tattletale. But how was Thom supposed to explain that a magical monkey was responsible for this?

"You don't have to take full blame for this," Mrs. Abbot continued. "If one of the other kids pressured you into it, you can tell me."

Thom swallowed and shook her head again.

Mrs. Abbot sighed. "I don't have much of a choice then, do I?" She gestured around at the mess. "I'm sending you to the Office."

◆ ◆ ◆

The Office. *Office* with a capital *O*. Where the principal, Mrs. Colton, lived. Thom sat, shaking, in front of the huge metal desk as she waited, not bothering to browse the neat bookshelves, ducking her face in case anyone saw her through the bright window.

"Thom," Mrs. Colton said, lowering herself slowly into her chair with as much effort and care as a spaceship docking. Even sitting, she towered over Thom, her shadow a looming, monstrous silhouette, dark against the brightness of the window behind her. "I don't often see *you* in my office."

Thom shook her head. If principals had a superpower, it was the ability to make everyone speechless and terrified. Anything Thom said could be misconstrued and used against her.

"Mrs. Abbot said you made a mess in her room. The desks thrown about, and you broke a calculator?"

Thom sank into her seat, her shoulders tense.

"Who was it, really?" Mrs. Colton asked, her voice dropping to a near whisper. It was clear she thought someone else had helped, at least, maybe even forced Thom to take the blame. Like they were in a movie and the real criminal had run away and Thom was the stupid one who was caught with her hand still in the jar. "If you tell me, I won't suspend you."

"What? Suspend me?" Thom bolted upright. A suspension would go on her permanent record! Universities would look back on the suspension and decide she wasn't good enough for their school. She would be forced to study even harder to make up for this mistake.

"I know you couldn't have torn apart that room alone. And the table . . . you couldn't have carried that to the middle of the room on your own. Mrs. Abbot said she was only gone for five minutes."

Suspension. Thom couldn't get that out of her head. Already, she could picture her life after today . . . First, suspension, then detention, not once, but every day, and ultimately expulsion. She would lose all motivation to study. It started with one bad grade—that's all it took—the gateway to a career of flipping burgers and living in Ma's basement.

Thom shook her head. No, that couldn't be her life. She was smart. She was a good student. She listened to her elders. She was filial and studious and *good*. She had to tell the truth.

But how was she supposed to explain that Mrs. Colton and Mrs. Abbot were right? That she hadn't messed up the room on her own, that it was the Monkey King they should go after. They would think she was crazy.

"Please don't suspend me." It was weak, but she had to say

something when Mrs. Colton was still waiting. "If it goes on my permanent record, I won't get into any good schools."

The corners of Mrs. Colton's mouth twitched. She looked like she was about to say something, then stopped and smiled. "I'm not going to suspend you."

Thom let out a breath.

"Only because you've been an excellent student so far, and I know you're still adapting to . . . life in Troy. Count this as a warning. But I will have to call your mom."

Thom's eyes flew wide open. No. No, no, no. This couldn't be happening. This was worse than suspension. Ma wouldn't understand. She would assume that Thom had done something wrong. Punish first, question after—that was the Vietnamese parenting method. Ma was going to make sure Thom never had the chance to misbehave ever again. Not that Thom had misbehaved before or even this time, but . . . she would never have the choice now.

"You can go," Mrs. Colton said, already turning to her computer. "You can probably still make it to second period. Here, I'll sign you a late pass."

11

AS THOM LEFT THE OFFICE, she bowed her head, hoping no one would see her, and almost walked into someone. Two someones. Wearing matching pairs of low-top pink Converse, jeans, and soccer jerseys.

Bethany and Sarah. Kathy's friends, and the stars of the soccer team. What were they doing out of class anyway, leaning against the overly cheerful yellow walls with their arms crossed, dressed almost exactly the same, in jean shorts that only barely met the school dress code and loose blue raglan sweaters? Bethany popped her gum and looked down at her shoe, where Thom had bumped into it, leaving a black smudge on the white toe cap.

"These are new," she said.

"What?" Thom rubbed at her cheeks. "Oh. I'm sorry."

But Bethany kept staring at Thom as if waiting for her to

do something. Thom inched away, eyeing the hall and wondering how she could escape.

"Well? Clean it," Bethany snapped.

Next to her, Sarah snorted and looked away.

"Your shoe?" Thom asked.

"No, your face."

Heat crept up Thom's neck. Bethany and Sarah eyed each other, and even though they tried hard not to, their laughs came out in breathy huffs.

Bethany kicked out her foot. "What are you waiting for? Clean it."

"It's just a smudge." Thom hated how small her voice was, whiny and high, like a baby's.

"I don't care if it's just a smudge," Bethany said. "These were brand-new and spotless before you showed up."

"Yeah," Sarah interjected obediently. "You ruin everything."

"Hey," Bethany said, and Sarah's face broke for a split second, as if afraid that she'd said something wrong. "She won that last game."

"Yeah, and hospitalized someone doing it." Sarah's grin morphed her face into something satanic, her white teeth flashing, sinking into her plumped, glossed lips.

Thom took a step back. They knew. First the Monkey King, and now them. Thom's life was officially over.

"Hey." Bethany snapped her fingers in Thom's face.

The door to the left opened, and Kathy walked out. They must have been waiting for her, but that still didn't explain why they were all wandering the halls when they should have been in class. Kathy looked at Thom with surprise, then at Bethany and Sarah.

"Hey." Even her voice was perfect, soft and melodic and not too sweet. She wasn't talking to Thom, but to her friends—Thom wasn't worth her notice. "Let's go."

Thom breathed a sigh of relief but caught herself when she saw Bethany still side-eyeing her.

"Not until she cleans my shoe."

"What?" Kathy looked down. "What's wrong with your shoe?"

"She got it dirty."

Kathy glanced at Thom, but it wasn't a nice glance. It was annoyed, irritated, like she couldn't believe she had to deal with this inconvenience.

"Come on, let's just go," she said. "We're already late."

"I said not yet." Bethany didn't take her attention off Thom. "You heard her—we're already late. Hurry up."

Thom looked at Kathy. She wasn't going to let this happen, was she? How could she just stand there and watch?

But Kathy turned away, walking a few steps from them, and crossed her arms.

Bethany didn't say anything else but waved a foot in the air.

"How?" Thom asked. This wasn't happening. Things like

this didn't happen. Any minute now, a teacher was going to make them go to class. This would have never happened back in West City, where security guards constantly monitored the halls. But not only that, this would never have happened because, back home, she would have had Thuy with her. She would have had her friends.

"Use your sleeve," Bethany said, as if it were obvious.

Kathy let out an annoyed sigh. "Whatever. I'll meet you guys there." She didn't look back as she disappeared down the hall.

Thom slowly pulled the sleeve of her hoodie over her wrist. She couldn't believe this was really happening, and Sarah was just going to watch it happen while Kathy slipped away like she couldn't be bothered, even though they both had to know it was wrong. Her eyes flooded as she tried to swallow the lump in her throat. What would Ma say if she could see her now? Ma was small but fierce, and there was no way she would have let some girls bully her, even if they were bigger and older. But Thom wasn't Ma. She wasn't that strong—not when it really mattered.

"Oh my God, just do it," Sarah said, grabbing Thom's shoulder and pushing her down. Her grip wasn't strong, so Thom moved, more out of surprise than anything. "Why are you so slow at everyth—Ow!" She let go of Thom and whirled around.

An apple—an apple?—rolled away from her foot. A red spot was already forming where it had struck her calf.

"What was that?"

Bethany and Sarah looked at each other, then at Thom.

Before any of them could do anything, a group of teachers came around the corner. Bethany and Sarah made a run for it, while Thom stood rooted to the spot.

One of the teachers—Mr. Charlton, who taught her Reading and Language Arts classes—made a beeline for her. Thom liked Mr. Charlton, even if he pronounced her name like it began with *th,* instead of the right way, like the name Tom.

"*Th*om," he said. "Shouldn't you be in class?"

That spurred her out of her shock. She couldn't think of anything to say, so she flashed her prison-blue late pass at him and ran away.

She was breathing too fast, her heart hammering, hands shaking. As she rounded a corner, sunlight spilled through the glass windows from the right. A door was opened at the end, and she ran through it, out into the courtyard.

Something pressed against Thom's shoulder, and she glanced up. The Monkey King was floating in the air beside her, one elbow resting on her head as he peered down at her. He was almost weightless, just heavy enough for her to know he was there.

"You could have killed those girls," he said, his teeth bared. "With your powers, you could have just—" He waved an arm, then punched a fist into his palm.

"Was that you?" she asked, still breathing hard. "The apple?"

"I could have hit her harder. Put a hole in that leg. Puny little girl didn't stand a chance."

"Don't hurt her," Thom said. That was the last thing she needed.

"Why?" He lifted off her shoulders and hovered backward, facing her. "You want to protect her even though she was going to beat you?"

"She couldn't beat me." It felt strange to say it out loud. Thom hated her superstrength, but it gave her a small thrill to know that Bethany really couldn't hurt her. At least not physically.

"That's right," the Monkey King said. He nodded, holding his fists up. "You could beat *her*. Show her—"

"No," Thom said, shaking off the thrill. "I'm not going to do that. I'm never going to do that. Besides, I wouldn't have run into them at all if you hadn't messed up that classroom— you threw a table at me! I had to go to the . . . principal's office." She said the last part in a whisper. Thom tried not to think about the fact that she was outside talking to the Monkey King instead of in class like she should have been.

"I wanted to prove that what I saw last night was real," he said.

"Real? Wait—" That was funny. She'd been thinking the exact same thing about him all morning.

"Yes. You are incredibly strong for someone so small. I've been alive for centuries, and girls like you are very rare."

Thom didn't know whether to take that as a compliment. On the one hand, it was a cool thing to hear, but on the other, she didn't want to be rare. She wanted to fit in and make friends. "What do you mean, girls like me? Are there others? Have you met others like me?"

He didn't answer. Instead, he leaned close and just batted his eyelashes. Thom took in a deep breath and let it out slowly. Why was she standing here, arguing with a monkey? She should be in class—she should get back before they noticed she was missing.

She turned around and started for the door.

"Wait." He appeared suddenly in front of her, and she had to stop, but she was so angry, she held up a fist.

To the Monkey King, her curled fingers must have looked like an infant's. A threat from a fly. A smile slowly spread across his mouth, eventually almost splitting his face in half. "It's only fair." He held out a cheek. "Go for it."

"What?"

"Hit me." His eyes sparkled; his giggles beat against her eardrums. "Use your power."

She dropped her hand, disgusted with him and with herself. Was she really threatening him? Had she really wanted to hit him, for real this time? "I'm never using my power."

His eyes widened. "Why?" he asked, horrified, like she had suggested she was going to steal candy from a baby.

"Because I could really hurt people. I really hurt someone already."

"Who?" he asked.

Thom swallowed. She should walk away; she shouldn't tell him anything.

But, no, she had a better idea. She should capture him and take him back to the temple, where he belonged. He was here now, and if she played her cards right, she could lure him there and no one would ever know she'd released him from imprisonment.

"This goalie." She told him about the soccer game, how Cassie Houghton was still in the hospital with broken ribs. That Thom had broken. The Monkey King listened quietly, his big brown eyes studying her face with concern.

"If anyone finds out . . . if Bethany or Sarah or Kathy or anyone knows, they'll tell the . . . the authorities. Or whoever. People who can take me away. Run tests on me. And the whole world will know. The whole world will think I'm . . ." She had only brought it up to gain his trust at first, but now she couldn't bring herself to finish the thought.

Something fuzzy touched her arm, and she jumped. It was only the Monkey King's fur. She looked up in surprise. He had leaned closer, one arm reaching around her shoulders.

A hug?

He was hugging her?

Thom didn't move. Ma rarely hugged her—it just wasn't

their thing. Vietnamese people bowed to one another a lot, and if there was an old person, Thom was forced to kiss them on the cheek, but they never hugged. It felt . . . weird—and he was a *monkey*.

But . . . it was also kind of nice. She'd expected him to smell bad, like Mochi when they hadn't bathed him in a while, but the Monkey King didn't. Maybe he had bathed, but he didn't smell like soap or flowers or anything obvious; he just smelled clean and . . . earthy. Like the forest. He was strong and sturdy as she let herself lean into him for just a second.

"I will protect you," he said. The lump in her throat threatened to grow larger and squeeze the breath out of her lungs. "If those girls try to hurt you, I will stop them."

But Thom pushed him away. He was a liar. A trickster god, a demon. She knew that she couldn't trust him. "It was your fault for getting me into trouble," she said.

Something flashed in his eyes, but it retreated when he smiled, the twinkle returning. "I'll make it up to you."

"How?" Thom asked, immediately suspicious.

"What do you want?"

She wanted her power taken away. She wanted to be normal. The Monkey King couldn't do that, could he? Besides, she wasn't about to make a deal with a demon-god.

But she could do something else instead. "Let's go back to the Thien Than Temple."

He smiled, close-lipped, eyes twinkling. "I can take you

anywhere on this earth, to the heavens even, and you want to go to some stupid temple?" He shook his head. "No. Something else."

"But you said you'll make it up to me."

He crossed his legs as he hovered a few feet above the ground, tilting his head upward. The set in his jaw told her there was no use arguing, and if she pushed it, he would know what she was trying to do.

"I can teach you to use your power. Control it," he said.

She didn't want to *use* it, she hated it! But if she could pretend to learn and then trick him back to the temple . . . "Okay. How?"

He scratched his chin, pulling out a few hairs in the process, but instead of tossing them aside, he shoved them back into his jaw. "Well? What do you hate most about your strength?"

"Everything."

"Impossible."

"It's like the worst thing ever. It's a curse."

"It is a gift!" He moved close, balanced as if on all fours in the air, still floating. Their noses bumped. "Hit me."

Thom didn't mean to actually do it, but he was way too close and he'd startled her. Her hand smacked his nose with a crunch, and he sailed to the ground, bouncing twice on his butt before skidding to a halt.

"Ah—sorry!" Thom cried. She reached to help him, but he bounded back into the air, giggling.

"Yes, yes! Again!"

"But . . . I don't want to learn to hurt people. I want to learn how *not* to."

"Before I can teach you that, I must assess the true extent of your power. Come on, hit me. I barely feel it. I am much stronger than you. To me, you are a mere bug. Your weak punches are like the buzzing of an insect—no, less. Like the flapping of a butterfly, or the ticklish crawling of a cockroach."

Now Thom found herself trying *not* to punch him.

A glint reflected in his eyes. "Do it. I know you want to."

She flexed her fingers and let out a breath. "No."

He cackled and flipped a few cartwheels. "I can show you how to control it. Teach you how to live with your power so you won't hurt people, even though some of them deserve it." He batted his eyelashes at her.

Ever since Thom had developed her freakish strength, she'd had no choice but to live with it, to touch things lightly, to avoid hugs and high fives, which sadly yet fortunately had been easier to do once she'd moved to Troy. But there'd been no one to teach her, because no one knew, and even if they did, how would they? The Monkey King was different. He seemed to relish her power, and he was just as strong, if not stronger. If anyone could show her how to live with this, it would be him.

He watched her closely, his eyes sharp and astute, and she had that sense that he was reading her thoughts. But that couldn't be one of his powers, could it?

"I know!" he said. "Toss me instead."

"What?"

"Hold your hands like this, like you are giving me a . . . a . . . What do you call it?" He mimed tossing something with both hands.

"A boost?"

"Yes! A boost! We'll see how far you can throw me."

That sounded, if not fun, at least less harmful and dangerous. "But you can fly."

"I won't. I want to see how far you can throw me."

"But what if someone sees?"

"I'll make myself invisible!"

"You can do that?"

The Monkey King beamed. "There is nothing that I cannot do! I am the master of the Seventy-Two Transformations! I can fly, I can breathe underwater, I can transform into any animal or being, and I can definitely make myself invisible."

"But *I* can see you."

"Of course, because I choose to let you see me. But no one else will be able to. Come on, come *on*! Where is your sense of adventure?" He skipped and tumbled weightlessly, too excited by his own idea. He grabbed her hands.

His energy was infectious, spreading a lightness over her, like she was the one who could float on air. Thom realized she was smiling, the muscles in her face relaxing and stretching, unused to the movement for so long. The Monkey King grinned back, positioned her hands into a scoop so he could place his feet on her palms, crouching down and easing his weight into her hands until she knew he was no longer flying.

"Ready?" Thom asked.

He chuckled, waving his hands. She took that as a yes and threw him. He burst upward but didn't go far, rising only a few feet above Thom before landing nimbly on all fours.

"Again! Put more strength into it this time."

She tried harder the next two times, though admittedly not her hardest—who knew where she could send the Monkey King? Into space? She hoped she wasn't that strong, and she knew he'd told her that she couldn't really hurt him, but it was impossible to let go of that instinct, that fear of seriously harming another being with her strength.

"Stronger!" he demanded as he stepped into her hands for the fourth time. "As strong as you can."

"What if I toss you so far you don't come back?"

"You won't get rid of me that easily." He ruffled her hair, and she shook her head, unused to such oddly affectionate behavior. Taking a deep breath, this time she tossed him much harder. She winced in fear, but she just launched him farther than before, higher than any of the nearby buildings, before he fell back down gracefully. This time, he walked back to her side, no more giggles or cartwheels. It was unsettling to see him so still and serious.

"You're still holding back." His tone had changed, his eyes intense. "Do not. Show me what you can do."

"But—"

"No more buts, Thom-Thom." He slashed a palm at her. "I am Sun Wukong, the Great Sage of Heaven, the powerful, handsome Monkey King, and I do not associate with weaklings." His shoulders square, his feet apart, he looked ready for a fight.

A shiver chased down her neck. He looked like the Monkey King she knew from the legends: powerful, tough, and undefeatable. Something about his stance and the way he looked at her, full of challenge, made her want to prove something.

"Okay." She clasped her hands together. "Let's do this."

As if she'd turned on a switch, his grin returned, and he skipped and jumped onto her hands.

"Brace yourself," she said, her chest filling with elation. He was about to see what she was truly capable of.

"I am bracing." He bounced. She lowered her hands and bent her knees. And then, with a shriek of laughter she couldn't hold back, she threw him as hard as she could. Her hands in the air, she watched as he rocketed up, up, up, becoming a small speck, until she couldn't see him anymore and the bright, clear sky became almost blinding.

It was a long time before the Monkey King returned.

12

THOM DIDN'T KNOW HOW LONG she had stood there waiting, when the bell rang shrilly, making her jump.

Oh God, oh no—she'd skipped the rest of her classes. She
was supposed to go to Social Studies, but she'd spent the whole
afternoon playing games with the Monkey King! What was
she thinking?

She hurried from the courtyard and joined the chaos of
students rushing out of the school. A teacher standing next
to the open door, making sure nothing too rowdy happened,
looked right at Thom. Did she know? Could she tell Thom
had skipped? Thom didn't have that teacher for any classes,
but all teachers seemed to have the superpower to smell out
misbehavior. She bent her head and shrugged her shoulders,
wishing she could become invisible like the Monkey King.

"Hey, Thom!" a voice shouted after her as she headed to
the pick-up area. It was Kha, who didn't seem to notice how

people turned and stared as he ran up to her. "What happened? I thought we were going to meet up in the library."

"Oh, I . . . forgot." She had never agreed to meet him in the first place, but at his hurt look, guilt washed over her. Maybe he wasn't such a bad guy. After all, he was the first person who'd shown any interest in being her friend since she'd moved here. "Sorry."

"That's okay," he said. Even though the expression on his face told her it wasn't okay at all. "I just wanted to give you this."

A gift? They hardly knew each other. She held out a hand, and he placed a piece of paper into it. It was thin but sturdy, almost like woven cloth. There were words on it, written in red calligraphy in a language she couldn't read.

"A bookmark?" she asked.

"A lucky token. My grandparents gave it to me."

She felt uneasy and tried to give it back. "Shouldn't you keep it then?"

"I have a couple." He grinned. He was being so nice—why? What did he want from her? Was it a trick? "I thought you could use it. Tape it over your bed, and it will bring you luck."

She tucked the token into a textbook inside her backpack. "Thanks. I, um, don't have anything for you, though."

"No worries." He looked up at the row of cars. "Oh, my ride's here. See you, Thom!"

His bright smile startled Thom into waving a little too

vigorously, so she tucked her hand into her pocket. It felt as if the whole school had seen that exchange between her and the new cool kid, and that they were still staring at her as she walked with her head down.

Ma was waiting for her in the designated pick-up lane. Something was wrong. Both hands gripped the steering wheel as she faced forward, not turning, when Thom slipped into the passenger seat. The air was thick with invisible explosives, air mines, as if any sudden movement would cause the car to combust. Thom was afraid.

"Hi, Ma," Thom said, reaching for her seat belt. Maybe she should make a bolt for it. She had nowhere to go, but the streets were probably safer right now anyway, judging from the clench of her mother's jaw.

Ma's breath rushed out her nostrils like steam, filling the car with red-hot tension. "You know who called me today?"

Oh no. Thom had completely forgotten, distracted by the Monkey King.

The silence stretched between them, and Thom kept wondering if she should say something, but nothing came to mind. Should she apologize? But that would be admitting she'd done something wrong, and, well, okay, she'd done a lot of things wrong today. But she wanted to know which one Ma was upset about the most before she apologized.

Should she try to explain about the Monkey King now? Ma was her ma—she wouldn't think Thom was crazy, would she?

Thom let herself imagine it. She wouldn't stop at just the Monkey King. She could tell Ma about her strength. It would be such a relief. Ma knew the answer to everything. She knew how to fix any problem. She would believe Thom. And if she didn't, Thom could prove to her how strong she was, and Ma would know how to make it disappear. She might even know why Thom was like this.

"They say you trash the classroom? Why, Thom?"

Thom winced. Ma hadn't called her cưng, which was never a good sign.

"The poor teacher probably spend lots of time to make the class neat and clean—and now you disrespect her? What will people think? And they say you never got back to your last class? Why, Thom? I don't understand."

Thom shrugged further into herself. Each time Ma said her name felt like a stab to her chest.

"You broke a calculator!" Ma burst out, and Thom jumped. Any thought of Ma understanding and fixing her problems disappeared. Ma believed in fixing your own problems, even if you were only eleven. "I know you're unhappy—are you sad about soccer? About moving?"

Thom opened her mouth to answer, but Ma kept going.

"There is adjustment period. You'll get used to it. Make new friends. No need to break expensive calculator! Those things cost more than your phone."

"I'm sorry." The words pushed at the seams of her mouth

despite how hard she'd tried to keep them in. She didn't have anything to really be sorry about, when the Monkey King was the one who'd done all of that, made the mess, broke the calculator. But Ma was in no mood to listen to anything preposterous, and that was exactly how Thom's story would sound to her. Ridiculous. Made up. "It was an accident."

Ma seethed quietly, the bones of her knuckles wiggling beneath the pale skin of her fingers. She'd forgotten to put on her driving gloves, which she wore more to protect herself from getting tan than from the heat of the steering wheel. As they navigated away from the school, Thom knew it was coming, but it still hurt when Ma said it out loud.

"I take away your phone."

Ma had gotten it for her in case of emergencies, but it was still cool to have, the one cool thing about her. She didn't want to lose it. What if she needed to talk to Thuy?

At the thought of her friend, her chest gave one of those painful twists, sending a sharpness down her veins all the way to her wrists.

"But Ma—"

"And you're grounded." She paused for effect, but Thom was still reeling from the news about her phone. Besides, being grounded in Georgia was a different story than being grounded in California. There was nothing to do here. She had no friends and never went anywhere except the library where her mom worked. "And you do more chores around the house," Ma continued, piling on the punishment like she realized it wasn't enough, "until you finish paying back the calculator."

Thom leaned closer to the window. Ma kept talking, launching into full lecture mode about embarrassment and lack of honor, about the shame Thom had caused. Thom looked at the sky. Something—a plane, a bird, too far away for her to see clearly—shot out of a cloud, leaving behind dots of white. It could have been the Monkey King, which made her smile. The fun moment they'd had when she'd tossed him into the air felt like it had happened a year ago, so distant now in the somber mood inside the car.

She stopped smiling. Shook her head. There was no reason for her to smile at the thought of the Monkey King. She still didn't trust him. Okay, so she'd had a lot of fun today. There was still something about him that made her uneasy.

But even though she knew this, she couldn't help looking up at the white spots of clouds, wondering if he would be back.

◆ ◆ ◆

Dinner was extremely tense. Usually, Ma peppered Thom with questions about school and homework and soccer practice, while Thom tried her best to answer with as few words as possible. But tonight, Ma was quiet. The scowl on her face was so tense it seemed to tighten the air between them.

Thom kept her head down. She held her chopsticks

correctly and ate every grain of rice and piece of soggy vegetable without complaining. Still, Ma didn't speak.

Thom glanced up. Ma wasn't eating. She hadn't even picked up her chopsticks. Her food was probably cold. A precious piece of meat had fallen off her bowl onto the table, and she didn't care. She did not care. About a piece of meat.

Things were worse than Thom had thought.

"Ma?" Thom's voice barely penetrated the shield of anger around her mother.

Ma looked at her. Thom had meant to say sorry. Again. But the scowl on Ma's forehead was contagious. The toxic atmosphere clouding Thom's lungs made her throat itch with frustration. She was always good, had always been as perfect as she could manage. She got good grades, behaved in class, even played soccer when all she'd wanted to do this season was quit. And yet, it was never good enough. *She* would never be good enough.

"Why did we move here?" Thom asked, the lump in her throat burning.

Mom tsked. "I told you already. I got good job."

"Not any better than your old job."

Ma now worked at Troy University Library, which wasn't much different than West City College Library, was it?

"This job better and pay more." Ma waved a hand dismissively and picked up her chopsticks. But she still didn't eat.

"How much more?" Thom asked.

Chopsticks clattered onto the table. "Why you talking back so much, hah? You didn't get into enough trouble today?"

The frustration Thom felt flushed away, shoved aside by the fear of Ma's wrath. Thom slumped in her seat, but try as she might, she couldn't completely push her anger down. She *hadn't* been talking back. That was just the term Ma used when she didn't want to answer Thom's questions. And Thom wasn't ready to let it go.

"You're not happy, either," she said quietly, as if speaking softly might keep Ma from getting angrier. "Are you?"

Ma covered her face with one hand. She couldn't be crying, though—she never cried. She took in a deep shuddering breath. "It's not about being happy or unhappy."

"Then why? Why did we move here? Why do we stay? We both hate it."

"*To keep you safe!*" Ma practically shouted. Then she sighed, placing both palms down on the surface of the table. "It's safer here. Schools are smaller. Teachers can pay more attention to you."

"Safe from what? There wasn't anything dangerous at home." And even if there was, Thom was pretty sure nothing could hurt her now that she was superstrong.

"How you know? You're just a kid. What if . . . what if someone . . ." Ma waved a hand, searching for the right words, or maybe making something up. "Someone try to take you away from me? Hah?"

"Who?" It was one of those paranoid Ma things. The dishes were never clean enough, the rooms too dusty; the carpet needed to be vacuumed every day because of the bacteria. Her daughter was never truly safe.

Except. Except maybe this was a real fear. Maybe someone *could* take Thom away. "Is it Ba?" she said.

"What?" Ma asked, too loud, too fast. Too scared. "Who say anything about your ba?"

"Does Ba want to take me away? Is that why we moved? Did he come looking for me?" Elation lifted the heaviness that had settled over her since the car ride home. Her dad had tried to find her! He still loved her, wanted her, wanted to be in her life.

Thom usually avoided asking questions about her father. She used to, but Ma would get annoyed every time she asked about him—and not just annoyed for a moment, but for *the whole day*, like any mention of him was a curse. Then, Ma always got a migraine afterward and had to lie in bed, grumpy and sullen.

Thom had learned to stop asking about him, and then to stop thinking about him completely. But now, all her questions, wondering about what it would be like if he had been in their life, flooded her. She wanted to know. Why couldn't Ma just tell her? Thom was old enough to understand now.

Would Ba have cooked for them? Would they be eating microwaved meals and frozen dinners if he were there?

"No! No." Ma stood, hands braced on the table. "That's nonsense. Your ba is not . . . He can't—" She stopped talking abruptly, her face full of horror.

"What do you mean, he can't?" Thom stood, too. If her father couldn't . . . whatever it was Ma had almost said, then did that mean he had always wanted to? That maybe he did want to be in Thom's life, but something was stopping him?

But what? He was a grown-up. They could do whatever they wanted. So why couldn't he be with Thom and Ma?

"Enough, Thom. I don't want to talk about this anymore."

"Did you make him leave?"

"No—why would I do that?"

"I don't know. You never talk about him." They were both breathing fast. Thom pressed her lips together. "Did you love him?"

"Who you think I am? You think I have baby with a man I don't love?" Ma started cleaning, picked up her chopsticks and bowl.

"So what happened? Did you kick him out?"

"You think I kick out your father and make it so you grow up without one?"

"I don't know!" Thom gripped the sides of her head. "I don't know what you would do!"

Ma stepped back, surprised by Thom's outburst. "I would never have done that," she said. "Not if it meant you wouldn't have a ba."

"So he just left then? He didn't want . . . to stay?" He hadn't wanted Thom.

"Oh, Thommy." But even though she used Thom's nickname, her words came out in a furious huff. Ma closed her eyes briefly. "We can't always do what we want. Sometimes, we have to do what's right. But he loves you. He loved both of us. He couldn't stay. That's all."

But that couldn't be all. It wasn't that simple. Why didn't Ma want to tell her? She was usually so honest, even brutally blunt at times. Thom's friends' moms had always sugarcoated everything, but Ma had always answered Thom's questions with frightening directness. It was probably the librarian in her, the need to give Thom all the information she had. Except when it had anything to do with Ba, of course.

Thom was drained. She sat down. Ma hesitated, then set her bowl and chopsticks on the table and walked around to Thom's chair. She placed a hand on Thom's shoulder.

"When I was pregnant with you, you know what I crave more than anything?" Ma asked.

Thom exhaled and shook her head.

"Lemon. Anything with lemon. Or sour. Cookies, star fruit, unripe mango. And you know what your ba did?"

Again, Thom shook her head, biting back the bitterness, the unfairness, because she could not know. Because her father wasn't here, and there was something Ma wasn't telling her.

"He would make me tea. Not just tea, but he set up

elaborate tea servings with the little cup and the teapot and saucer. He bake lemon cookies. He was always baking new things, trying new recipes, coming up with his own creations."

Thom looked up at her, absorbing the new information, tucking the details somewhere safe so she could replay them later. Ma had never spoken so much about Ba before.

"He loved to make me lemon cookies. He cut up star fruit for me. He even bought peaches, giant peaches the size of cantaloupe."

"Peaches?" So random. They never kept peaches in the house.

"Oh, yes, he loved peaches. Always smelled like it, too." Ma sighed, squeezing Thom's shoulder. "If he was here, he'd make you tea and bake you cookies, too. He just . . . can't be."

Thom wanted more. It was like a sip of milk tea and boba. She couldn't stop with just one taste—she needed the whole cup.

But Ma was done. Her hand left Thom's shoulder, and Thom could hear her footsteps padding softly out of the dining room. Thom could only keep wondering at what life with her father might have been, why he had left, and what made Ma so scared that she'd moved them to the other side of the country.

13

AT LUNCH A FEW DAYS later, someone set a tray in front of her—right in front of her, even though the entire table was empty, and they could have sat at the end. Thom looked up. Kha, her neighbor. They had classes together, but Thom still hadn't really talked to him. Mostly because she still felt weird about what people might think if they hung out: that just because they were both Asians, by default they had to be friends. The cafeteria quieted down, like everyone had turned to watch them, as if Thom and Kha were performing in some stage play.

"Ham sandwich, huh?" he asked.

Thom nodded.

"Rice and beef," he said, indicating the packed lunch on his tray. "I keep telling Grandma to stop cooking with fish sauce, but she says fish sauce is the backbone of our culture."

He opened the paper bag and wrinkled his nose. "No wonder no one wants to eat with me."

Thom's mouth was glued shut. Seconds ticked by, and she couldn't think of a thing to say, even though she knew he was being extra nice. She had seen Kha in the cafeteria before, sitting with the more popular kids, like he had been their friends for years. So why was he here now, talking to her, lying about not having anyone to sit with?

"You can just nod," he said, as if reading her mind. He smiled. "Or go 'hmm.' So I know you heard me."

She nodded.

"Ugh." He popped the lid of his Tupperware, and the smell of fish sauce wafted out. "How come your mom doesn't make you bring Vietnamese food?"

Because Thom had asked her not to, because Thom thought that not eating rice dishes would make her more normal, because she'd wanted one less thing to be made fun of about. But she didn't want to explain that.

"She doesn't cook," she said. "It's one of the reasons she doesn't have a husband."

Kha snorted through a mouthful of rice. "What?"

Thom shrugged. "It's just something she said. Her mom always told her that to catch a good husband, she had to learn how to cook—and she hates cooking. So she decided she didn't want a husband and had me instead."

He paused. "What do you know about your father?"

"I don't have one," Thom said.

"You mean you don't know who he is."

"I mean I don't have one." Thom was usually eager to talk about her father, but that was only with Ma. For some reason, talking about it with Kha was agonizing, especially after the last conversation she'd had with her mom about Ba.

"Everyone has a father," he said, peering at her.

"I don't," Thom said, clenching her jaw. "Do you?"

She immediately felt guilty. She was pretty sure he lived with his grandparents. She had seen them out exercising a lot, swinging their arms while speed walking up and down the street. They were spritely for people who looked like they had lived through the Vietnam War, but they were definitely too old to be his parents.

Kha nodded, but he was stuffing his face, so he couldn't answer. Where were his parents? Working? Thom knew a few kids in West City whose parents still lived and worked in Vietnam while their kids grew up in America without them. Something about being better for their future. Which was probably true, but she doubted Ma would send her to live in a country alone, even if that meant Thom would get better grades.

"I've been meaning to ask you," he said, breaking the awkward silence, "do you have a partner yet, for Culture Day?"

She'd completely forgotten about Culture Day, and now her skin was all tingly from the dread of presenting in front of her classmates. The teacher who came up with this idea must have hated kids and loved seeing them suffer. "No, not yet," she admitted.

"Me neither!" Dimples poked in on his plump cheeks. Of course on top of being confident and stylish, he also had to have adorable dimples. His canines were sharper than normal, giving him the scary but cool appearance of a wolf, or a vampire. "Want to be partners?"

A multitude of feelings rushed through Thom. Relief—she wouldn't be that loser who had to be assigned a partner—but then, suspicion. Why would someone like Kha want to partner with someone like her? The loner sitting at an empty lunch table?

She looked down at the few grains of rice that had spilled out of his bento box, and it clicked. He wanted to partner for Culture Day because they were from the same *culture*. Duh. She was surprised at how disappointed she felt.

"Okay." Her voice was small.

"What?"

"Yeah. I mean, sure, let's be partners," she said. It would be an easy A at least.

"Oh, great! I have lots of ideas. We could perform a play or a dance. Or maybe recite a poem?"

She sat up straighter. "Um, I thought it was supposed to be an art project?"

"Those are forms of art," he said, laughing.

"Can't we just do a poster? Or a diorama?"

His smile faded. "But . . . I mean, sure, but everyone else will be doing the same thing."

She exhaled. "Good!"

"Can we dress up at least?" he asked with an eyebrow raised. He grinned.

Thom wanted to groan. "Um."

"Just think about the extra credit!"

Thom didn't need the extra credit with her grades, but she couldn't resist the allure of it, either, like salted-caramel chocolate-fudge cake even when she was already full.

He popped open a box of green-tea panda cookies. "Want one?"

She hesitated. He smiled, his dimples deepening. He held out a panda cookie, its eye-crinkling smile matching his.

"Sure."

◆ ◆ ◆

Maybe the Monkey King was gone for good.

Thom had waited at her window every night, hoping for a sign of him. She hadn't been able to stop thinking about how he'd taught her to use her strength, how she'd been able to toss him a bit higher each time, how maybe, just maybe, she could learn more about her power—how to control it, use it. Maybe her superstrength wasn't so bad after all. Maybe she could learn to live with it, with his help.

Things at home weren't too great, what with Ma still angry about the calculator. Thom had to do all the dishes, and Ma was serious about *all* of them. Usually, Thom only had to load the dishwasher after dinner, but now she also had to put the clean dishes away, rescrub the ones that weren't clean enough, and reorganize the utensil drawer.

Ma checked her homework every night and made her turn over all her graded quizzes. She got one wrong on a spelling test, and Ma added an extra hour to her study time, which meant she had about five minutes of freedom before bed every night.

Life was exhausting.

To make matters worse, soccer wasn't getting any better. At practice that afternoon, they formed two lines for a drill where two players passed the ball back and forth, ending with the player on the left taking the scoring goal.

At her old school, Thom and her friends always lined up so they would partner with one another, but here, there was no point. Thom didn't bother checking the line to see who she would come up against. The scent of freshly mown grass had filled Thom's nostrils, the wind blowing through her hair and transporting her to a different time.

She'd imagined herself back on the field in West City. Her team's uniforms were red and black instead of blue, white, and gold, and older than the ones they had at Troy. The West City jerseys didn't have their names printed on the back, just the number so that the school could reuse them next year. But she didn't need to see TRAN printed on the back of Thuy's jersey to know when her best friend was running in front of her.

"Ball!" Thuy would call, and Thom passed to her without hesitating, weaving through the opposing players and emerging with no one blocking her.

"Ball!" she'd call to Thuy, who passed to her at lightning speed. Thom dribbled down the field, her own name in her ears as other players and the moms sitting in the bleachers cheered her on. She knew Thuy was right behind as she pulled her foot back and shot the winning goal.

Thom couldn't stop grinning, turning, jumping, hugging all her teammates, high-fiving her best friend, waving at Ma in the crowd.

She was so lost in the memory that she didn't realize it was her turn for the drill, didn't see Sarah until it was too late, didn't see the ball until it loomed in her vision, too big, too fast for her to dodge. It smacked her in the nose.

She was more shocked than hurt, stumbling. Her foot slipped on a wet patch of grass, where that one broken sprinkler never shut off, and she fell, landing on her back in something squishy and wet.

Clumps of mud dripped off her neck and arms, and water soaked into her T-shirt. She touched her hair to inspect the damage.

Snickers started behind her, small at first, then louder,

stronger. Soon, the entire team was laughing. Sarah pinched her nose like Thom had fallen into poop and not mud, and ran back to the others.

Thom froze. What was she supposed to do now? She couldn't finish the drill without Sarah, and the other girls had given up altogether, clutching their middles like they were trying not to pee. Coach Pendergrass's mouth was all pinched, but she kept her composure. Finally, she cleared her throat loudly.

"No, do you have something else you can change into?"

Thom nodded.

"Okay, get cleaned up. But," she added as Thom turned stiffly toward the lockers, "if you don't . . . Why don't we call it a day, yeah? You can have your mom pick you up early if you want."

Thom took a deep breath. Going home early would show that Sarah had finally gotten to her, but the idea of coming back to the field made her mouth dry.

"Just . . ." Coach seemed to run out of words. She waved at Thom to leave, shaking her head.

◆ ◆ ◆

Thom ran fully clothed into the showers and turned the heat up full blast, gritting her teeth to fight back the lump in her throat. Even though the locker room was empty, she kept hearing laughter, echoing off the walls and hitting her in the gut until she was gasping for breath, water barely drowning out the sound of her sobs.

"Thom?" a voice called from outside the shower curtain. She bit her lip and wiped at her eyes. "Thom?" She huddled against the faucet and didn't answer. "It's Kathy."

Somehow, that didn't make her feel better. Kathy might not have joined in with Bethany and Sarah in tormenting Thom, but she'd done nothing to stop them. None of her teammates did, but Kathy would have been the one Bethany and Sarah listened to.

"I brought you a towel," Kathy said, her voice hesitant. "I noticed you didn't have one on the hook."

Thom wiped the hair off her face and down her back, wringing it out, her movements robotic and numb. She reached for the faucet and twisted it off. Water dripped, the only sound for miles. And Kathy's breathing. Her eagerness to get out of there as palpable as rain. What was she doing here? Coming to pick on Thom some more, to finish what her friends had started?

"Why are you here?" Thom asked.

Kathy didn't respond at first, like she was shocked at Thom's tone. Thom hadn't meant to sound sharp, but she was cold and embarrassed, and wanted to be alone. When Kathy spoke, her voice wasn't exactly kind, just weary.

"I wanted to make sure you were okay. It sucks, what Bethany and Sarah are doing."

At least she had noticed it. Acknowledged it. At least Thom wasn't crazy or ten times clumsier than normal. But this still wasn't going to help. Not unless Kathy did something about it or told her friends to stop. And she wasn't going to do that. She wasn't going to risk her popularity and her friends' loyalty for someone like Thom.

"You shouldn't make it that easy for them," Kathy said.

"Yeah? How?" Thom asked.

"Don't pay attention to them. Ignore them when they laugh."

"You think all this time, I've been *letting* them bully me?" Thom was tired. She wanted Kathy to leave so she could call Ma to come and get her. So she could go home and curl up in her bed.

Kathy sighed. Thom practically heard her rolling her eyes. "No, obviously. But you . . . are just so . . ."

"I don't get it," Thom said. "If they hate me because I'm Asian, why are they friends with you?"

Kathy made a funny sound, as if to remind Thom that she was crazy if she thought she could compare herself to someone like her. "It's not because you're Asian. It's because you're so . . ."

"So what?" Thom's wet clothes were getting colder, making her shiver, so her words came out wobbly.

"*Weird,*" Kathy said.

Weird? Thom stayed quiet. She was smart but not too nerdy, she never bothered anyone, or at least not deliberately.

All she'd wanted was to play soccer and make new friends, or if not that, then at least to *fit in*.

"And it's annoying," Kathy went on. "You make it easy to—"

"To what?" But Thom knew. She made it easier for them to hate her.

Kathy exhaled loudly again. "To pick on you."

Thom's teeth started chattering together.

"Here, just take the towel before you get sick or something," Kathy said.

Thom reached for the curtain, but she pulled too hard, and the metal rod broke off the wall. Kathy shrieked as it fell toward her, but Thom yanked on the curtain before the rod hit her head. It flew away and clattered loudly on the ground.

They stared wide-eyed at each other. Kathy's gaze fell to the rod on the floor, then to Thom's hands, mouth open. She clutched the towel to her chest, looking small in the oversized T-shirt and shorts she wore to practice. Water had splashed onto her knee-high socks.

"Are you okay?" Thom asked. *It was an accident. Please let Kathy think it was a normal accident.*

Kathy looked at the spot on the wall where the rod had broken clean off.

"That thing must have been, like, so old," Kathy said, but her voice wavered.

"Yeah," Thom agreed quickly. Neither of them said

anything else. Water dripped off Thom's clothes, each drop like a ticking clock counting the awkward seconds of silence.

"Here," Kathy said, holding the towel with outstretched arms, as if trying to stay as far from Thom as possible. "I better get back to practice."

Thom took the towel and wanted to call out to her, to make up more excuses about the broken curtain rod. But Kathy had sprinted away, her cleats clicking on the floor.

14

KATHY KNEW, SHE MUST HAVE figured it out.

But, no, it was an accident. Curtain rods break all the time.

Then why had Kathy looked so scared?

Thom didn't know what to do. She dreaded school the next day, dreaded facing Kathy, who must have told Bethany and Sarah everything. Thom needed to talk to Kathy alone, explain that it really was an accident.

Thom's nose was dripping later that night, and when Ma took her temperature, it read 103 degrees, which let Thom off the hook for doing the dishes. It also ended their feud. Ma was back to being overworried. She tucked the blankets around Thom and placed a cup of cocoa on her nightstand.

"My poor cưng," she muttered as she fluffed Thom's pillow. "I get you another hot water bottle, okay?"

"No, it's too hot," Thom whined.

"It burn out the fever," Ma insisted.

"Ma, I will die," Thom said, weakly batting Ma's hands away.

"*So* dramatic."

"Please. I just want to sleep."

Ma tsked, but took the hint, tucking Thom so tightly in her blankets she felt like an overstuffed burrito. Ma turned to leave the room, but something caught her eye. "What is this?" she asked, her tone full of delight. Thom glanced over to see her books scattered across her desk, Ma holding up a piece of paper with cursive lettering on it—the bookmark from Kha. She'd forgotten about it. "Where you get it?"

"Kha gave it to me."

"Your friend?" Ma looked like she was about to hug her. "You make friend at school?"

"Uh, I mean, maybe. He's our new neighbor."

"Vietnamese?"

Thom couldn't remember the last time Ma looked so happy. Maybe when she'd wanted to shop for a new áo dài.

"This is a lucky token," Ma said, grabbing some tape. "It will help protect you from bad spirits and demons." She stuck it to the wall above Thom's head, the only decoration on the otherwise barren walls. Instead of arguing, Thom closed her eyes. Her body was achy, and her head felt as if she'd been dunked underwater for too long. Ma turned off the lights and closed the door.

Thom tossed and turned for most of the night. She looked

up at the lucky token taped on her wall. Ma said it protected from demons. Was that why the Monkey King hadn't been back? Was the token keeping him away? She hadn't seen him since Kha had given it to her.

That was silly—the token couldn't be strong enough to keep out someone as powerful as the Monkey King. But she reached up and took it down anyway, turning it over in her hands. Then she ripped it in half, to be safe.

Suddenly completely exhausted, she fell back into bed.

Just as she was drifting off, a voice startled her.

"Poor sweet Thom," the Monkey King said, his words punctuated by monkeyish *ooh-ooh*s.

Thom sat up, smiling. "I thought you were gone forever," she said.

"Me? Leave you?" He giggled. "Of course not. But what's wrong with you? You're all hot."

"I have a fever."

"Sickness?" His hand pressed her forehead. "Will you die?"

She laughed. "No, weirdo. It's just a cold. Maybe a few days."

"Days? No, no, no. You should get better now. I need your help with something."

"I'm sick," she protested.

"I know how to make you feel better, little Thom. Thom the Strong. Instantly better. Not in days."

She tried to sit up, but her body ached with each movement. The touch of the sheets on her feverish skin made her groan.

"There is a magical waterfall. My home. It has healing powers. It will make you one hundred percent again."

She closed her eyes. The world was spinning, but her bed was warm and the Monkey King was here to keep her safe.

His eyes caught the moonlight for a moment as he hopped down to the floor. "Shall we go?"

"Where?"

"To my waterfall. So you can drink from the healing waters."

"But . . . I can't go," Thom said.

"Why not?"

"I . . . My mom . . ."

"She's asleep. I checked," he said, waving a hand dismissively.

"You . . . what?" The idea of the Monkey King hovering in her mom's room was horrifying. Intrusive.

"Just to make sure you are both safe. I was watching over you."

"Safe from what?" What did the Monkey King need to protect them from?

He didn't answer. "Come with me. You feel like fire." He touched her forehead, the hair on the back of his hand cool and soft. "I will make it better."

It was difficult to think of a good argument. Her thoughts were like slippery fish, darting quickly out of reach. "It's cold," she said.

He grabbed a coat from her closet and threw it over her shoulders. A scarf and a beanie followed—Thom had forgotten she owned them. She looked like she was dressed for Antarctica, when it was probably at least 60 degrees outside.

Still, as he pulled her out of bed and opened the window, the half of her face not covered by her scarf and beanie felt chilled. He placed her arms over his shoulders and made her clasp her hands together.

"Hang on tight!" he called, and before she could stop him or protest or even think about what to do next, he launched them both out of the window.

Thom clung to his back so hard, it should have hurt. As they lifted into the air, her stomach dipped and her heart climbed to her throat. They floated through the dark, over her backyard, which was huge compared to the one they had in West City.

Something caught her eye, a movement in a tree.

Thom looked over her shoulder as the Monkey King flew. Someone was there. She knew it. A boy. Her age.

Kha?

What was her neighbor doing in her backyard?

He was holding something in his hands, torn scraps of red paper, his face turned up. He saw them. He could see them. No one had ever spotted them before. Thom knew the Monkey King could become invisible, so she'd assumed he hid them both from view. But Kha had stared straight at her, had seen past the enchantment.

Thom turned to tell the Monkey King, but they were rushing forward so fast that all she could do was grit her teeth and hang on. The wind froze her hot skin; the cold seeped through her scarf and beanie. Her teeth chattered. She buried her face into the back of the Monkey King's neck.

Just when she thought she couldn't take it any longer, the wind wasn't as cold or strong anymore. The air had grown warmer.

She looked up and gasped. They were flying above fluffy white clouds, the sun breaking across waves of mist.

The Monkey King slowed enough that the wind no longer deafened her, and she breathed out in awe.

"Beautiful, right?" he asked.

"Where are we?"

They broke through the wall of white mist. Below them, a green mountain, hills stacked against one another on an island surrounded by the bluest, clearest water she'd ever seen, even in pictures. The island was full of luscious greenery, trees with beautiful leaves. Something about it just seemed *alive*, like beneath the canopy lived a world of creatures.

"This island is called the Mountain of a Hundred Giants,"

the Monkey King said. "My home is just over there, the cave behind the waterfall."

"Why is it called that?"

He *ooh*ed curiously. "That's a good question."

"Did a hundred giants live here?" she asked.

They must not have been too gigantic or maybe there hadn't been many of them, because the island wasn't a big island. It reminded Thom of Catalina, near Long Beach—Ma had taken Thuy and her there once—except this island didn't have any houses or docks or people. No one was around.

That creepy-crawly feeling went up Thom's neck, and she fought against the fuzziness in her mind. "Why are we here?" she asked. Now that the wind wasn't freezing her cheeks, she grew hot again, sweaty in her coat and scarf and beanie. Her nose was still stuffy, and her head felt like enormous hands were squeezing from both sides, threatening to pop it like a grape.

"So you can drink from the healing waters and be cured of your sickness. Hold on tight."

She threw her arms around his shoulders and buried her face into the slope of his neck once again. His fur was warm and smelled surprisingly pleasant, faintly like peaches and a bit like sand and salt.

She opened her eyes just in time to see the waterfall they were about to crash into. "Monkey King! Watch out!"

"Don't worry!" He laughed. "We're finally home!"

Before she could ask him what he meant, the freezing-cold water hit her in the face, soaking into her beanie and scarf. She gulped in breath after breath as they emerged on the other side of the torrent. She slid off his back, sputtering. The Monkey King giggled and bounced off the stone walls, shaking water off his fur every time he paused long enough.

"You could have warned me!" She snatched her hat off, then grabbed her scarf, but it was stuck in a wet tangle around her neck. "I thought we were going to crash into a cliff or something!"

"Here, let me help you before you strangle yourself." He reached for the scarf slowly, as if approaching a wild animal, and unwound it, then held the soaking cloth out with both hands. She glared at him, grabbed the scarf, and wrung it out. Luckily, her coat was water-resistant and had kept the rest of her dry, but her hair was drenched.

It was only then that she stopped to take in their surroundings. They were in a tunnel. Light was reflecting off the waterfall behind them like crystals, glowing on the damp walls. It wasn't even that cold.

The Monkey King must have seen Thom's anger disappearing, turning into awe, because he took her hand in his surprisingly warm and dry one, and pulled her down the tunnel. They stepped into an underground clearing, a brightly lit cave with holes in the roof, where sunlight filtered through.

The sound of flowing water echoed throughout, bouncing off the stone walls, and Thom had the sense that they were somehow inside a river, or maybe underneath it. Water fell in shimmering curtains all around them. Green moss cushioned their steps, and colorful flowers decorated their path, broken only by a small babbling stream that disappeared somewhere between the tall, lush trees at the edge of the cave. A rainbow— an underground rainbow!—arched over the stream, and butterflies fluttered all around, landing on the flowers and grass.

Bright daylight now illuminated the cave, shaded by the broken patterns of the pocked roof, even though they had just come from night. But Thom was sure not much time had passed, less than an hour since they'd left her bedroom.

But that wasn't even the strangest part. The clearing was full of monkeys.

She looked from the Monkey King to the others. They walked a bit like the Monkey King but couldn't stand completely upright, like he could. And while the Monkey King had always seemed more human, like a man dressed in fur, these monkeys didn't have the same sharpness in their eyes.

Five of them bounded up to Thom. The Monkey King lunged and began wrestling with all of them at once. He shrieked and giggled as they pulled him to the ground.

Others came over to sniff and poke at Thom. One pulled up strands of her hair and blew on it. The other padded his paws against her puffy coat. One stole her scarf, and another took her hat. She would have run after her things, but then they tried them on, and it was cute and funny to watch, so she just stood there and laughed.

This place was magic. That was the only way to explain everything. Rainbows and butterflies—just like the song. Here, intelligent monkeys and . . . superstrong girls like her were real. She half expected more people to come out, to hug her and welcome her home. There was a sense of rightness to this place, like she could curl up in the grass and never leave.

"Well?" The Monkey King was back at her side. He held the hand of a monkey who looked older than the others, judging from the gray hairs sprinkled among the brown ones.

"I feel like I'm Jane. You know, from *Tarzan*."

The Monkey King gave her a weird look, then gestured to the elder monkey. "This is my older brother, Shing-Rhe."

"Oh." She hadn't thought about the possibility that the Monkey King might have a brother. "Hi," she said, and bowed, crossing her arms in submission because she didn't know what else to do.

"Thom," the elder monkey said, making her jump. She hadn't expected him to talk when the others only made *ooh-ooh* sounds. "Wukong has spoken a lot about you."

"Only my closest friends can call me that," the Monkey King said to Thom. "You still must show me respect. After all, I am the Great Sage of Heaven, with the strength of—"

"Oh, stop." Shing-Rhe slapped the Monkey King's palm, and

the Monkey King burst into giggles, jumping onto his brother's shoulder. Shing-Rhe gave Thom a look, exasperation and affection rolled into one. "Okay, okay, stop," he said. He grabbed the Monkey King's ankle and pulled him back to the ground. "Let's get your friend some healing water before she collapses."

"What?" Thom followed him past a group of sleeping monkeys. "I feel fine."

"You're delirious. Pink as a sunrise. Come, little one. I know any trip with Wukong is enough to kill a person. You must be incredibly strong."

How did he know? But maybe . . . he wasn't talking about her physical strength. She couldn't be sure, though if anyone knew about why she was this strong, it was probably this wise old monkey. He just had that all-knowing vibe about him.

Thom and Shing-Rhe crouched together by the babbling stream. The rainbow arched over the entire length of the water, like one short but wide bridge, no matter how you looked at it. Usually, rainbows disappeared if you moved and the light changed, but this one stayed forever. It almost looked solid, except that when she reached out a hand, her fingers passed through it and part of the rainbow bridge disappeared.

The Monkey King bounced back to them, holding out a large gourd that had been hollowed out for use as a water bottle. Shing-Rhe dipped the gourd into the stream, his furry arm breaking into the rainbow. When the gourd was full, he handed it to Thom.

"Drink all of this before you leave," he said, sitting cross-legged at the water's edge. She sat with him while the Monkey King flew off again to play with his friends or brothers or whatever they were to one another. "Go on." Shing-Rhe gestured to the gourd.

She still wasn't too sure about drinking water from a stream—Ma always warned against bacteria and stuff. But it seemed rude when the wise old monkey was staring at her expectantly, his sharp eyes full of concern. Besides, this place was magic. How could rainbow water hurt her?

She took a sip. The liquid was slightly sweet and refreshing, and as the coolness flowed down her throat and hit her belly, relief spread over her hot skin.

"It's good," she said, smiling.

Shing-Rhe nodded, grasping his knees and rocking back and forth.

"How come you don't share it with the world?" she asked. It seemed like a waste to hide the healing waters when others were sick and dying.

"We did, once," he said sagely. "And the

world drank the river dry. That's how some demons were created."

Thom clutched the gourd. "Wait, you mean this will turn me into a demon?" She started to hand it back to him.

"No, no, of course not. You are young and healthy, and despite choosing to be friends with Wukong, I can see your heart is good." He chuckled. "No, no. The water heals, but there are some wounds that are not meant to be healed. Some lives aren't meant to be lived forever. People should die, and when they don't . . . it is against nature, and when you challenge nature, *that* is how a demon is born."

Thom looked down at the stream, then at the gourd, tempted to dump the contents out. She wanted to believe Shing-Rhe, but her ears burned, like her fever was getting worse.

"It is fine." He nudged the gourd, reading her hesitance. "Drink. Finish it. Or you will be sicker than sick, and regret it."

She did feel a little better from the one sip she'd had. And if she was going to turn into a demon, it seemed too late now anyway. So she drank. Her fever and stuffy nose disappeared gradually, until she realized that her body no longer ached and her head felt lighter than before. A question sat on the tip of her tongue, but Thom hesitated, not wanting to insult anyone. Then again, Shing-Rhe seemed friendly, one of those grown-ups who couldn't wait to teach you something. "Are you . . . a demon?"

"Yes, child."

"But you're not evil."

Shing-Rhe smiled, nodding. "No. If we were, we wouldn't be allowed in this sanctuary. It is a haven, protected from those who would steal from the healing waters and do us harm."

"We? So . . ." She looked at the other monkeys. One rolled around in the moss, giggling happily as his friend sprinkled dandelions on his belly. "They're demons, too? But I thought demons were all evil. In the movies, they are."

"There are good demons and bad demons. Just like there are good people and bad people."

"So, what happened?" she asked, resting the gourd on her knees. "If other demons, the evil demons, drank the river dry, how did you take it back?"

"It helps to have the Monkey King on your side." He leaned close. "Sometimes," he added with a nod. If he'd had a beard, he would probably have stroked it.

"The Monkey King helped you take back the river?" In Thom's mind, a huge battle played out: thirsty, greedy demons against the Monkey King and his gentle, playful brothers. The monkeys weren't fighters. She looked around at the ones dozing under the sun, swatting lazily when butterflies landed on their noses.

It was possible that the Monkey King alone went up against the bad demons. In the legends, he was stronger than a hundred oxen. She had no idea how strong oxen were, but she had fought the Monkey King herself and knew he probably could beat her in a real battle.

"My brother has done many things for us," Shing-Rhe said. "He protects us. That is why we call him the Monkey King."

"Not because he's the Great Sage of Heaven?" She grinned.

"He is that also."

"Oh." Thom had thought the Monkey King was just exaggerating about his many assets. She didn't expect the wise old monkey to confirm his bragging rights.

"Drink."

"So you're afraid of the other demons?" she said. "You're not evil like them. Is that why you stay hidden behind the waterfall?"

"We are here to protect the healing waters. And Wukong protects us. Many centuries have passed since we won back control of the cave behind the waterfall. Many have forgotten about this place, but we are always fearful of an invasion," he said. "For a long time, Wukong was gone, and we lived in uncertainty, always wondering when the other demons would return. They also live on this island, you know. Only the peaceful among us are allowed in this clearing, but the island is home to many demons who have been banished here, kept guarded from the rest of the world. Once you released Wukong from the temple, he came back. And we are safe again." His smile crinkled his eyes.

Warmth filled Thom down to her toes, not the feverish warmth but the tingly kind you get when you drink hot chocolate on a cold day. "That's right. I did release him. But why was he there in the first place?"

She had never completely gotten rid of that feeling that she'd made a terrible mistake by taking the Monkey King's hair from the temple. Every day, she'd expected someone to show up, some magical creature seeking her out to punish her for setting the demon-god free.

But the more she got to know the Monkey King—Wukong—the more she realized he wasn't as bad as the myths said he was. He wasn't an evil guy. Yes, he'd made some trouble for her at school, but that was all a misunderstanding. He'd been curious, and after that, he'd saved her from Bethany and Sarah, and he was helping her learn the extent of her power. And now, he'd brought her here to heal her from her cold. His monkey brothers loved him, and Shing-Rhe talked about him like he was their savior. A protector. Someone who used his powers for good.

Which was better than what she was doing with her superstrength. Maybe she could be like him—learn how to use her power so she could protect others. She could be an actual superhero, like Superman or Wonder Woman.

"An enemy," Shing-Rhe said, in answer to her question. "Someone meant him harm. He was wrongly imprisoned. The Monkey King is extremely talented and powerful, and he wanted to help others. He asked for a seat in the heavens among the gods, but instead of giving him an honorable position, the Jade Emperor made him Master of the Horses. The other immortals made a mockery of him."

"Master of the Horses doesn't sound bad," Thom said. "I like horses."

"You have never seen the horses of the Jade Army. They are magical creatures, ten times the size of a mortal horse, almost deities themselves. They refused to show the Monkey King the respect he deserved, and the other gods treated him like a servant."

"Because he wasn't one of them? Because he's a demon, not a god?"

"He is both, child. He was created in the heavens but fell to this land as a crystal egg and hatched here, raised by us, his demon brothers. There is no one else like the Monkey King. He is the only one of his kind, and the immortals of the heavens have never accepted him."

The Monkey King was an outcast, different, just like Thom. She knew what that felt like—to be shunned when all she'd wanted was to belong.

"So what happened?"

"He worked hard to prove that he was worthy of a higher position, but the Jade Emperor never saw his full potential. And the immortals were jealous of Wukong. They feared he would upstage them, so they complained to the Jade Emperor, spread rumors, made up stories about him. The Jade Emperor took the immortals' side and banished Wukong from the heavens."

"And imprisoned him?"

Shing-Rhe nodded slowly, his eyes glistening.

"But that's . . . that's so unfair!"

"'Unfair' is a word we demons are quite familiar with."

His words stirred feelings of anger in Thom, on behalf of the Monkey King and his brothers, but also made her feel better about what she'd thought was a mistake. She hadn't done anything wrong by setting the Monkey King free then. She had maybe even done the right thing.

By the time she'd finished the water in her gourd, her fever was completely gone, her nose cleared, and her head no longer felt like a balloon threatening to pop. Several of the monkey brothers bounded over to play, but Thom was too tired, and unable to suppress a loud yawn. She was tempted to lie down in the warm oasis and close her eyes.

The Monkey King flew over, giggling as he poked her playfully in the stomach. "I told you I would make you feel better."

"It's nice here. But now I want to sleep," Thom said.

"Come, I'll take you home."

She didn't want to leave the comforting atmosphere of the sanctuary, but she could barely keep her eyes open, so she nodded.

The monkeys returned her hat and scarf, now dry from lying out in the sun, and they all patted her puffy jacket affectionately as she and the Monkey King prepared to leave.

It wasn't until she was back in bed, the Monkey King tucking the blankets around her just right, that she wondered if Shing-Rhe could tell her more about her superstrength if she asked.

15

"WHY YOU ALL BETTER ALREADY?" Ma asked the next day, as if it were a bad thing and Thom's fault that she wasn't sick anymore. She touched Thom's forehead, tsking, and then set a glass of orange juice on the kitchen counter. "Drink anyway, just in case."

Thom rolled her eyes at Mochi, who wagged his tail and ran to her, but then cowered, as usual lately, when she reached for him. The microwave beeped, announcing their breakfast of warmed-up dinner trays.

Ma grabbed some plates from the cabinet as Thom reached for the oven handle. The door broke off, the hinges ripped clean from the rest of the unit.

"Thom," Ma gasped. "Be careful!"

Thom looked at the door in her hand, then up at Ma. "I'm sorry! I don't know how . . ." Only she did know *how*. She thought she'd gotten a little better at controlling her strength, and being sick had made her feel slightly weaker. But now that she was okay again, maybe she was even stronger than before. Was her superpower getting worse?

Or had it been the healing waters from last night?

The doorbell rang. Mochi launched into a frenzied furball of barking and tail wagging, unsure whether to be excited or angry.

"Mochi, stop," Ma snapped. "Be quiet. Stop it! Bad dog!"

She threw Thom an exasperated look. "Here, give that to me." Ma took the microwave door. "Go see who's there."

Thom rushed to the front of the house. She stood on the tips of her toes to look through the peephole, dropped back to the floor, and almost latched the dead bolt. But there was no way she could pretend they weren't home. Kha's grandparents might be old, but the whole county had probably heard Ma yelling at Mochi to stop barking.

Thom sighed and unlocked the door. It swung open. She crossed her arms and lowered into a bow.

"Chào bà. Chào ông," she said. *Hello, Grandma. Hello, Grandpa.* Everyone was related when you were Vietnamese; she had to call them by the titles of whatever she assumed they were. Once she'd called an older girl cô, meaning *aunt*, and had gotten in huge trouble because the girl was offended that Thom thought she was older than she was. "Would you like to come in?"

"Oh, hello, little Thom," Kha's grandma replied in Vietnamese. Usually Thom got annoyed when strangers called her little, but it was hard to be angry when Kha's grandma smiled with those deep, wrinkly dimples and especially when she held up a tin of cookies. "Yes, please," she said. "Is Mother home?"

"Yes, we're just eating breakfast," Thom said. "Please join us." She stepped aside, and it wasn't until the older couple moved out of the way that she realized Kha was with them. "Oh. Hi."

He wore a black-and-white-striped T-shirt over whale-print shorts, and somehow managed to look casual but dressed up at the same time. Thom tugged on her cutoff jean shorts and the soccer T-shirt from her old school, which she only wore around the house.

He held up a clear box full of markers and a trifold poster board. "I wasn't sure what you have, so I brought my own stuff."

"For what?" she asked.

"For our Culture Day art project, remember?"

How bad would it look if she just made a run for her bedroom and locked the door, escaping to the sweet relief of not having to deal with Kha, or be friendly or act polite to anyone? "No," she said. "I've been sick."

Ma rushed into the entrance, all smiles and bows, like she hadn't just been snapping at their dog. "Oh, what a surprise!" she said, and the three older people started talking in rapid, sweet, and polite Vietnamese. Kha's grandparents had brought over cakes—they said they'd realized they'd lived next door for weeks but hadn't gotten the chance to say hi, and Ma apologized profusely: She was younger so it was her fault for not making time for them, blah blah blah.

Kha and Thom looked at each other with equally dazed, bored gazes. "Where's your room?" he asked.

She eyed the box in his hands but didn't see any way out of this, and didn't exactly want to stick around to listen to the grown-ups.

"Upstairs."

"Can I please see Thom's room, Auntie?" Kha asked Ma sweetly, and of course Ma almost melted. "We're partners for the school Culture Day project."

At the sight of those dimples, hearts almost appeared in Ma's eyes. "Culture Day project?" she asked Thom, widening her eyes as if to say *Why haven't I heard of this before?*

"Yeah, remember, I have to do an art project?" Thom said. Ma had probably been fixated on the áo dài–wearing part of Culture Day, which was just extra credit anyway. "Kha and I are partners. We're going to do a poster."

"I really want to do a dance—" Kha started.

"No," Thom said, cutting him off. "Just a poster."

"And wear áo dài."

"Is it okay if we work in my room?" Thom asked quickly before Ma caught that last part and really pushed the idea of dressing up. Thom would do anything if she could get out of looking like a dork in front of the whole school when no one else was going to dress up.

"Yes, but keep the door open," Ma said to her with a serious look.

The grown-ups nodded and waved at them to go away. A little suspiciously happy, Ma grinned at Kha.

"Cute," he said, inspecting Thom's decor, which was nonexistent. She was suddenly aware of how plain her room was, the white walls bare, the desk spotless, books stacked neatly on the shelves. The beige sheets on her bed and white duvet made the space look like a hotel room. "You're very . . . clean."

"Yeah. Have you met my mom?"

"I can get on board with the asylum vibe." He nodded, too vigorously. She wished she could blame the stark decorations on the fact that they'd just moved, but they'd been at the house for months, since before summer, and her old bedroom had been exactly the same.

"Um. Why are you really here?" she asked.

He looked a bit hurt, but she had never been good at faking it or hiding what she was thinking. She'd probably have more friends if she was.

"I mean," she added, "it's Saturday. Don't you have, like, things to do?"

"My grandparents wanted to meet your mom. And I don't have anything else to do, because I have no friends yet. That's why I'm here. To make one?" A flash of perfectly white, perfectly straight teeth, a twinkle in his eye, the perfect hair flip, making his bangs cascade ever so casually over his eyelashes.

He was like a walking, talking, live anime character.

And the way he'd said "yet." *I have no friends yet.* So confidently. Thom wondered once more why someone like him would want to be anywhere within breathing space of her. Then again, he was here, wasn't he? And that meant something, after all. So what if he only wanted to be friends out of a sense of loyalty to his culture? It was probably the only chance she'd ever have.

"So what do you think we should do for the project?" Thom asked, taking the trifold poster board and propping it on her desk. Kha laid out the markers while Thom turned on her laptop so they could research ideas.

"What about something to do with our mythology?"

"Like monsters and stuff? Dragons and snakes?"

"Or gods," he said.

"But there are so many."

"We'll focus on a group. Like the Four Immortals." He watched her closely, as if gauging her reaction.

"Hmm." She kind of wanted to go with the monsters and dragons.

"Come on, they're cool, these mortals who did something amazing and ascended into the heavens to become higher gods. The Sage, the Mother Goddess"—he ticked them off on his fingers—"the Mountain God . . . and the Boy Giant."

"Oh, I know him! Ma told me about how he ascended to the heavens after he defeated some invaders."

"Awesome." Kha uncapped a marker and leaned over the poster board.

"But . . . what if we do something different?"

"Like what?"

"I don't know. I feel like the immortals always get the spotlight. People talk about them all the time. Even temples are always about gods or Buddha."

"So . . . what are you thinking?"

She toyed with the bar-code sticker on her laptop. "What if we did our presentation on the other guys? Like the demons?"

Kha paused, the small muscles in his face twitching, like he was trying to find a way to turn her down gently. "Do you think we're allowed to? Wouldn't it be scary to do a presentation like that at school?"

"We can ask for special permission." Thom opened a browser on her computer. "I was thinking something on . . ." She felt Kha's scrutiny and hesitated. "On the Monkey King?"

He didn't respond. She stared at the cursor in the URL bar, but couldn't think of what to write, so she focused on what his reaction might be. Ma had brushed the Monkey King off as a mischievous troublemaker, but Thom knew he wasn't as bad as everyone made him out to be. He deserved better than what people always said about him—he wasn't evil, he was kind, he used his powers to protect his brothers, and he was even helping her find out more about her own. People should know about that side of him, the good side, not the stories about his mistakes. She could use Culture Day to show people how wonderful the Monkey King could be.

"Thom," Kha whispered.

"Yeah?"

He paused, and then his voice dropped dramatically low. "*I know.*"

"You . . . know what?"

He went to the door and closed it. "I *know.*" As if that explained everything.

"Um. Okay." She didn't really have the patience to humor him. "Cool."

"No, no, Thom." His gaze dropped directly to hers. "I know. About everything."

Her chest gave a horrifying lurch.

He knew. He *knew. Knew* knew. Wait. But . . . what did he mean by *everything*? Her strength, or . . . or the Monkey King? And even weirder, he wasn't freaking out. He still looked at her like he always had—like he had found a long-lost sister.

Play it cool. She didn't know what he was talking about yet, or if he'd just gone completely insane.

"About what?" Her voice was surprisingly calm and steady, despite that *she* was freaking out. How did he find out? She would have to move now. Again. Make up an excuse to tell Ma. Find a corner of the world where no one could see her and she could never touch a thing, lift an object, face another human being.

He leaned closer to whisper in her ear. "About the Monkey King. About you and your power."

She stood up. "How?"

"I saw you last night. When you left with him."

"That *was* you, wasn't it? In my backyard."

Stalker! Creeper! Spying on her. She was so going to tell Ma. She reached for the doorknob, but as she swung the door wide open, the knob snapped off. She stared down at it, then at Kha. There was no way he didn't notice that she'd ripped the thing clean off with nothing more than a light touch.

But he didn't seem to care. "I was looking out for you!" Kha said, holding out a hand to stop her. "I thought he might come back."

"Come back? Wait. You've seen him before? Why didn't you say anything?"

"That's why I gave you that token. I thought it might keep him away."

Thom looked at the space above her bed, where a piece of tape had broken off and still stuck to the wall. "Are you going to tell anyone?" she asked quietly. That was all that mattered—if he could keep it a secret while she found some way to convince Ma to move to a dark corner of the universe, everything would be okay. She could keep hiding her powers, be more careful.

"No, of course not. But if the Monkey King comes back, we need to capture him."

"We can't. I've tried." Guilt made her look away. She was the one who'd released the Monkey King. And while she did try to capture him once before, she hadn't been trying very hard since. She hadn't been trying at all. "He's too strong—"

"You're stronger."

She shook her head.

"You are. You can defeat him," Kha insisted.

"He hasn't done anything wrong. Why do we need to catch him?"

Kha's mouth opened in shock. "He's a demon-god!"

"But that doesn't make him *bad*. And even if I *can* catch him, then what?" Thom asked.

"We give him up to the heavens."

But she couldn't betray the Monkey King like that—he was her friend.

"I'll take us there," Kha said, standing up straighter. "I'm a dragon."

Thom's jaw dropped. "What?"

"I'm a dragon. A guardian. Of the Fifth Order, under the command of the Dragon-King of the Jade Army's Seventh Legion."

Her head began to throb.

"Someone sent me here," he continued. "To protect you."

It would have been just a little believable—he knew about the Monkey King, after all, and he knew about her power and didn't think she was crazy—except that the story seemed too familiar.

"Like . . . Mushu?" she asked flatly. "From *Mulan*?"

"I'm better than Mushu. I can fly."

Despite herself, Thom was a bit offended. She loved that movie. "Mushu breathed fire."

"I can turn invisible."

"He helped save all of *China*."

"I can turn into a human." He spread his arms and gestured down at himself, like this ended the argument.

"Kha, you can't be a dragon. You're, like, five feet tall." Vietnamese dragons, called rồng, could fly, turn invisible, and breathe fire, and they had other magical abilities, but they were huge serpentine creatures.

"Wow, look who's talking. You're shorter than me, and I *saw* you throw a seventy-pound table."

"I didn't throw that table. I caught it." She slapped a hand over her mouth. Up until now, she'd admitted to nothing, but the words had slipped out before she realized that she might as well have confessed everything.

"It's okay, Thom. I know about that, and that's why I'm here, to help you. The Monkey King is more dangerous than you think he is."

"He wouldn't hurt me. He can't. I'm strong, too, remember?"

"There's more than one way to get hurt."

"Like what? You think he'll hurt my *feelings*?" She snorted.

"I don't know what he's planning, but it's nothing good. He's a *trickster*. But we can figure it out together."

She shook her head. "I don't need your help."

His face reddened. "*Thom.*" His voice was high. Frustrated.

"Thom?" Ma stood in the doorway, frowning. "Everything okay?"

Thom thought about telling Ma then and there about Kha creeping in their backyard, but then she'd have to explain about everything else, or Kha might tell—about the Monkey King, about her strength—and she had no idea if Ma would believe her or how she would react. "Yeah. We're just—"

"What happened to the doorknob?" Ma asked, looking at the round hole in the door.

"It . . . broke," Thom said lamely.

"We're trying to decide on what to wear for Culture Day," Kha jumped in. "I was thinking of matching áo dài."

"Really?" Ma looked like she was about to hyperventilate, her breathing too fast, her smile splitting her face. "I would *love* if you and Thom wear áo dài together!"

Thom closed her eyes briefly. Oh yeah, that sounded like a wonderful idea. The two of them in matching outfits. Then Bethany, Sarah, and Kathy could make fun of both of them— two for the price of one.

"Yeah, this is the one I really want to buy," Kha said, whipping out his phone and pulling up a picture of a flashy black men's áo dài with a swirly golden print.

Ma clapped her hands together. "That look really good with the one I got for Thom!" She pulled out her own phone and they compared pictures. "What do you think, cưng?"

Thom plunked down onto her bed. "Sounds great," she said, but they were too distracted with their phones to hear the distress in her voice.

16

AT SCHOOL ON MONDAY, THOM redoubled her efforts to avoid Kha, whom she'd secretly nicknamed Crazy Creeper. No matter what he claimed about being her guardian, he'd been stalking her. Following her around school, sneaking into her backyard. That stuff might seem cute and sweet in movies, but in real life, it was pretty scary. She checked behind her every second, looked over her shoulder, constantly felt a tingly sensation on her neck like someone was watching her.

On top of that, soccer season was in full swing, with one or two games per week keeping her busier than ever. Not that she ever got to play. Practice was brutal, with Coach running drills like she meant to kill them with exhaustion, but during the games, Thom sat alone on the bench. Sometimes, Coach would put her in, but on defense, which wasn't her position, and then only for a few minutes before pulling her back out again.

Then there was the dynamic trio. Bethany and Sarah never missed an opportunity to trip Thom, bump into her with elbows protruding, pass the ball hard enough to injure a normal person. Kathy didn't join in, but the way she watched Thom now had changed. Ever since that day with the shower curtain, Kathy no longer looked at Thom with pity, but with suspicion.

Did Kathy know about Thom's superstrength? No. No way. She hadn't seen anything; Thom was just being paranoid. The curtain rod incident was clearly an accident. But then why did Thom always catch Kathy watching her on the field now? And when Thom moved to pass the ball, Kathy always stepped back, like she was afraid. Afraid that Thom might hurt her.

What if Kathy knew? What if Kathy told everyone?

Thom wasn't one to ditch practice—soccer used to be one of her favorite things ever—but the idea of putting up with Bethany, Sarah, and Kathy . . . only to get benched again made her want to throw up as she walked toward the locker room. Her feet dragged, and she hesitated for a split second. Then she took an abrupt turn and darted out of the building.

Other teams were getting ready for practice, dragging equipment and buckets of ice to the fields. Before the softball coach could see her and ask her what she was doing, Thom ducked behind the bleachers.

Already, relief flooded her. Would it be so bad if she

skipped today? Did it make her a weak person if, just this once, she gave herself a break?

She missed Thuy. She needed someone to talk to—about Kha and the Monkey King—and Thuy would know exactly what to think.

She looked up at the clear blue sky. "Wukong?" He hadn't shown up the whole weekend, and she was starting to wonder if Kha didn't even have to worry about him anymore.

Then his nose and whiskers appeared, followed by his giggle. "I thought I told you only my friends call me that."

"Aren't we friends?"

The rest of him materialized, upside down, legs crossed. Excitement ballooned in Thom's chest. She was surprised to realize that she had actually missed him. "Do you want to be? It takes a lot to be friends with someone like me, you know. Not everyone makes the cut."

"I don't know," Thom said.

At her serious tone, he flipped right side up, legs untangling, feet padding softly on the pavement. "Then why did you call me?"

"Kha . . . The new kid next door." She paused, and the Monkey King flew into the air, leaning his head back on his hands. "He said you're a demon-god, that you're . . . bad." Kha wasn't the only one—Shing-Rhe had confirmed that the Monkey King was part demon. But Shing-Rhe was a demon himself.

"Hmm. He did, did he?" The Monkey King giggled, tilting his head. "He's right. The only demon-god to ever exist."

"But does that mean you're bad?"

"What is 'bad,' really? What does that mean? Don't you think, perhaps, we all have a bit of bad inside us?" He was in a mischievous mood, and talking to him was like trying to get Mochi to let her pet him again. "How good do you have to be to be considered good? How much goodness do you need to have? Half goodness? A quarter goodness?" He twisted his legs into a pretzel and sniffed at his feet. "What if only nine of your toes were good but one was bad? Does that make this foot a bad foot?"

He stuck his foot under her face, wiggling his toes. She shoved it aside.

"You know what I mean," she said.

The Monkey King turned onto his side, floating at eye level with her. "I have never pretended to be something I'm not."

Thom didn't know what to think. *Was* the Monkey King bad? Was Kha lying? Or maybe Kha just didn't know the Monkey King like she did. Kha believed all the stories that said the Monkey King was a bad guy, but Thom *knew* Wukong.

She needed someone else's opinion. She needed to talk to someone she could trust. She checked her phone, which Ma had finally given back to her, for a text from Thuy, but her last three messages remained unanswered. It had now been three weeks since Thom had asked Thuy if everything was okay.

What if Thuy wasn't okay? What if something had happened to her? If only she could see her BFF face-to-face.

"You're sad," the Monkey King said in a bewildered tone, like he couldn't understand why anyone would choose not to be happy. "Why?"

Thom couldn't answer, looking westward, or what she thought was west, toward her old home. She missed it so much. Missed her friends, missed who she used to be: just a girl who liked soccer and boba with popcorn chicken, whose toughest decision had been whether to get red socks with or without stripes as part of the team uniform.

"What can I do, Thom-Thom?" the Monkey King asked, touching her cheek with his knuckles. "We can do anything you want."

But there was nothing to do in Troy, at least no one to do them with. Back in West City, there'd always been boba, ice-skating, beach picnics, movies. Here in Troy, she had three stops—school, home, and the library.

"We can go anywhere," the Monkey King added.

"Anywhere?" An idea formed. A strong craving for a place, to see her friends.

"I am the great and handsome Monkey King who has mastered the Seventy-Two Transformations!" He bounded above her. "I can take you anywhere you'd like!"

"Anywhere," she repeated, taking a deep breath. "Okay. Let's go to California."

◆ ◆ ◆

As they rose high into the air, Thom shut her eyes, clinging on to the Monkey King's shoulders, gripping his coarse hair so tight her fingers grew cold and numb.

The wind blew past her ears and tugged on her hood, whipping her hair all around her face. Her teeth were clenched, the muscles of her mouth pulled back in fright. But then, they reached a height just beneath the clouds and suddenly leveled out. After a few minutes passed and she still hadn't plummeted to her death, Thom relaxed her body, her muscles loosening just a fraction. She would never get used to flying like this.

It took a long time before her pulse slowed to a normal rate, and she found the courage to force her eyes open.

They couldn't have been in Georgia any longer. For one thing, there were too many buildings. Georgia, or at least, the part that she knew, was full of greenery and nothing but trees and miles and acres of land. She was reminded every day how far from any city she lived.

But now, beneath them, houses cluttered the area, rooftops bare and deserted. They were in West City. Cars moved slowly on the freeway like tiny ants crawling. She had missed the sight of traffic, as weird as that was.

She couldn't hear anything through the roar of wind, and she still was too busy trying not to die to notice much else. If she hurt the Monkey King by holding on to his neck and shoulders too hard, he didn't seem to care. His giggle echoed back at her every few minutes as he ran through the air, his legs cycling beneath him like he was riding an invisible bicycle. He spread out his arms and jerked sideways, and Thom shrieked loudly, afraid he was about to show off with some tricks. He then righted himself and patted her hand apologetically.

Cars honked in the distance. No one looked up, but if they did, they didn't seem to notice a monkey piggybacking a girl.

Music blasted from speakers as they floated closer to the ground. Buildings grew bigger, going from unrealistic boxes to skyscrapers with colors and details, the frame of a window, the carved edges along a rooftop. There was the corner shop where she and Thuy would buy Flamin' Hot Cheetos before school so their parents wouldn't find out. As she got closer, she recognized the Boba Queen, where Ma would take them for milk tea and popcorn chicken after school.

They landed in a field connected to West City Middle School. In the distance, she could make out the empty basketball courts. At this hour, the students would be gathered in the cafeteria for lunch.

Thom's feet barely touched the ground before she was off running, not knowing or caring if the Monkey King followed. As she reached the buildings and ran past the rows of portable classrooms, familiarity hit her, along with a deep feeling of sadness that threatened to knock her down. She kept going. She was here. She was home. Thuy would be so happy to see her. She would be at lunch—all Thom's friends would be there.

They'd be talking about the latest shows they were watching or whatever trouble Thuy had gotten into at her Catholic weekend school. Thom's spot would be empty, but she was here now, back to fill it.

Her heart thundered as she neared the cafeteria. Students' laughter and conversation filled the air. No one noticed her as she blended into the crowd of kids shoving to get to their food, the groups gathered at tables, some sitting to eat, some standing and hanging out. No one looked at her weirdly or moved out of the way when she walked toward them, or stopped talking to whisper behind hands, like they did at DeMille.

She made her way through the room, squeezing between backpacks and cliques of students who barely noticed her. Some smiled, recognizing her from last year, even waved, but her friends weren't there. She knew exactly where they'd be, at their usual table in the courtyard.

As she pushed the door open, sunlight blinded her, seeping across her vision and setting a glow over the scene. Maybe this was all just a dream, or a hallucination. That would explain how she had been in Troy just an hour ago and was back in West City now. That would explain the Monkey King, too. Had Thom finally snapped, the shock of moving across the country too much for her?

Her eyes adjusted to the bright daylight. The door closed behind her with a *thump*. The courtyard was full—it always was. The area was popular, with its patches of grass shaded by cherry trees. They weren't in bloom until spring, but the branches arched up and encased them in a fairy-tale-like oasis.

She spotted them immediately. Third from the left, where the shade fell just right during lunchtime, with just enough sunlight to keep them warm and for taking the perfect selfies. Thuy and her friends—Emily and Hannah—were there. With Thom, they made the perfect foursome, and all the best things came in fours. The Incredibles—if you didn't count Jack-Jack. The Fantastic Four, obviously. Even the three musketeers were actually the four musketeers when you remembered to count D'Artagnan. Without Thom, their group just didn't make sense.

Except it did.

Because in Thom's usual place was another girl.

Amber.

Thom recognized her from last year's science class. She hadn't wanted to be Thom's partner—which was fine because Thuy had later changed her schedule to be in that class so she and Thom could hang out more.

And now Amber was sitting there. Next to Thuy, the girl who'd rejected her best friend. In Thom's own spot. And worse, the two of them were taking selfies, Thuy's arm outstretched, as they grinned and tilted their heads just right. The same exact way Thom and Thuy used to, the lighting perfect, casting warm glows on their skin.

Thom felt the strange urge to rush at her best friend and push the other girl away. And yet at the same time, she wanted to run, and never talk to Thuy again. She thought about it for a second, just leaving, even though she had come all the way here, even though the Monkey King had flown her across the country just so she could see that her best friend was okay. Instead, Thom reached for her phone with shaking fingers. She found Thuy's number and hit DIAL.

Thom watched as Thuy laughed at something Amber said while they looked at the selfies they'd just taken on her phone. Thuy's smile froze for a second. She must be seeing Thom's call.

Thom held her own phone up to her ear. "Pick up," she whispered, her chest throbbing painfully with hope.

Thuy pressed a button.

In Thom's ear, the ringing stopped, leaving behind a low, echoing drone.

Thuy had rejected her call. She turned back to Amber and said something else that had them both cracking up.

Thom had been replaced.

Something in her chest twisted sharply. What had Thuy said to Amber? Was it about Thom? Were they making fun of her, the same way Bethany and Sarah whispered to each other, then glanced at her to make sure she knew? This explained everything. Why Thuy could never talk when Thom called. Why she didn't text back. She was probably hanging out with her new BFF, her new Thom. The girl who had never been nice to her was now in her spot.

This hurt more than all the times Bethany and Sarah had tripped her, a bone-deep, buried ache she couldn't reach.

She thought about marching up to them. Demanding that Amber leave. Accusing Thuy of not picking up the phone.

But what good would that do? She didn't live here anymore. She didn't go to this school. She went to DeMille Middle now, and there, she wasn't one student among many, she was the sore thumb, the weirdo who stood out, who would never fit in.

That wasn't Thuy's problem. Thuy had her own problems, her own life, her own friends. She had moved on.

And maybe it was time Thom did, too.

17

THOM DRAGGED HER FEET ACROSS the grass, but she didn't care that her sneakers would get caked with dirt after how hard she'd struggled to keep them clean. She turned to look back at her old school, feeling silly and embarrassed about how excited she'd been to see it.

Who got excited about a school? Why had she missed this place so much? The portable classrooms were gray blocks on black concrete, the brick buildings crumbling. The basketball courts were missing actual baskets, and the tennis nets drooped.

Even the cafeteria courtyard she'd loved seemed decrepit now, the cherry trees dead, the branches like claws waiting to snatch kids and steal them to a dark corner of some fairy-tale forest.

And her friends . . . They didn't miss her at all. They had probably forgotten about her by now. She'd spent the past months in Georgia wondering about them, thinking about what they were doing without her, and all this time, they hadn't given her a moment's thought. She was gone; she might as well be dead to them.

A gust of wind flared, making her stumble, blowing dirt into her eyes, and she screwed up her face. One thing she didn't miss—the Santa Ana winds rushing through with their dryness and heat, stirring up dust. She pressed a fist in her eye to rub out whatever had gotten in, and her knuckles glistened with something wet. It was just the wind, though, she told herself, making her eyes water.

"Have fun?"

She whirled, squinting because her eyes still burned. "Oh," she said. The Monkey King lay on his side in the grass, a pinky finger digging into his ear.

"Did that cheer you up, seeing your old friends again?" he asked. But with a closer look at her face, he didn't need an answer. To her surprise, he stood up slowly and pulled her into a hug. "It's okay, Thom-Thom. Some friendships aren't meant to last forever."

"How did you know?" What she really meant was, how had he known to say that? She hadn't told him what had happened. She was tempted to bury her face in his fur, which now smelled like flowers and, weirdly, the cold but fresh quality of snow. Where had he been?

"Believe it or not, I've had many friends." He held her

shoulders, his grin crinkling his eyes. "And enemies. Friends who turned into enemies. Enemies who became friends." He giggled. "Friends who are also enemies."

"How?"

"When you're a demon and a god." He shrugged and didn't explain further.

"Has anyone ever betrayed you?" she asked, thinking of Thuy and Amber together in her usual spot.

"Oh, many. Too many to recount."

"Shing-Rhe told me how the Jade Emperor made a mockery of you by making you Master of the Horses, and how everyone laughed at you."

He nodded. "It was humiliating. The horses never did anything I asked. And they were bossy. I was not a master, but a servant! To horses! Me! The Great Sage of Heaven! The handsome Monkey King!"

He puffed out his chest and stood tall. Thom couldn't help snickering. The Monkey King deflated, pouting at her.

"Why did you want a seat in the heavens so much anyway?" she asked. "Weren't you happy on the Mountain of a Hundred Giants? Weren't your demon brothers enough for you?"

He considered the question carefully. "It wasn't fair. The gods and the fairies, you should see where they live. Elaborate temples made of jewels—everywhere you go, everything is beautiful. And the food! Feasts of meats, and peaches for dessert, the sweetest peaches you will ever find. Servants to serve you, soldiers to protect you, and all day just lounging and having fun." He shook his head. "And what did demons get? Most of us are banished to the hells. Only the lucky ones, the ones you've met, got an island."

"But your island is beautiful," Thom said, thinking of the blue waters and the lush green cave.

"It wasn't always. It was chaos at first. Too many demons. Always fighting."

"But your monkey brothers are so peaceful," she said. "They wouldn't really hurt each other."

"They're not the only ones who live on the island. They're the only ones allowed in the sanctuary, but there are others. They live in harmony now, but it wasn't always like that. The strong picked on the weak. The weak stole from the strong and did none of the work. It was a nightmare." He wiggled his eyebrows. "Until I came along, of course," he boasted, "and made everything better."

He leaned back and kicked his legs as if he were floating in a pool. "It wasn't easy, you know. Why should they have listened to me? My monkey brothers only wanted to be lazy. They weren't willing to work. They're not strong like you. They're not warriors."

She felt a small thrill at his compliment.

"And the demons," he said. "They only respect power."

"Was that why you left?" she said. "To learn how to grow more powerful?"

He sat up and crossed his legs. "No, I was sick of them. I had no intention of coming back. But after I left, I met the Lotus Master. He's a Taoist legend, the only master willing to show me anything about the Seventy-Two Transformations, and he taught me there was so much more to the world, so much power to be gained. I only wanted more."

"So you went to the heavens."

"The looks on their faces!" He cackled. "They were so shocked—I had broken in, and no other demon had before, you see, but I was not to blame. Their defenses should have been stronger, considering they have giant horses in their army. I declared myself the Great Sage of Heaven, because I was smarter than all of them. You should see the court, Thom-Thom. So many bright colors and gold and jade and diamonds. The gods and goddesses of the council sit on crystal seats." He mimicked sitting bolt upright, making his voice high and pompous. "'I declare we must have sunshine today. And flowers, pretty flowers, so that the birds may sing. The peaches—I worry they are not growing in wisdom. The horses—they are worried their new master does not brush them with love.' They discussed very silly things. No one wanted to hear about the lives of demons."

Thom smiled at his high-pitched mimicry of the fairies. She imagined them as dressed-up versions of Bethany and Sarah, wearing silly hats and bossing everyone around. "What did you ask for?"

"I wanted my brothers to have the same benefits as the fairies. You know, entrance into the heavens, freedom to roam the gardens, maybe a few peaches here or there. They deserve pretty things, too."

"The immortals said no?"

His lips curled over his teeth. "They laughed." He seemed faraway, his eyes glazed. "They laughed. And they banished me from the heavens."

His voice was tight and full of hurt, and Thom wanted to reach out and hug him like he'd done when he knew she was sad, except she didn't know how exactly. She was about to give him a stiff pat on the shoulder, but he moved away at the last minute, giggling as he flipped into the air, all smiles again.

"So I returned to the Mountain and lived happily ever after!" He skipped and twirled, and eventually settled on his side, resting his head on his hand.

Thom tried to match his grin, but something still weighed her down. The Monkey King's story did not have a happy ending, no matter how cheerful he pretended to be. The demons were still isolated on an island, and the Monkey King had been imprisoned. Everything he'd fought for remained unchanged.

"I'm sorry I couldn't help make you feel better," he said, reading something in her face.

"Don't be sorry." She gave his shoulder a playful punch, as soft as she could manage. It landed with a *thunk*, and he took several steps back. His eyes gleamed.

"You're still holding back," he said.

"I wasn't really trying to hurt you, you know." She smiled and looked down at her hands. It was nice to be with someone and not have to worry about breaking their bones.

"Why not? It might help you feel better."

"Is this what you do with your friends? Fight them?"

"Only the ones I like. Come on, as hard as you can." He pointed to his shoulder.

"Can't I just toss you?"

"Last time, I almost got lost."

"More reason to do it again."

He giggled. "Just once, please? Please!" He held his hands together and batted his eyelashes. "Please, Thom-Thom!"

"Okay." She laughed. "Just once."

He stood with his legs apart, braced for impact. As she pulled her elbow back, he gave her a reassuring nod, cackling his monkey cackle. She let her fist fly, but at the last second— she just couldn't help it—she held back. Still, her fist collided, and the Monkey King sailed backward. He dug his feet into the grass, ripping up chunks of dirt until he skidded to a stop. Thom was horrified. Sure, this was the Monkey King and he had asked for it, but that would definitely leave a bruise.

To her surprise, he launched into the air. "Wooo-hooooooo! Let's see what else you can do!" He reached down for her hands and swung her around in circles.

Thom giggled.

The Monkey King stopped over the basketball courts. He dropped her at one end and curled up into a ball in front of her. "Think you can make it?" he asked.

"What do you mean?"

He floated, knees against his chest. "Isn't this a silly game you mortals play? With a ball?"

She looked from his curled-up body to the basketball hoop on the other side of the court. "You want me to shoot you?"

He cackled gleefully. "Yes, yes! You are strong, but you must also be disciplined. Here. I'll make it easy." And right in front of her eyes, he shrank, his body constricting into a sphere. His face grinned at her through the circle of his arms.

"Okay," she said hesitantly. She touched him with careful movements, holding him between her palms. He was no bigger than a basketball now. "Okay, but like . . . but what if I hurt you?"

"We've been over this, Thom-Thom. I am the great and powerful and invincible Monkey King. I am unhurtable."

Thom smiled. It did look sort of fun. The basketball court wasn't as big as a soccer field, but she was used to kicking the ball, not throwing it. She held the Monkey King up to her face, and he let out a giggling shriek as she tossed him straight at the basketball hoop.

Her hands flew up to her mouth as he was about to sail over the backboard, but right before he whizzed past it, he burst into his full form, arms and legs spread wide. His toes touched the top of the backboard lightly, and he landed with the grace of a cheetah. Then, like an acrobat, he flipped, arms outstretched, and, cartwheeling through the air, he dove into the hoop.

Thom clapped as he bowed and bounced back to her. When he reached down, she also reached up, and their hands met, fingers interlacing before he pulled her onto his back.

"Where are we going?" she asked as he lifted them both into the sky.

"You'll see," he shouted over the wind. "You'll see!"

They were zooming along too fast to be able to talk as they flew up inside a cloud of mist and fog. Then they burst into the clear blue expanse of the sky. A dark flock of crows flew ahead of them, and the Monkey King cawed loudly, as if mocking them.

The birds suddenly changed formation, banking to the right, and swarmed her and the Monkey King, and Thom gripped the fur on his shoulders even tighter.

"Ahhhhh," she shouted, but she wasn't sure he could hear, because the crows had started cawing at them from all sides. Their aggressive cries, the wind in her ears, the flapping of wings, the Monkey King cawing back just as loud: They were going to die. He was going to drop her, or the birds would peck her to death.

"Wukong!" she cried, ducking when a crow dove for her head.

Just before it reached her, the Monkey King darted, flipped

in the air, and twisted his way out of the formation. The crows followed, but the Monkey King stayed just out of reach, letting them catch up before zipping away, and then laughing maniacally when their cawing got even louder, more menacing.

Eventually, the Monkey King descended, and they landed in a junkyard, surrounded by piles of metal, parts left over from abandoned vehicles.

"Are you insane?" Thom cried, slipping from his back and shoving him away. "We could have died."

"What? Because of a bunch of birds? One snap of your fingers, and they would drop like flies. You're stronger than you think you are. How many times must I tell you?" Then he turned abruptly and surveyed the junkyard he'd dropped them in. "Pick that up," he demanded of her, pointing to an old car.

She had trouble catching her breath. "What if someone sees?"

"There isn't a mortal around for miles. Come on, take it."

The mountains of scrap metal hid them from view. It was better than having to punch him. And she wanted to learn; she needed to control her strength if she was going to have to live with it. Thom took a deep breath, but the Monkey King didn't give her a moment to hesitate, pushing her to the car. He took her hands and guided them to the bottom of the car.

"You can do it, Thom-Thom," he whispered, and then disappeared.

Alone, Thom faced the car. It was small, one of those

egg-shaped compacts, the white paint covered in dust. She lifted it. Easily. She held it over her head, surprised at how effortless it felt. The Monkey King popped up next to her under the car, grinning at her beneath its undercarriage.

"Excellent," he said. "Now this one." He pointed to something bigger, an SUV. It was only slightly heavier to her than the car had been. The Monkey King's giggles led her around the junkyard as he instructed her to pick up one vehicle after another, each heavier than the last.

When they got to the giant eighteen-wheeler truck, Thom leaned back and shook her head. The truck was missing a few tires and was hunched to one side like an animal with an injured leg. That rush of wrongness was back, the guilt that had overcome her when she'd accidentally used her strength. But this wasn't an accident. No one had been hurt. "I don't think I'm *that* strong," she said.

"Yes, you are," the Monkey King said. "You are stronger than you think, stronger than anyone I've met, stronger than a Jade Soldier. *You* could be a soldier, a true warrior."

"A warrior." She was no warrior. She was just a small middle schooler. But the idea of it, of being a great fighter, of being someone strong—really strong like a soldier, not clumsy like her—seemed so *cool*.

"I can teach you to be the greatest warrior there ever was," the Monkey King said. "I can train you to control your strength."

Thom wanted it. She wanted to be able to use her power, to not be afraid of it. She nodded.

He pointed to the truck again. "So pick that up. And then we can go home."

"I don't know . . ."

"You can do it. Show me what you are capable of."

Thom clenched her fists. She crouched next to the truck, positioned her hands underneath it, and pushed upward. At first, it didn't budge. The metal where she gripped it bent beneath her fingers. The truck rumbled and creaked, threatening to break apart, but then when she'd thought about giving up, the entire thing eased up. She held it above her head and turned to the Monkey King.

He laughed and clapped so loud she almost didn't hear the crunch of metal as she set the truck back down.

"You're strong, you're strong!" the Monkey King shrieked, somersaulting so fast he became a blur. His excitement was contagious, washing away Thom's uneasy feeling, along with the sad weight dragging her down, deep in her chest. She felt light, elated.

Their laughter was drowned out by a dog barking, and they both stopped as a wiry-haired mutt appeared between two piles of scrap metal. Thom grinned and held out a palm, but the dog growled at her, hackles raised.

Lowering to all fours, the Monkey King growled back.

Thom laughed, and that seemed to egg him on, because he grinned and barked at the dog. The dog sniffed at him, confused. They circled each other.

The Monkey King barked loudly, and the dog jumped, backed up, then moved forward, as if unsure whether to attack or run away. The Monkey King giggled and rose in the air before launching toward the dog.

"Wukong, no!" Thom grabbed the back of the Monkey King's robes before he could attack. She dragged him away.

The Monkey King barked a few more times at the stray, but he couldn't keep it up for long, because he was laughing so hard.

When he calmed down, he turned around and grabbed Thom's hands.

"You are strong," he said over and over, swinging her around and around. "You. Are. Strong."

Thom closed her eyes, dizzy and excited and . . . proud. "Yeah," she said. "I am."

18

KATHY STAYED HOME SICK FROM school the next day and couldn't play in the game against Comer Middle School. Dressed in their soccer uniforms—blue-and-gold striped jerseys and white shorts with matching knee-high socks—Thom and the other girls waited on the field as Martha counted the players, again and again, as if hoping that the next count would yield someone new.

Bethany dribbled the ball, rolled it onto her foot, tossed it into the air, and began bouncing it with her knees. Show-off. But she had a right to be. She didn't miss and kept going until Thom lost count.

Coach Pendergrass called Thom over. Coach's hair was a fluffy mess, curling like uncooked ramen noodles around her face. She scribbled furiously on her clipboard, crossed out what she'd written, and muttered to herself.

Kathy usually played middle or right forward, two of the

most important positions on the team, and it was unthinkable that Thom could replace her. Which meant shuffling a lot of players.

To her surprise, Thom was placed in the left center. A weak spot, but at least she wasn't useless in defense. The girls glanced back at her with uncertainty and a bit of fear, but whether actual fear of her or just fear of losing the game with her on the field, she couldn't tell.

She thought of Cassie Houghton, who, according to Coach, had finally come home from the hospital but would have to wear a brace for a month while her ribs healed. She let out a sigh of relief that Kathy wasn't there, watching her with suspicion.

The game started. The ball hardly ever came to Thom's side, but she still got to run up and down the field with the rest of the team and pretend she was important. She couldn't help grinning, relishing the fact that she was playing! She'd missed this, missed the way her feet pounded on the grass, her pulse racing, her teammates by her side, all eyes on the ball. She glanced at the bleachers, where some of the other girls' moms sat, sharing bags of chips and plastic bins full of cupcakes and cookies. She missed having Ma there, but once again, Ma had to work.

"No!" someone shouted, and Thom looked up just in time to see the ball head toward her. "Kick the ball—that way!" Coach waved frantically at the opposing goal. Bethany and

Sarah, who usually scored, were too far upfield. Thom was the only one on the team anywhere near the ball, and the other team was closing in fast.

Thom looked at their faces. She could do it. Send it flying. Gentle, though, so no one got hurt.

Her foot shot out—but it was too late. A red jersey pushed past and stole the ball, a blur as she ran down the field and scored. The other team erupted in cheers. Thom's team moved back into position, shoulders slumped. Pinpricks of heat traveled on her skin from all the dirty looks. Sarah shook her head, and Thom knew the rest of the week's practices were going to be dangerous.

As the referee set up the next play, someone giggled to her left. But there was no one there. She was the player farthest left, and the bleachers were on the other side. She shook her head and focused on the ball.

Spurred on by anger, Bethany rushed forward and claimed the ball, dribbling it down the field.

As Thom followed, she heard another giggle to her left. This time, she was sure she hadn't imagined it.

"Wukong?" she whispered under her breath.

"Oh, are we really on a first-name basis now?" the Monkey King's voice spoke out of nowhere.

"You're here." This made her feel better, like she had an ally, and relief wrapped around her. She wasn't alone. She didn't have to do this alone.

"What is the purpose of this game? Running around like horses, kicking a random object."

"We need to put the ball in that goal." Thom ran with her team, but whenever the ball came close, another player got there first.

"Well then, put the ball in the goal." He giggled. "You can do it. Why did you stop earlier? You're better than everyone here. You can run faster than them. You don't get tired. You can kick farther than any of them, too."

"I can't. If I kick too hard, everyone will find out about my strength."

"Then why play at all?"

"Because . . ." She searched for the right answer. In West City, it had been something to do with Thuy and her friends. Here, she had joined out of habit, a way to get to know the other students, maybe even make friends. And the truth was, Thom loved soccer. She loved being part of something, part of a team with a single objective. Sure, it was tough, but when they scored or won, it was the best feeling. "Because I love it," she said.

He was quiet for so long, she thought he'd left. But then she noticed that the ball was doing strange things, making its way toward her, slowly but surely, despite her own team's efforts to stop it. If someone kicked it away, it came to a sudden stop, gravitating toward her like she was at the bottom of a downward slope.

"Go, Thom. Now's your chance." The Monkey King's

voice was pushing her forward. No. *He* was pushing her forward, his hands at her back. She wanted to stop, but it would have looked too funny to everyone watching, so she let him move her. "Kick it! Go!"

She couldn't. Everyone was watching.

Something knocked against the back of Thom's leg, and her foot connected with the ball, sending it down the field.

The Monkey King's giggle bounced off her eardrums as he ran with her, his shrieks drowning out any other sound. Each time she came close to the ball, he moved her leg so that she kicked it with just the right amount of strength.

Even though the Monkey King was the one controlling her strength, forcing her to use exactly the right amount, Thom felt the rush of understanding, the excitement that came with mastering a new skill. She had always either used too much power, usually breaking something in the process, or she'd held back altogether. Now she realized that she didn't have to—that if she was disciplined enough, she could actually play and live and do the things she wanted.

Thom had left her teammates and the red jerseys behind, and it was just her, the goalie, an invisible demon-god, and the thrill that she had never come this far before.

The Monkey King giggled and said, "It's all yours." And Thom thought he was gone, but he wasn't gone, he didn't leave her. Still, this time, she was the one who controlled the kick. Her foot connected with the ball, and it flew into the air, rose above the goalie's outstretched arms, and hit the net.

The buzzer sounded. The referee blew his whistle.

Thom had won the game.

◆ ◆ ◆

Even though she'd scored the winning goal, the girls didn't treat her any better. Whispers echoed in the locker room, and she heard snippets of the conversation.

"Did you see the way the ball flew?"

"Yeah, like there was a ghost or something."

"Do you think she did it?"

"Maybe, but how?"

"Who knows. She's such a freak."

Thom hid her face in her locker, breathing in the smell of old sneakers and the chemical singe of chlorine. The elation she'd felt from the game was quickly diluted with shame and guilt and confusion. If she avoided the ball, she was a coward, but if she won the game, she was a freak. What was she doing wrong? She wished Ma wasn't working late again. She wouldn't be by to pick Thom up for another hour.

After everyone left, Thom found herself back on the soccer field. A dewy mist had settled over the grass, and she felt the chill seep in through her sweats and hoodie.

"Monkey King?" she whispered, hoping he was still there. Silence. The field was empty. The boys' soccer team had gone home; the track-and-field runners were long gone. She would practice alone then. The Monkey King had shown her that she could still play soccer even though she was superstrong. With more practice, she could play better, score more, become an excellent teammate. She grabbed a ball from the storage bin and placed it in front of the goal.

Out of habit, she glanced left and right before pulling her leg back and delivering a kick. The first shot was too strong. The ball crashed into a goalpost, which skidded back by a foot.

The second shot was way too weak. The third was better. After a few rounds, she realized she had to keep it at about a tenth of her actual kick strength, and then she decided she needed to divide that in half again.

"Not bad," a voice said out of nowhere.

She jumped. The Monkey King giggled. "You really need to stop the invisible thing."

"What if someone sees me?"

"Can't you change into a man or something? Isn't that one of your powers?"

"I can transform into other animals, yes, but humans are so ugly. Why would I want to hide this face?" His furry head popped up in front of her. He batted his eyelashes and then disappeared. "Let me see what you can do."

Thom took a deep breath. "Okay." She kicked the ball but got nervous, now that she knew she was being watched, and miscalculated. The ball rolled forward a few feet.

"Weak. You underestimate yourself."

She tried again.

"Better, but stop holding back," he said.

"I have to hold back. I'm too strong."

"For this world, yes. For the mortals. But not with me."

She wished she could see his face. There it was again—that tease, a glimpse, a mention of this other world, one she might belong to more than the one she was in. She wanted to ask more about it—no, to see it. "Are there others like me?"

"Like you?"

He hesitated, and hope rose. Maybe she wasn't alone.

"No. Not like you," he said. "You're different. Better than anyone I've ever met. You and I—we make a great team. You're strong, almost as strong as me, and with my cunning and magic, we can do anything!"

Thom beamed. That wasn't the answer she'd hoped for, but it still felt good. No one complimented her like this—not her teachers, not even Ma—and he knew about her strength and praised her for it when most people would have been afraid.

She tried the ball again, and with the Monkey King whispering advice, made the goal ten times in a row. She jumped up and down, her fists in the air, a grin on her face.

Then a tingly feeling chilled the back of her scalp—like she was being watched. She stilled, turned.

Kha stood on the small row of bleachers at the side of the field.

"You should go," she said softly to the Monkey King.

He sniffed in Kha's direction. "That boy is not what he says he is."

The back of her neck tingled more. Mochi hadn't liked Kha, either, had barked and growled at Kha for no reason when her dog was usually friendly with strangers. Then again, Mochi hadn't let Thom pet him for months, so she doubted her dog was a good judge of character.

"Don't trust him," the Monkey King whispered. "He's deceiving you."

He stopped speaking, but she had no idea if he was really gone.

Kha took Thom's gaze as an invitation, jumped down from the bleachers, and approached her. He looked incredibly grown-up, in ankle-length chinos and a plaid button-up shirt, his hair stylishly rumpled, his bangs swept casually over his brow. He held up a palm, and she slapped at it but missed and had to try again. Smooth. Her hand came away hot—*she* felt hot, standing this close to Kha. She stepped back, and the evening air cooled the flush on her skin.

"Hey, what's up?" Her voice was too squeaky, her words too fast. Had he noticed the Monkey King? Could he see him when he was invisible? "What are you doing here?"

"I came to ask about your dress," Kha said. He smiled, and his cheekbones reflected the light in that pearl-like shimmer she'd seen before, but when he tilted his head, it disappeared. Weird.

"My what?" she asked.

"Your dress. You know, for Culture Day."

Thom groaned. She had forgotten all about that. She'd only agreed to dressing up and matching with Kha to get her mom off her back.

"Are you wearing white pants or black pants?" he asked, whipping out his phone and pulling up pictures to show her. "White would look better with your áo dài, but black is better with mine."

"Black then."

"Really?"

Thom shrugged. No matter what pants she wore, Culture Day would be disastrous. But maybe she could get out of it somehow. She still had time to think of something.

"Sweet!" Kha tucked his phone away. "Hey, great job earlier at the game!"

"You watched my game?"

"Yeah." An awkward pause. "It was the Monkey King, wasn't it? That's how you scored."

Thom opened and closed her mouth. *Lie. Make something up. Kha didn't understand the Monkey King—how could he?*

She laughed. "Come on," she said. Her laugh had sounded fake, even to herself. "You don't think I could have scored on my own? I'm good. You saw all this, didn't you?" She waved at the soccer ball, abandoned in the goal.

"I knew it was him. Thom—"

And thank heavens her phone buzzed.

"My mom's here," Thom said, glancing at the screen.

Kha tucked his hands in his pockets, looking hopeful and expectant.

Don't trust him, the Monkey King had whispered. But he looked so innocent and puppylike, and she didn't want to be rude. Plus, he'd watched her game, and he was being nice to her. He had always been nice to her. She hesitated. "Do you want a ride home?"

She hoped he would say no, but his megawatt grin lit up his face, those sharp incisors gleaming. "That'd be great!"

"Where are your grandparents?" she asked as they walked to the front of the school. If the Monkey King was following them, he was completely silent.

"Probably hanging out with their friends."

Thom laughed—old people had friends?—but realized Kha was serious. "Really? What do they do?"

"Play mahjong, mostly. Or Thirteen."

"I love Thirteen!" It was a popular strategy card game where players had thirteen cards and followed a set of rules to get rid of them. She had something in common with Kha. Well, with his grandparents.

"We should play it!" Kha walked with a bounce, like he was always about to make a flying leap. "You should come over. It's better with four people."

"When Ma and I play," Thom said, "we pass out the whole

deck, so it's more like Twenty-Six. But it makes it easier to guess what the other person has."

"I used to do that with my dad." It was the first time Kha had volunteered information about his parents.

"Did he let you win?"

"That's not really his style." Kha looked down at his shoes. "He likes to win. He thinks something's only worth doing if it means beating someone else."

"Even his own son?"

"If he let me win all the time, how would I learn to beat him?"

"Beating someone isn't the whole point of the game. Not always, as long as you're having fun."

"My dad never has fun." Kha still hadn't looked up, and now he shrugged his shoulders like he was trying to shrink into himself. Thom almost reached out to pat him.

"Maybe you can play against my mom. She always lets me win. Until I really started winning. Then she got more . . ."

They'd reached the car. Ma leaned over to smile and wave at Kha.

"Ruthless?"

Thom opened the door and gave Kha a strange look. "Fair."

19

TO THOM'S HORROR, MA INVITED Kha over to dinner, which he accepted after a short stop next door to get permission from his grandparents. And then to Thom's surprise, dinner wasn't as terrible as she'd thought it would be.

"Thom won the soccer game today," Kha announced, and Ma clapped. "How come you didn't watch the game?" he said.

"That mean coach kick me out, said I'm not allowed anymore. Sometimes, I still sneak in, but then I have to be verrrry quiet or they kick me out again. I wanted to be there today, but I had to teach a course at the library, so I couldn't come." She leaned over to plant a kiss on the top of Thom's head. "Good job, cưng!" Thom was pleased—Ma rarely hugged, much less kissed—but she was also embarrassed at the way Kha smiled at them. "See," Ma said. "I told you soccer would get better."

"Ma," Thom whispered, ducking so her hair hid her face.

"Wait, Coach Pendergrass banned you from the games? Forever? That's kind of harsh," Kha said.

"I scold one girl." Ma held up her index finger. "One time."

"She screamed at her," Thom said. "For like ten whole minutes."

Ma shook her head, but Thom leaned closer to Kha. "People were too shocked to stop her until the girl started bawling."

No wonder Bethany, Sarah, and the team didn't like her. Maybe they were just terrified of Ma.

"Was it someone on your team?" Kha asked.

"No, it was someone from Cocopa Middle, but the girl hates me, and Coach said she won't put me in the game when we play against them again." Not that Coach put her in the game much to begin with.

"One time," Ma repeated, shaking her head.

Thom and Kha looked at each other. His lips twitched. She almost choked trying to hold back her laugh.

Usually it was Thom's job to do the dishes, but Ma took over when it was time to clean up. "Go, go play with your friend." She took the sponge away. "Or do homework, or whatever you like for fun."

"Are you sure?" Thom stepped off the step stool she used to reach the kitchen sink because she was so short, folding it up and tucking it in the space next to the fridge.

"Yes, I clean up. Go have fun." Ma started humming as she soaped the sponge, and Thom headed back to Kha, wondering if her mom had been replaced with a more cheerful look-alike. Lots of weird things had been happening lately, so it wasn't impossible.

She stopped. Kha was crouched down, petting Mochi. Mochi, who usually shook so hard he almost fainted around her, was snuggling up to Kha as if Kha were made of treats. She approached slowly so she wouldn't scare her dog away. Mochi looked up, ears perked. He hadn't let her come this close in months.

"I guess he just needed time to get used to me," Kha said, scratching Mochi behind the ear.

"Weird." She leaned down and held back a gasp when Mochi nudged her hand with his nose. He was still shivering fearfully, but he actually let her pet him. Thom and Kha huddled together, playing with the dog until he got bored and ran back to his carrot chew toy. Kha didn't move, and for a few moments, everything was quiet and peaceful and Thom let herself forget about everything else—soccer, the dynamic trio, the Monkey King, and her superstrength—and focus on the fact that this was the first friend who had come over in a long time, who had stayed for dinner and laughed with her mom and played with her dog.

"Do you want to stay a little longer?" Thom asked. "We can work on our project."

Kha's eyes widened, and his mouth opened into a grin. "Yeah, for sure! We never decided on the topic."

"Let's go with the Four Immortals."

Kha looked surprised. "Are you sure? I thought you wanted to go with demons."

"You were right—demons might be too scary." And she would have to admit where she'd gotten all the information on them. Kha might know about the Monkey King, but she wasn't going to expose Shing-Rhe and the monkey brothers.

While Thom went upstairs to collect their art supplies, Kha ran next door to get some books from his grandparents. They spread out the poster and markers in the living room this time, and Thom began cutting and coloring while Kha flipped through the books and read out loud.

"First, there's the Sage," he said. "He has a hat and stick that combines into an umbrella and can fly."

"Oh, like Mary Poppins."

"Who's Mary Poppins?"

"She's like this magical nanny who has an umbrella that helps her fly." Thom propped the poster against the carpet.

"Magical nanny? What powers does she have?"

Thom considered that. "She can clean up very fast."

"Your mom must love her."

Thom chuckled. "And I guess she can make medicine taste better?"

Kha frowned, as if it had never occurred to him that these were enviable gifts. "I don't think the Sage is like that at all. He was this poor dude. Like really poor. Apparently, he and his father owned one loincloth. They had to share it."

Thom frowned over the poster at him. "Ew."

"That's what the book says." Kha hid behind the cover. "He married Princess Tien Dzung. The princess's father was super upset when he found out his daughter had married a commoner, so he sent soldiers after them. Instead of fighting back, they chose peace or whatever, and because of that they ascended into the heavens and became high immortals."

"How come he's called the Sage?" Hadn't the Monkey King called himself the Great Sage of Heaven? Was this the same person? Was it the Monkey King in disguise?

"He apprenticed with a sage, who gave him the hat and stick."

"How come only *he* got to become one of the Four Immortals? What about his wife? She ascended with him, right?"

Kha looked up from the book. Mochi's chew toy gave a squeak from the corner. "Maybe it's because she didn't study with the first sage? I don't know. I'll ask the next time I get a chance."

Thom wasn't sure if he was joking or not, but she cut out a triangular hat in yellow, and a stick. "Maybe we can add real straw to the hat."

"Good idea. Okay, next is the Mountain God. He was involved in a love triangle with the Lord of the Waters. They both wanted to marry Princess My Nuong, and the Mountain God won the challenge for her hand."

"Like a contest? Like she was a prize?"

Kha shrugged, looking harassed. "This was a long time ago, okay? Women's rights weren't a big deal back then!"

"I'm wondering if we should go with the demons after all."

"*Anyway*," Kha continued, "the Mountain God won, so the Lord of the Waters was enraged, and he flooded the world with storms and stuff. To protect the people, the Mountain God raised the mountains and saved them."

"So he was already a god? I thought the Four were mortals who ascended to become gods."

"He was a god of a mountain. A lower-level god who was in charge of a small area of the mortal world. His protection of the people allowed him to ascend to the heavens and join the greater immortals."

"Okay, cool," she said. "Who's next?"

"You'll like this one. She's known as the Mother Goddess. She was born in the heavens, but she was a troublemaker, and after breaking the Jade Emperor's favorite teacup, was banished to the mortal world."

"Must have been an expensive teacup." Thom cut the shape of a teacup out of some origami paper she'd never used. "Look!"

"Cute!" Kha grinned. "She lived her life as a mortal punishing bad people and rewarding good people, and every time she died and went back to the heavens, she begged the Jade Emperor to send her back so she could keep up her vigilante ways."

"Like a superhero."

"Yup."

"She's definitely my favorite. Okay, who's the last one?"

"The Boy Giant."

"Oh yeah." Thom picked up a new piece of construction paper. "The small baby who didn't talk or grow for a long time until invaders . . . um, invaded, and then he suddenly grew powerful and gigantic and beat them."

"Yup."

"But he wasn't a god before he ascended to the heavens?"

"No, I think he was a normal mortal."

"So how did he get so strong?" How did *Thom* get so strong? She paused in her cutting. She'd never made the connection before, even though Ma told the story all the time, because it was just a story. But if the Monkey King and demons were real . . . was she like the Boy Giant? Was she—

Ma yawned loudly, making them both jump. She'd been reading so quietly on the couch behind them that they hadn't even noticed she was there.

"Ayah, it's so late, you two." She looked at her phone. "Nine o'clock already."

Thom held back a yawn herself, stretching her neck.

"We got a lot done," she said, getting to her feet. Maybe Kha wasn't so bad after all. They looked down at the poster, a mosaic of construction paper depicting each of the Four Immortals' stories. "I think we can probably finish it tomorrow."

"Want to walk me home?" Kha asked.

Thom glanced at Ma, who nodded. She'd probably be watching from the door the whole time anyway.

The cold air felt good after such a long homework session, and Thom bounced on the balls of her feet. She hadn't had a night like this in so long, hadn't had a friend come over, and even though it had been for homework, she'd still had fun. She felt exhilarated, like she could do anything, but as she stopped at Kha's door to say goodbye, the serious expression on his face wiped the smile off hers.

"What's wrong?" she asked. "Are you worried about the project? We'll get it done in time. We have more than a week."

"No, that's not it." He wouldn't look at her.

She had a feeling what this was about. The excitement leached out of her, filling with heavy dread. "It's the Monkey King, isn't it?"

"You can't trust him," Kha burst out.

"That's funny. He said the same thing about you."

"What? Why? I haven't done anything."

"Neither has he." She lowered her voice, even though they were alone. "Why don't you like him? Have you even met him?"

"Because . . . you don't know what they say about him, about what he's done."

Thom hadn't trusted the Monkey King at first, either, from all the stories about his mischievousness, his reputation as a troublemaker and a trickster. But after hanging around him, she knew he was different.

"You said yourself that the Mother Goddess was a troublemaker," she pointed out, "but she was given many chances and reincarnated lots of times, and she became a superhero."

"That's different."

"How? Because she was a princess and Wukong is a demon? That's not his fault."

Kha shook his head. "I don't know what he has planned, but he's using you. That's why I'm here—my dad sent me to stop you from helping him."

A sharp pain twisted its way from her chest to the bottom of her stomach. So she'd been right all along. Kha wasn't there to be her friend. Why would someone cool like him want to be friends with a loser like her? Of course he was hanging out with her because he had to. He had been assigned to her, like she was a chore.

Something in Thom's stomach soured. What a bad way to end the night. "You're right," she said. "You *don't* know. The Monkey King's my friend. He's never asked me for anything, but if he needs my help, then of course I'll help him."

Kha's face went red. Was it just her imagination, or did it suddenly get much hotter? "He's manipulating you, and you're falling for it."

She stepped back, away from the searing heat of his body. She wasn't imagining things. The air was much cooler the more space there was between them. "*He's* my friend," she said.

"He's a demon-god. He doesn't have friends. He doesn't

even know what friendship means!" Kha's face was tense, the skin around his nose scrunched. That shimmer was back on his cheeks, not just a trick of the light anymore.

"Oh? And you do?" she snapped.

Kha looked confused. His skin stopped shimmering, and the temperature cooled.

"*You're* not my friend, either," Thom said. "*You're* the one who lied to me."

"Thom?" Ma called softly across the yard.

"Maybe we should find different partners for the project," Thom said.

Kha clenched his jaw and looked like he wanted to say something else, but Thom didn't want to hear anymore. She walked away.

20

THOM PUSHED KHA'S WARNING OUT of her head. He didn't trust the Monkey King, but the Monkey King didn't trust him, either. She wasn't sure who to believe. Kha was the first person who'd wanted to be her friend since she'd moved to Troy, while the Monkey King was the one who'd helped her, taught her to control her power, shown her that she could use her strength after all.

But Kha didn't really want to be her friend, did he? He'd admitted it—he had another motive. Was anything he said even true? *He* was the one who'd lied and manipulated her. The Monkey King had always told the truth, even when it made him come off as the bad guy. At least he had always been honest with her.

And the Monkey King knew why she was like this. He hadn't told her so, but little things he said when he visited, almost every night now, convinced her that he knew exactly why she was superstrong. Hints about another world, other magical creatures.

Ever since discussing the Four Immortals with Kha, she couldn't help wondering about the Boy Giant and how they were so much alike. But he was a god, who ate a bunch of rice to grow and defeat the enemy. Thom was just a mortal girl, who continued to grow stronger every day for no reason.

If the Monkey King didn't have the answer as to why she was special, at least he could take her *to* the answer.

"I want to go back," she said one night when he popped in through the window, "to the Mountain."

"My home? Why?"

"I've been thinking—about how you're training me to control my power? I could get better if I knew more about it, and I could ask Shing-Rhe—I'm sure he knows."

The Monkey King flipped through a textbook from her desk. "Useless teachings," he muttered. "Where's the magic? What good will this do you?" He opened to a diagram of the ecosystem. "I hope everyone knows that lions eat other animals. Who would be stupid enough to test that theory?" He tossed the book over his shoulder.

"Can we go?" Thom hopped off her bed and pulled a jacket from her closet. But as she shoved her arms through the sleeves, she stopped. The Monkey King looked odd . . . serious.

His brows drawn in a way she'd never seen. When he noticed her staring, his grin broke the effect, and his eyes gleamed with their usual mischief.

"Fine. The brothers will be happy to see you."

Thom glanced at her bedroom door. Ma had tucked her in a couple hours ago, but she sometimes came back to check on her, or just opened the door to peer in when she thought Thom was asleep.

Just to be sure, Thom fixed her bed so that it looked like she was buried under the covers, just like she'd seen in movies about rebellious teen daughters.

It was kind of thrilling, like she was a different person, someone who got in fights, who snuck out at night, someone who hung out with the Monkey King.

◆ ◆ ◆

Her hat and scarf keeping her warm and no fever threatening to make her faint, Thom found the flight to the Mountain much more enjoyable this time. Despite it being pitch-dark when they'd left her house, the Mountain was bathed in sunshine, like a magical paradise perpetually in beautiful weather and full of green life.

This time, it wasn't empty. They landed in a forest clearing filled with animals. But these animals looked odd, like someone had chopped up different animal parts, mixed them up, and pieced them together. Thom didn't immediately slide off the Monkey King's back when he released her legs.

"Um, Wukong? What . . . who . . . ?"

"Friends. It's okay." He patted her hands, but she didn't release her death grip on his shoulders. "I'll keep you safe."

If anyone could, it would be him. Still, her hands shook when she let go and turned to survey the herd circling them. They were demons. She knew without asking. Animals shaped like humans, like a pig that stood upright in a man's body, with a snout for a nose and sharp horns above his ears. A cross between a hyena and some sort of bear with a plump, fluffy body, and a mean sharp-toothed jaw.

Hiding behind the Monkey King didn't help. No matter which way Thom turned, there were more, at least twenty or thirty of them.

A white-furred figure stepped forward. A girl. Her eyes were large and doelike, full of curiosity and framed with thick black lashes that contrasted with the pure white of her skin and fur. Her nose was elongated almost into a fox's snout, but not quite. She sniffed at Thom, crouching low to observe her from head to toe.

Thom should have been scared, but something about the fox demon made her want to pull her into a hug instead, maybe because she reminded Thom of Mochi.

"This is Concao," the Monkey King said, pulling Thom forward. "Concao, the mortal girl I told you about."

Concao sniffed Thom again, then leaned close to the Monkey King to whisper something.

He brushed her aside, beckoning to Thom. "Meet the rest of my friends." He turned to the demons and growled, a hissing sound, complete with bared teeth.

Thom jumped and jerked away. She'd never seen the Monkey King like this. The muscles of his face taut, spit flying. He really did look like a demon. His growl lingered, becoming words in a language too old for her to understand, and the demons shrieked in return. Thom forced her hands to stay still instead of doing what she really wanted them to do, which was to cover her ears. It was too loud, animals everywhere, crying, howling, jumping.

And worse, some looked at her with a hunger like they wanted more than just to eat her, like they wanted something else, something deeper. Solid ice formed in her veins. Had the Monkey King tricked her? Taken her just to feed her to his demon friends?

And then, the Monkey King's growl erupted into laughter, his staccato giggles cascading over the crowd like bees spreading pollen. The other demons broke into laughter, too. One tackled another, and pairs teamed to wrestle and roll across the forest floor.

"They're demons," the Monkey King said, as if that explained everything. "Here." He grabbed the pig, who was wrestling a smaller creature, with bovine legs but a manlike torso. "This is Pax. Pax, my friend Thom."

Pax snorted. "Girl flesh," he grunted, moving closer to her like he was ready for a feast.

"Not dinner," the Monkey King said, stopping him. "Just play."

"Play?" Pax eyed Thom with his thin black lips pursed. "Pax no play with weaklings."

"Oh, but she's no weakling. Show him, Thom."

"Show him what?" This was getting too weird. She'd wanted the waterfall, the cave, the monkeys' oasis. Not demons who had to fight the urge to eat her. Sure, they'd resisted so far at the Monkey King's request, but what if they decided they didn't want to anymore?

"Your strength."

"No." An automatic response. She didn't want to use her power, not if she could help it. She wanted to find out more about it, about where it had come from. She needed to talk to Shing-Rhe and find out what he knew about her: her background, the source of her power.

The Monkey King was next to her, an arm around her shoulder, head bowed like they were sharing secrets. "Listen, these demons value strength over anything. Like pack animals."

"Like wolves."

The Monkey King nodded. "You have to show them you're the alpha."

"But . . . I've never shown my strength in front of anyone

else before. At least not on purpose." The Monkey King was the only person she trusted enough to use her power around because he was strong enough to withstand her strength. The other times had all been accidents and ended with broken things or injured people. Her strength was a curse.

"You want to learn how to control it, don't you? Then you must use it. Just show them you're not a weak girl, Thom. You're strong." He punched her shoulder playfully.

She took a deep breath. It went against everything she wanted, but the Monkey King had brought her here to his friends, and if she backed down, she would embarrass not only herself but also him. What would it hurt? These were demons, they looked strong, and they wouldn't hesitate to hurt her if the Monkey King didn't stop them.

At her nod, the Monkey King bounced away giggling. "An arm wrestle, to start," he announced gleefully. The animals shrieked and formed a circle around Thom and Pax, who propped his elbow on a tree stump. She faced him, bringing her palm to his. "And . . . go!" the Monkey King shouted.

The shrieks and growls grew louder as Pax shoved at Thom's hand. It didn't budge. He must have been pretty strong—he was three times her size and looked like he could charge down a car or a train. But her hand stayed where it was. The demons went quiet, and the awe washed over them, filling her with pleasure and . . . pride. She was good at this, at being strong. By default, but still. Too bad it wasn't something she wanted to be good at, but at least she could have some fun before she figured out how to get rid of it.

With a smile, she took in Pax's shocked, slack-jawed expression, and easily brought his arm down to the tree stump.

The animals rolled with laughter. Pax's bovine friend pointed a finger at his face and guffawed until Pax tackled him.

The hyena stepped up to Thom, growling in her language, then placed her elbow on the tree stump.

"Your turn?" Thom asked.

She nodded, or at least Thom thought she nodded—the demon bobbed around a lot.

A line formed behind the hyena, other demons eager for their turn. The Monkey King floated above them, giggling and flipping through the air.

Thom arm-wrestled one demon after another, each win resulting in rounds of laughter and animals lunging playfully at one another. It was the first time she'd been able to use her strength for fun. And it felt . . . well, a bit wonderful. The demons were still kind of terrifying, but she also found them

endearing. Like how you know panda bears could bite your head off and they were, like, hungry all the time, but they were also so adorable and fluffy. She laughed as a small fox—not quite as old as the Monkey King's friend Concao—came up next.

As the growling, shrieking demons kept fighting one another for a chance to get closer to Thom, a warm sensation settled over her, something she hadn't felt in a long time. These creatures accepted her for who she was, didn't question her strength or think anything was wrong with her. Instead, they seemed to love her for her power, just like the Monkey King had. This must have been why he'd brought her here, to show her that she could belong, that there was a world that would accept her for who she was, even if she couldn't. Not yet.

It took her a while to realize that something was missing. It wasn't exactly quiet, with all the animal sounds.

But the Monkey King's giggle was gone. *He* was gone.

By now, all the animals had had their turn arm-wrestling her, and they were rolling around fighting with one another. As she walked through the crowd, a few punched her shoulder. Some rolled back, a feral offer to wrestle, but she shook her head and moved on. Where was the Monkey King?

Once she was away from the crowd, the trees muffled the chaotic growls. Leaves and twigs crunched beneath her feet; the scent of flowers and fresh dew filled her nostrils. An insect buzzed next to her ear, and she waved it away. She made out the *ooh-ooh* of the Monkey King, and the occasional chuckle. He was hopping around Concao, who sat on her hindquarters, head raised high, like a sophisticated, elegant snow fox. She was so unlike the other demons, her movements soft, flowy, well-mannered, and quiet. She could almost pass for human, except for her thick white fur.

Thom moved toward them, but then stopped when she heard the Monkey King's next words.

"Where is it? You know, don't you? But you won't tell me."

Thom knew she shouldn't eavesdrop. In movies, it always ended in disaster, but she couldn't move. They'd see her if she tried to slip away now.

"I only discovered recently," Concao said, her voice low and husky. "It's in the heavens."

"The heavens?" The Monkey King didn't look happy, his face blank.

"That's all I know."

"Who told you?"

She lifted her head, refusing to answer.

"They'll keep it in the armory," the Monkey King said as he punched his right fist into his left palm. "We can break in, get it back."

"Break into the heavens?" The tip of Concao's tail flicked. "Wukong. That would be suicide."

"I can get us in. I've done it before."

"And you can do it again. Alone."

"Come with me."

The fox demon's tail swayed. "Ruin my chances for good?"

"Chances? What chances? You don't believe they'll actually make you a fairy, do you?" He laughed, but his laugh was full of meanness, not because he thought what he'd said was funny. "Look at you! You're a demon. To them, you'll never be anything else."

Concao rose to her feet, lips pulled over sharp fangs. "I won't help you. You can't trick me into doing it. Not this time."

The Monkey King *ooh*ed softly at her. "Sorry. Sorry, my friend." He nuzzled her neck and shoulder. Concao closed her eyes, settling into the affectionate embrace. Thom looked away, embarrassed.

"You know I'm useless without my cudgel, Concao," the Monkey King said. "I need it. And I need your help to take it back."

Concao's eyes opened, her jaw tight.

"Please, my friend."

But Concao was done with the conversation and slipped lithely away from him. She didn't rejoin the demons but ran off into the forest.

Thom caught the Monkey King's expression before he went back to the clearing. For just a brief second, she saw him without the mischievousness he kept up when others were around. His face was creased with worry and loss.

But when he saw her, his face immediately brightened. "Come," he said. And he pulled her onto his back, giggling the whole way to the sanctuary behind the waterfall.

The oasis was just like they'd left it, bathed in sunshine and full of butterflies, the rainbow arching over the babbling stream. Birds sang in the distance.

Shing-Rhe greeted them with tired but happy warmth. He looked even older, his whiskers gray and dark circles under his eyes. He sniffed at the Monkey King and shook his head but didn't pull away when the Monkey King hugged him.

"You've been with the others," Shing-Rhe said.

"They're my brothers, too, brother." The Monkey King cackled.

Thom tried to catch Shing-Rhe alone, but the Monkey King stuck close to his brother's side, talking with his voice lowered, and stopping and grinning at Thom every time she came close.

"What is it, child?" Shing-Rhe asked. The Monkey King

was watching her closely. "You look like you've got something on your mind."

"Do you know why I'm like this?" she asked, tired of waiting for the right moment. "Why I'm so freakishly strong?"

"The gods have bestowed upon you a gift. Like they did with Wukong."

"But Wukong chose to learn those skills, right?" She turned to the Monkey King. "You left and studied with a master and learned how to do magic."

The Monkey King giggled. "Who told you that? Your pet dragon?"

"You did. The night we met. You called them the Seventy-Two Transformations."

"What else has that dragon told you about me?" The Monkey King hovered close, batting his eyelashes.

"So it's true, then?" she asked. "He really is a dragon? He's not lying?"

"All dragons are untrustworthy," Shing-Rhe said. "They pledge their loyalty to the Jade Emperor."

"He's lying about something," the Monkey King said. "But not about being a dragon."

Thom bit back a groan. "So what am I then? Why am I like this?" When neither of them answered, she added, "How do I control it?"

"With discipline and practice," Shing-Rhe said.

"How long will that take? How long did it take you?" Thom asked the Monkey King.

"Centuries."

"Centuries?" She didn't have that long! She had another soccer match in a couple days, and it was already getting harder to avoid hurting anyone, not to mention how closely Kathy had been watching her lately. "Isn't there some way to . . . like, skip that?"

"You can't cheat what can only be accomplished with discipline," the Monkey King said.

"Then can I just get rid of it?" She held out her hands like she could just give her strength away as easily as that.

"We don't know, child," Shing-Rhe said.

It wasn't his fault, but she couldn't help the frustration that gnawed at her insides, a biting, stinging sensation, followed by the poisonous, numbing effect of isolation. No one else was like this. No one else knew why or how or what it felt like.

The Monkey King put his arm around her shoulders and led her away, bending his head close to hers. "Don't be sad, Thom-Thom. I know how you feel."

"No, you don't," she snapped, then felt bad for snapping, an apology already forming. But he just nodded silently.

"I may not be exactly like you, but I'm the only one of *my* kind, too, remember? The only demon-god to ever exist. Belonging to neither the heavens nor the mortal world."

Her anger melted slowly. He was incredibly strong,

too—he was actually stronger than her, despite what Kha had said, and he had a bunch of other powers as well.

"How do you deal with it?" she asked.

"Deal with it? That's the problem, Thom-Thom. You act as if it's a curse, but it doesn't have to be. It's what makes you special."

"But I don't want to be special."

"You want to be just like everyone else?"

"No, not . . . exactly. Just normal."

"Look at my brothers." The Monkey King pointed at a group of five monkey demons snoozing in the shade. One rolled over right under a small water stream, which shot up his nostrils. He sat upright, blinked, and lay back down, only to roll over and land back under the water stream again. "If I was like everyone else, that would be me."

Thom loved the monkey brothers, even though they seemed a bit . . . listless . . . at times. She wasn't going to insult them out loud, but the Monkey King had a point.

"I thought you wanted to be a great warrior," the Monkey King said. "And you can't be that without your strength." He patted her on the top of her head. "Here, sit here." The Monkey King led her to a perfectly round and smooth boulder. "This is the Thinking Stone. It will help you conquer your greatest doubts."

"How do I use it?" She rubbed the stone, but nothing happened. That knot in her chest was still as tight as ever. "Is it magical?"

"No. Just hug it and meditate."

"Hug it?"

"Like this." He plopped belly-down onto the boulder and extended his arms over the side. Feeling awkward, Thom tried not to laugh as she copied him, taking up the other half of the giant rock. "Good. Now stay like that until you achieve clarity."

"Um, okay." She wanted to ask where he was going, but he'd bounded back to Shing-Rhe before she could speak up. The rock was warm from the sun, and even though she felt silly, she relaxed against it, resting one cheek on the smooth surface. Her eyes drifted shut.

"What has he promised you?" a hoarse female voice said above her.

Thom jumped, flopping onto her butt, surprised to see Concao the fox demon sitting on top of the boulder. She hadn't even heard her approach. "Are you allowed here?"

"Why shouldn't I be?" Her fluffy white tail swayed back and forth, but not in the playful way Mochi's tail sometimes wagged. Concao's was like a careful warning to stay back.

"I thought this was the monkeys' sanctuary."

Her eyes narrowed. "Then why are you here?"

"I'm the Monkey King's friend."

"Are you sure about that?"

Thom didn't know how to answer.

"Wukong doesn't believe in favors," Concao said.

"What do you mean?"

"He protects the monkeys, but in return, he's declared himself their king. They have to do whatever he says, even if they don't want to."

"But Shing-Rhe said they *made* him their king."

The fox demon didn't reply; she just studied Thom with sharp intensity.

"What is it he wants them to do?" Thom asked.

"I'll tell you if you tell me what bargain you've struck with him."

"But I haven't struck a bargain."

There was a long pause, like the fox demon was trying to determine whether she was lying. "You must want something, don't you? Something he can help you get." Concao got to her feet silently. "Don't let him use it against you."

After she left, Thom looked back at Shing-Rhe. He was laughing at something the Monkey King had said, and their brothers surrounded them, jumping and *ooh*ing and wrestling one another. Was Concao just jealous of her friendship with the Monkey King?

Thom couldn't get it out of her mind: the image of the Monkey King and the fox demon standing so close, looking at each other with focused attention. They had been talking about some cudgel in the heavens.

Then it came to her. That's what had looked so strange about the Monkey King the first time she saw him. In the stories, he always carries his cudgel, a staff made of iron that can change size. It could grow as tall as one of those skyscrapers in downtown, or small enough to tuck behind his ear when he wasn't using it to fight.

And it was missing.

21

WHAT WAS THE FOX DEMON to the Monkey King, really? Thom found herself replaying the scene in the forest as she got her gym bag ready for her game the next afternoon. They had seemed closer than friends.

"You're going to do great."

She was used to the Monkey King's voice speaking out of nowhere now, even when he chose not to be visible. A faint outline sat on the edge of her desk. He knew they were playing against Monrovia tomorrow. A different goalie this time, or so Coach had told her. The first one was still benched, her ribs bruised, but at least the brace had come off.

"I'm nervous, but I think I'll be okay, with all the practicing we've been doing." She zipped her bag.

Things were getting better lately. She'd been practicing her kicks every day, sometimes on her own, sometimes with the Monkey King's help. She was ready to play—Coach had even put her in a couple games. All in the left center, but still better than sitting on the bench.

The Monkey King appeared, cross-legged on her bed right above where her knees were, but she felt no weight. She studied him. The missing cudgel was glaringly obvious now that she'd noticed. Like Harry Potter without his round glasses or Sherlock Holmes without his plaid hat. Why hadn't she noticed before?

"How's your friend?" she asked.

"Which friend?"

"Concao."

He picked up the ball next to her nightstand and bounced it on his head. "Who?"

Thom sank into her mattress, energy leaving her like air out of a balloon. "The fox demon. I don't think she likes me."

"Oh. That one. Hmm. Why so curious?"

"Just wondering."

"Haven't seen her since," he said.

"Doesn't she live on the Mountain?"

"All demons do. The ones that don't live elsewhere." He giggled. "It's the only place they're not imprisoned, forced into a magic gourd, or exorcised."

"What's 'exorcised'?"

"Like . . . when a demon possesses a mortal and a monk forces him out."

"Wait—demons do that?"

"The truly evil ones, yes. Oh, don't worry," he added, seeing her face. "None of my friends would even think of it. They know where their place is. On the Mountain. The ones who stay in your mortal world are the ones you need to worry about."

He tossed the ball high and flipped upside down. It plunked off his bottom and bounced across the room, while he flopped down onto the mattress.

Thom laughed as he flew into the air again. But she couldn't stop thinking about the missing cudgel. She blurted out, "Wukong, where's your staff?"

He stopped somersaulting and narrowed his gaze at her. "Why do you ask?"

"I just realized you don't have it."

"Did *you* take it?" His face clenched with fury, making Thom's blood run cold.

"N-no. Why . . . would you think that?"

For a moment, she thought he didn't believe her, crouched like that, like a spring ready to bounce.

And then he broke into gales of laughter, rolling and tumbling toward her. He gripped her shoulders. "Your face!" He wheezed and choked until there was no air left, then wiped his eyes.

She pushed him away.

"Oh, Thom, sweet little Thom, were you scared? Did I scare you?"

"Well." She didn't want to admit it, but he had looked ready to attack.

"I would never hurt you." He surprised her by pulling her into a hug. It was warm and close and furry. "You're my friend."

A sense of comfort rolled through her stomach when she heard him say it out loud. "You're . . . my friend, too," she said softly.

He gave her a final pat. "My cudgel is in the heavens. Someone—whoever locked me in the temple—took it, and gave it to the Jade Emperor. Probably for good points."

"Good points?"

"Maybe the Jade Emperor rewarded him. A chance at immortality, at becoming a fairy, living in the heavens. But who would want that?" He made a face and stuck his tongue out a few times like he'd bitten something bitter.

"You did," Thom pointed out.

"When I was no more than a baby. But I learned the hard way that life in the heavens is worse than life in the hells."

"You've been to the hells?"

"Just for a short stint."

She frowned. "What were you doing in the hells?"

"Rescuing some friends."

"But . . . how did you get in? Or out?"

"I am the invincible, handsome Monkey King, remember? I still had my cudgel with me then."

"Can you get it back?"

"Me? I'm not allowed in the heavens anymore." His voice was almost sad. Then he giggled and flipped backward so fast he became a blur and disappeared.

The ball dropped onto her bed. She looked in the direction he'd gone.

"You could get into the heavens, though," he said as his body re-formed above her.

"I can't do that. I'm mortal."

"Are you sure about that?"

She zipped her gym bag. "What does that mean?"

"Concao said that you're not . . . completely mortal."

So that's what the fox demon had whispered in the Monkey King's ear.

"You're something else," he said.

"Something else?"

A breeze next to her, a weight on the mattress. "She said you might even be . . . part god."

Thom shook her head. "No, that's stupid. I'm not."

"It would explain your incredible strength," he said. "There's only one I know as strong as you are. And he's a god."

The Boy Giant. Maybe she could meet him. Ask him about his strength, how he lived with it.

"You can do it," the Monkey King said. "Get into the heavens. Learn about your true self. That's what you want, isn't it?"

Thom turned to face him. But he was gone.

• • •

Thom's team won the next game, but without her of course, so when Coach treated the girls to dinner at a famous barbecue restaurant, she wanted to call Ma to pick her up as soon as possible.

"Nonsense, No," Coach said when Thom asked if she could go home early. "You're part of the team. You need to celebrate with us."

Finding a seat among the other soccer players was more stressful than being in the cafeteria at lunchtime. None of the girls looked at her; they only huddled closer, spoke louder, and pretended she didn't exist. The only ones who did acknowledge her were Bethany and Sarah, but their glares weren't at all inviting. Kathy also made eye contact, but she inclined her head slightly to the right, as if to tell Thom to get lost. Or maybe it was a warning. Thom couldn't tell.

She sat with the coaches instead. Coach Pendergrass dug into her food while Martha recounted the highlights of the game. Thom was pretty sure she ate, but later she couldn't remember what the food tasted like, and she was more than grateful when they packed up and headed back to the school. She'd texted Ma that she was on the way, but even so, she found herself as one of the last ones to be picked up. Everyone else was gone but Kathy.

After away games, which usually ran a little later, Coach waited until the last girl was gone, but tonight she had an emergency and left Martha with them instead. They stood outside at the school pick-up area, shivering. The wind had picked up, cold and sweeping, and the moon was hidden behind thick clouds, the streetlamps barely lighting up the dark parking lot. A strong gust of wind almost knocked Thom over; she managed to stop steps before stumbling against Kathy.

Martha guffawed. "We might have to put rocks in your pockets, No!"

Thom, who'd always been smaller than most kids her age, was used to people telling her that, but Martha kept laughing like it was the funniest thing anyone had ever said. Kathy rolled her eyes.

"Ooh, this weather's chilly," Martha said. "I'll be right back, girls. I'm just going to run and get a thicker jacket right quick."

Thom stood closer to a streetlamp, bracing one hand on it in case another gust hit. To her surprise, Kathy followed, looking cozy inside her thick fur-trimmed coat, which she'd draped over her soccer uniform. Somehow, this managed to make Thom feel frumpy in the hoodie and school-issued sweats she'd put on over her own jersey.

Kathy surprised Thom even more when she spoke to Thom voluntarily. "Sorry you didn't get to play today."

"Oh. I mean . . ." Thom coughed. "I never get to play? But . . . thanks." Her ears burned, and she gripped the lamppost harder, wishing it were big enough to shield her from any other awkward thing that came out of her mouth. "I mean thanks for saying that."

"You must really like soccer if you're still willing to stick around after being benched and everything." Kathy flipped her hair over her shoulder, somehow managing to keep it from whipping into her face in the wind.

"I did. At my old school, I was pretty good."

"Really? What happened?"

Ouch. But Thom couldn't defend herself without spilling everything she'd worked so hard to keep secret. "I tried to quit, but Ma says I have to finish out the season."

Kathy nodded. "My parents won't let me quit, either."

The sound of metal grinding caught their attention, but it was just a nearby pole rocking slightly from the wind. Thom couldn't talk for a bit when her hair blew into her face. Kathy handed Thom a scrunchie, and memories—a hundred of them—slammed her all at once, of all the times Thuy and her old teammates had done the same thing.

"Why do you want to quit?" Thom finally asked. "You don't like it?"

"I don't know. I only joined because Bethany talked me into it, and like, my parents have this thing where I have to keep busy all the time. It was either this or piano lessons, which ugh." Kathy rolled her eyes. "It's like just because I'm Asian I have to play the piano, you know?"

"My mom never made me play the piano." But Thuy's did, and her ex–best friend used to complain about it, too.

"You're lucky."

Thom could only stare at her.

Kathy exhaled. "Yeah, so now I'm stuck with soccer."

"Would you choose piano instead now if your parents let you?"

"Ugh, no. That's such a cliché. If I was going to play an instrument, it'd be something that's actually cool, like the drums or the guitar or something. They're really mad, though, because they bought the piano but no one uses it, so now it's just in our house."

"Yeah. My best friend"—Thom left out the *ex* part—"had a choice between piano or violin."

"That's even worse—violins are so depressing."

"I like them."

Kathy gave her an assessing look that Thom couldn't dissect. "If you didn't play soccer, what would you do instead?"

"Ma would probably find me an SAT tutor. They offered pre-high-school sessions back where I used to live, but they don't have anything like that here. Thank goodness."

"Right? It's like we're not even in high school yet and they already want us to prepare for college. I don't get it. Bethany's and Sarah's parents don't do stuff like that. They're *so* lucky."

Was she really bonding with Kathy? Over the exhausting pressure of having Asian parents? She had never really thought about how strict Ma was before. Compared to her friends' parents, Ma had always seemed like the more lenient one, except for certain things—always having the dishes done and a clean room and an organized bookshelf—but that was a Ma thing, not an Asian parents thing. She huddled closer to the lamppost. "I know, right?" was all she could think of to say.

"Maybe—"

But Kathy didn't get to finish, because a strong gust shoved Thom forward. She grabbed the lamppost, but instead of steadying her, the metal bent under her hand. The pole pitched sideways, electric sparks exploding. The light went out as the lamppost fell toward Kathy's head.

Thom grabbed it and pulled it upright before it landed.

"Oh my God." Kathy's eyes widened, going from Thom's face to her hands on the pole. "*I knew it.*"

Thom didn't know what to do. She followed Kathy's gaze to her hands, then let go.

The lamppost swayed once more, then slammed to the ground with the noise of a thunderclap. Thom and Kathy stood on either side of the fallen pole.

"Oh my God," Kathy muttered again.

Martha ran outside, screaming, "What was that? Good Lord, are you girls okay? Get back, get back!"

A car pulled up that Thom didn't recognize, but she figured it was Kathy's parents, coming to pick her up.

Then Ma arrived. She leaned over to shout out the passenger-side window as she drove up.

"Thom, I'm sorry I'm late. There was car accident, and—"

"Ma, look out!"

She slammed on the brakes. Her car stopped an inch from the other car.

Kathy bolted toward the first car. Thom called out to her—to explain, to make an excuse, to lie—but Kathy slammed the car door, and the car drove off.

Thom couldn't move. Martha was still flittering about, apologizing, and Ma was trying to get Thom's attention, but all Thom could see were the taillights of Kathy's car, the red lights blinding her vision. That was it. It was all over. She'd worked so hard to hide her secret, and all for nothing.

Her life was finished.

22

THOM WENT UP TO HER room, giving short answers when Ma kept trying to explain why she had been late. She offered to bring Thom something to drink, but Thom could not think about food at a time like this. Her mouth felt like she'd tried to eat chalk. Her skin was tingly and numb all along the back of her neck.

She couldn't stop picturing Kathy's reaction: the shock, the wide eyes, the dropped jaw, the fingers flexed like she was reaching for help, like Thom might hurt her.

If Kathy hadn't known before, she definitely knew Thom's secret now.

How long would it be before she told Bethany and Sarah? Because of course she would tell, they were her BFFs. And then the team would know—they already thought she was weird. Then the school. Then the world.

What was Thom supposed to do now? She couldn't go

back to school, couldn't face Kathy and the others. It would be easy for them to prove how much of a freak she was—she could barely control her strength now, even after all the coaching from the Monkey King.

Why was she like this? Why *her*?

She had to get rid of her strength. Then they wouldn't be able to prove anything. Then no matter what Kathy said or who found out, Thom could show them that she was normal.

But how?

She needed the Monkey King.

While she sat waiting for him, her leg jiggling, something clicked. She knew what she needed to do. Warmth rushed back into her veins as she came up with a plan.

◆ ◆ ◆

When he finally popped into view, sitting on the windowsill, swinging his legs, she stood up and rushed to him.

"What could you do if you got your cudgel back?"

In legends, the Monkey King was unstoppable with his cudgel, so powerful even the immortals hadn't been able to defeat him. He could fix this. He was the only one who understood her power, who had known how to help her. The fox demon had said that the Monkey King could get Thom what she wanted. All she had to do was make a deal.

"All sorts of things," he said. His eyelashes fluttered. "Why? Have you an enemy you want me to obliterate? Those girls at the school—the ones who always trip you? Just tell me, and I'll—" He punched a fist into his other palm.

"No—not that. Can you . . . Would you be able to get rid of my strength?"

For the first time since she'd met him, he seemed surprised. "Why?"

"Because I hate it."

"But you're learning to control it. I'm training you to be a fighter. A warrior." When she didn't respond, he studied her face. "Your power is a part of you—"

"No, it's not." She cut off whatever else he was going to say—something just to make her feel better about what she was. She was sick of it, of adapting, of compromising. She would change things, control something for once. "I hate being like this. I want you to make it go away. If you had your cudgel back, would you do it?"

He studied her face like he was scanning a book. "If I had my cudgel," he said, "there is not much I cannot do."

"But would you? Would you take my power away?"

He nodded, looking serious. But not for long. His contagious grin spread. "Of course. But how can I when I don't have my cudgel?"

"You said it was in the heavens." He would do it, take her power, fix everything, just like she knew he could. She almost hugged him. "What if I sneak in and get it for you?"

He bounced in front of her like he was on an invisible

trampoline. "Yes! You can sneak in, find it, bring it back to me."

Thom felt a lightness she hadn't felt in a long time, like she was the one who could fly. "Okay. So how do I get into the heavens?"

He giggled and bounced high, then higher, until he floated and circled her head. He grabbed her hands and pulled her up, her legs leaving the ground. They swung through the air in a wide dance.

"I will take you," he said.

"But you said you can't get in."

"To the Gate. I'll show you how to get through and where to find the staff."

Her body felt weightless. The Monkey King's hands gripped hers tightly, securely.

"When?" she asked.

"Tonight. Now."

"Now?" Too soon. She thought she'd have time to plan and prepare.

"You want your power gone, don't you?" He stopped spinning and lowered her back down.

"But what about school? Ma—"

"You will be in and out quickly. No one will notice. But . . ."

"But what? Tell me. I need to know everything that could go wrong if I'm going to do this."

"If you stay in the heavens too long," the Monkey King

said, his fingers lacing and unlacing, "you may get stuck there."

"*Get stuck there?*" Thom's voice came out squeaky. "How long?"

He hid his hands behind his back. "Forever."

Thom tried to gulp, but a lump stayed stuck in her throat. "So I would die. Basically."

The Monkey King scratched his armpit, pulled out a hair, and held it up to his face. "You have a few days at least before that happens."

"A few days . . . Like one or two or what?"

He stuck the hair into his other armpit. "I don't know."

"What do you mean, you don't know? What if I can't come back? Ma would go crazy!"

"I don't know because I don't know how mortal you are. A full mortal would only have one day at the most, but you are not—"

"Not normal." Thom was starting to freak out. He was right, though; she must not be full mortal. How else could she explain her strength? But that didn't mean she could just stay in the heavens or come and go as she pleased. If the heavens knew, if the gods caught her, if she stayed too long by accident, then what?

"Don't worry." The Monkey King touched her cheek, the pads of his palms rough compared to his fur. "They won't catch you. I will teach you exactly what to do."

"What happens if they do catch me, though?"

"They won't. Come on." He opened her closet and riffled through her things. "Change into something warm but
stealthy."

"Stealthy?"

"Yes. You will need to be quick, invisible. Because, Thom-
Thom, you are about to become a thief."

◆ ◆ ◆

Someone was following them. She'd thought she was imagining it at first, but she and the Monkey King were flying above
the clouds, and the flicker of a large blue-feathered tail was not
something she could have made up twice.

The tail itself was white, but covered in pearly scales that
shimmered. The feathers cascaded down the top, a cerulean
blue, the kind her mom would have chosen if áo dài came in
that color, and if Thom were
milky-complexioned enough to
pull it off.

"Wukong!" she shouted
over the wind. "Someone is following us!"

His ears twitched, and he
looked to the side. He nodded.

He went faster, flying up, then down, diving into the white sea of mist.

A shadow moved in the cloud, a huge shape, long and serpentine.

The Monkey King charged toward it.

A dragon—a rồng—emerged. Its face was furry, its whiskers blue. Scales grew from the top of its head and trailed down to its tail. Thom didn't get a good look at its eyes, because just then the Monkey King thumped the dragon hard on the nose.

The dragon's head dropped, and it dipped several feet. Its tail lashed out, but the Monkey King dodged, shrieking with laughter.

"Begone, dragon! Or I will pummel you into dust."

"I'm not here for *you*." The dragon spoke, but its voice belonged to Kha.

Thom almost lost her grip on the Monkey King's shoulders. "Kha! What—"

"Go home, dragon," the Monkey King said, gripping Thom around her knees to keep her from sliding off.

"Not without Thom."

"She's with me now."

"She doesn't know what she's doing."

Annoyance pricked Thom's throat. "I know what I'm doing!" she said.

"He's tricked you," the dragon said. "Like he tricks every-one."

"This is *my* idea."

The dragon—Kha—shook his head. "Come with me, Thom. I'll explain everything." He turned so his back was close enough that she could climb on.

Fly on the back of a dragon? For a moment, she was tempted. Or maybe she could reach out, just to touch his feathers, to see if a dragon was really there.

"The Monkey King promised to make me normal," she said. "It's what I want."

Kha peered at her through the eye on the right side of his face. "You'll never be normal, Thom."

Her throat ached, like she'd been punched there. The Monkey King hissed, baring his teeth.

"And you call yourself a guardian?" He flew away, but Kha followed. "Leave us alone, snake!"

"Thom," Kha shouted, but the Monkey King flew faster, so fast that she couldn't hear whatever else Kha said over the roar of the wind. Her eyes watered until she couldn't see him anymore. She buried her face in the Monkey King's neck and hung on.

23

THE GATE OF THE HEAVENS was not a gate, but a temple, its red roof curving and sharpening into points that pierced the plush white clouds. The building was decorated in gold carvings that pulsed with light. Thom stood next to the Monkey King, her heart pounding. This was it. The Gate. A way into paradise. A heavy building that sat on a field of white mist, floating impossibly in the sky.

It was bigger than her school, from what she could see. The entrance itself was ten times the size of the school's entrance, the doors red and smooth.

"This is what you're going to do," the Monkey King said, pulling her into a puff of clouds.

That was another thing. They were walking on clouds.

At first, when the Monkey King had set her down, she'd clung on, refusing to let go. She was sure she would sink right through. He could fly—but she would fall to her death. But

he made her let go, and to her surprise, her feet had found solidness beneath the mist. It was soft, sort of like stepping on sand, her foot sinking into it, but it held.

"You will go through those doors and meet with the Gate-keeper, Xuan-Ling. Tell him you are a Lotus Student, freshly appointed, and that you must speak to the Lotus Master."

In her imagination, Thom had seen herself sneaking in and out of a building—an armory—taking the Monkey King's cudgel, and sneaking back out. She hadn't realized she'd have to talk to people, to lie. She'd never been good at lying, especially to grown-ups. Especially not elders—she couldn't disobey them. The thought made her mouth dry.

"Then once he brings you to the Academy, you get your robes and go to the Jade Palace, and find the armory. It's in the basement, three floors down—"

"But where is the Jade Palace?"

He giggled. "It's the tallest temple on the highest cloud. Trust me, you will know it when you see it."

The plan seemed more complicated the more she pictured herself going through the steps. People would notice her—they always stared. They would stop her, question everything.

"Won't they ask why I'm going to the armory?"

"If anyone stops you, tell them you're on an errand for the Lotus Master. They're all afraid of him."

"Why?" If everyone was afraid of the Lotus Master, then Thom certainly should be.

He waved a hand. "He's nothing but an old man—don't worry about him. Listen. Basement of the Jade Palace, the armory. You will sneak in, find my cudgel, and get back out. But remember, the staff is very heavy."

"Seventeen thousand pounds." She nodded, then stopped. "You're the only one who can wield it because it's so heavy."

"You are strong enough to carry it. Don't worry. You picked up a truck, and it's . . . almost as heavy as the cudgel. I know you can do this."

Thom wasn't as sure, though. The whole scheme was much more complicated than she'd imagined. She'd thought it would have been like sneaking candy out from a store, not *Ocean's Eleven*-level thievery. "How big is the staff? In the legends, in your . . . stories . . . sometimes it's as tall as a building and sometimes it's as small as a pin."

"I don't remember."

"Don't remember? This is important. How am I supposed to carry it out if it's bigger than me?"

"It'll be the same weight no matter what size it is."

"Wukong."

"I don't remember, all right? I don't know anything about why I was in that temple or who took my staff from me."

Thom narrowed her eyes. "I don't like this plan. I want to go home."

"No, no—listen." The desperation in his voice surprised them both. *Desperate* was not a word that could be used to describe the Monkey King. He was calm, cool, collected, full of giggles and tricks. He cleared his throat, blinked rapidly, and manipulated his expression into its usual carefree mischievousness. "You want me to take your power away, don't you? Make you normal?"

Yes, more than anything, she wanted that, and the fact that she could have it, so close if only she could do this one small thing, made her dizzy. She nodded.

"Then you'll have to get my cudgel."

She took several deep breaths, but that still wasn't enough to calm her nerves. She couldn't go home yet. The Gate was right there. The heavens . . . somewhere beyond. And the idea of seeing it all, seeing immortals and fairies and the Jade Palace . . .

"I'll tell you a secret," the Monkey King said in a whisper even though they were the only ones in a sea of clouds. "Something no one knows. Not my brothers. Not Shing-Rhe. Not even Concao, my closest friend."

A thrill ran through her. The Monkey King trusted her enough to tell her something no one else knew. "What is it?"

He beckoned for her to lean closer. "The cudgel is not that difficult to control. All you have to do is ask it to change sizes, and it will."

Whatever she'd been expecting him to say, that wasn't it. "Ask it? Like a spell, you mean. Like in *Harry Potter*?"

"No, not a spell. Just ask it, like you would an old friend. Its name is Ruyi Jingu Bang."

"It has a name?"

"Of course it does. All magical things do. But no one remembers, which is why it doesn't listen to anyone but me. And you, now that you know its secret." He paused, his brown eyes warm and sincere. "You'll keep my secret, won't you?"

Thom had spent enough time with the Monkey King by now that she was starting to be able to distinguish between moments when he was being honest and when he was playing games. There was something in his eyes—that twinkle when he was his usual playful self, and a deep earnestness when he was being genuine, a depth like you could drown yourself in the darkness of his pupils.

She trusted him.

Kind of.

No, of course she trusted him. He was her friend; he had taught her to control her power—or tried to anyway—and now he understood why she didn't want it. He was the only one willing to help her, the only one who *could* help her.

"You must promise, Thom."

"Okay, yeah, I promise to keep your secret."

"And you'll go?" His eyes were like puppy eyes, turned down at the corners, a little wet and shiny with tears. A monkeyish sound echoed from his throat, like a whimper. Begging.

Thom took a deep breath. She turned toward the Gate.

"Wait," he said. Then he plucked out a hair from the top of his head and held it out to her. "For luck."

◆ ◆ ◆

She leaned back to look up at the Gate, which was at least fifty feet tall, its red surface engraved with gold etchings. No handles jutted out from the surface; there was no obvious place to knock or get in. She glanced around her, but the Monkey King was gone, or at least, not visible. Since he wasn't allowed in the heavens, he probably couldn't even go near the Gate.

Thom raised a hand to the Gate and pressed her palm against the glistening surface. It was warm, and to her surprise, it shifted as soon as she touched it. There was no shudder, just a silent movement, a swirl of mist as the Gate moved inward, across the cloud where the temple sat.

Mist clouded her vision. She should have been scared, not being able to see what was inside, but all she felt was a sort of nervousness, and not even the bad kind, but like the kind she'd had right before she'd stepped through the entrance of Splash Mountain. Excitement.

She crossed the giant threshold. The fog swallowed her. Beneath her, the ground solidified. She no longer walked on clouds but on marble, and yet her footsteps were silent. When she stomped her foot to see if it would make a sound, the surface swallowed the noise.

She walked. And walked and walked. How much time had gone by? How far had she gone?

Thom stopped, and her mind cleared. She blinked and shook her head, trying to see through the mist. Objects, faint outlines of statues on pedestals, pillars of gold marble. At one end, an archway.

She started toward it, but the clouds moved in, the fog swirling until her head was thick with it, like she'd breathed in poison.

"Hello?" she called out. If this was the Gate of the Heavens, shouldn't there be guards? The Monkey King had said there'd be a Gatekeeper. "Is anyone there? Guards?" She lowered her voice back to normal. "Immortals? Monsters?"

"There are no monsters here."

Thom jumped, spinning around and around and throwing up her hands defensively, automatically. Nothing but mist. The voice sounded like several men had spoken at the same time.

"Who are you?" she asked.

"It is more important that I ask you that question. You are, after all, the intruder here."

Thom stopped spinning, stopped trying to look for him—them. The mist made her dizzy; trying to see through it made it worse. "My name is Thom Ngho and I . . . I'm a Lotus Student." What else had the Monkey King said? "I need to . . . to see the Lotus Master."

The voice didn't respond for so long Thom thought whoever it belonged to had abandoned her.

Then the mist cleared, enough so she could make out a long hallway, the archway she'd seen before at the end of it, and a tall figure walking toward her.

It was a soldier, armored from head to toe in gold and purple plating—royal colors. On his head was a funny-looking helmet, not really a hat but a round black knob that perched on the crown of his head, with long feathers sprouting from it, swaying like a peacock.

"A Lotus Student?" His voice no longer sounded like several people at once, but she knew it had been him. "You?" He looked her up and down and walked around her. Thom started to turn back, but he tsked, so she stayed still, subjecting herself to his inspection. Whatever he saw must have been extremely disappointing, judging from the scrunch of his nose.

"Please." She tried to sound polite, not desperate. "Can you take me to the Lotus Academy?" Find some robes, the Monkey King had said. Pretend to be a student. Sneak into the Jade Palace. Find the armory, steal the staff, and hightail it out of there. Easy.

She could do it. Step one, trick the Gatekeeper.

"It is not my job to take you anywhere except through the Judgment Veil, and to banish you should your soul be deemed unworthy of entering the heavens."

What on earth did that mean? The Monkey King hadn't said anything about a Judgment Veil.

"Follow." He turned toward the archway. Everywhere he stepped, the mist cleared and closed in behind him. When he became a faint outline, Thom lurched forward, jogging to catch up.

"Whoa," she breathed when they stopped before the archway. It was a work of pure, solid white gold, with flowers etched into the surface and words written in ancient characters she didn't understand.

In the archway itself, the fog grew thicker and shimmered with some sort of magic. Colors danced on the surface of tiny water droplets, but she could see it only if she unfocused her eyes or turned slightly away.

"This is the Judgment Veil," the Gatekeeper said. "You will pass through it, and if you are found worthy, you will enter the heavens."

"And if I'm not?"

"You will be sent to the hells," he answered in an annoyed tone, as if the answer were obvious.

Thom's eyes widened. The Monkey King had said nothing about that. Her palms were sweating. She couldn't go to the hells. For one thing, she was still alive, and for another, Ma would kill her. She still had to graduate from middle school and high school, take the SATs, and become a doctor, lawyer, or engineer. Her whole life was ahead of her.

She took a step back, but the Gatekeeper stood behind her, and his face, while mostly unreadable, let her know that it was too late now. If she ran, he would catch her and figure out that she was up to something.

"Go," he said.

She stepped forward. Was she worthy of entering the

heavens? Was her soul pure enough? It was like the days before Christmas all over again, her mom taunting her with the question of whether she'd been naughty or nice, even though they both knew Thom was just going to get a bunch of socks and lots of books.

Was she good enough to enter the heavens? What did that even mean anyway? *Good enough.*

And then she was under the Veil.

A cold but gentle cascade of water splashed over her. Each particle of magic dusted over her skin like droplets of rain rolling down a glass window.

It wasn't unpleasant, but her breath caught, and she gasped for air. In first grade, before she'd developed her strength, she'd been punched in the stomach by a mean boy—and this felt something like that. Not pain but absence: an absence of air, of life, of thought, until her entire body was focused on being awake, on being here, on being, on not not-being, on staying, staying, please let her stay—

And then air filled her lungs, and the sensation was gone. She fell to her knees, sinking into the mist.

"You," a voice said, making her jump. The mist had cleared, and Kha stood over her, in human form, nostrils flaring. "Are in so much trouble."

24

"I NEED TO GO TO the Lotus Academy," she said, getting to her feet. "Can you show me the way?"

Kha's mouth opened. He had trouble finding a response, and Thom didn't blame him. She was surprised by her own brazenness, but she didn't have much time. She didn't know how long she had in the heavens—a day, maybe two.

"If you think for one second," he said, "that I'm going to help the Monkey King—"

"You're not helping him. You're helping me."

"No. No way. You're coming with me." He grabbed her hand, but she yanked free, sending him bouncing across the fluffy cloud.

"Oh, oops, sorry!" Thom said, scrambling to help him up.

But just as she reached out to him, he started to change shape. His skin took on a shimmer, the same glow she'd mistaken for makeup before, spreading over his cheeks, down his neck, and along his hands. His body stretched, his legs elongating and merging into one serpentine limb, his mouth forming a snout with long blue whiskers, and his skin turning into shiny scales all along his body. Fully grown in his dragon form, his body twice as thick as before, stretching at least ten feet long. Light reflected off his scales, which were white at first glance, but shimmered like mother-of-pearl as he moved closer. Thom was so transfixed by his beauty that she didn't realize he was wrapping his serpentine body around her like a snake around a mouse.

"What are you doing?" she demanded. Heat blossomed over her torso, where he touched her. Sweat broke across her nose.

"I'm taking you to my father. He'll know what to do."

"No." She nudged at his coils, but he was stronger as a dragon than she'd expected, and the multiple layers of muscle formed a wall that was closing in, tighter and tighter. "No . . . Kha . . . stop . . . I . . . don't have time for this."

He didn't stop until he was wrapped around her in a snug fit.

"Let me go before I really hurt you," she warned.

He huffed, smoke trailing out of his nose. "You're strong, but you're not fireproof."

Her skin was now so hot it felt like she was developing a fever.

Something caught her eye in the distance. At first, she couldn't make out the shapes until they came closer. Soldiers, some on foot and some on the backs of flying horses the size of elephants.

Were *these* the horses the Monkey King had been put in charge of? They were huge! The sun reflected off their jade helmets and golden saddles as they galloped in the air, heading straight for her and Kha.

Kha saw them, too, and swept toward them, dragging Thom within his coils.

She panicked and shoved harder at him, and this time, he winced, unwinding just a little. She sucked in a breath and, with enough space now, kicked. Kha cried out and uncoiled entirely, and she used the moment to drag herself out of his grip.

And straight off the cloud.

Someone was screaming. It was her. She flailed her arms, as if that would stop her fall. Above her, sky. Below her, endless mist.

"Why are you screaming?" Kha's voice cut in.

"I'm falling!"

"No, you're not."

She looked over her shoulder, to prove her point, and discovered that he was right. He peered at her from the cloud she'd just fallen off, which was actually right above her still.

She was floating. "Why *aren't* I falling?"

"This is the heavens. That's not a thing here."

"So I can . . ." Thom did an awkward frog kick and glided forward, sort of like swimming. "I can fly," she said. She looked up and saw the Jade Palace, covered in jewels, the tallest building on the highest cloud. A glow appeared around the palace, as if its jewels were illuminated from the inside. If she could just make it up there.

"Oh, no, you don't." Kha zipped toward her so fast she reacted out of instinct and swung her fist, hitting him in the side of his dragon head.

"Ouch!" she shrieked, shaking out her scalded hand. His scales were burning hot, like a car door handle that had been parked all day in the sun. He jerked to the side, blinking slowly. She used the moment to swim-fly away and found that when she focused on an object in the distance, she seemed to go faster. But the Jade Soldiers were getting closer, and it was only a matter of time before Kha caught up with her.

She landed on the nearest cloud, which housed a white building several stories tall. She ran up the steps and through the door, slamming it shut behind her. She was inside a huge lobby, and everything was made of white marble. Above her, a glass ceiling opened into the heavens, casting the building in bright daylight that reflected off the stone and made everything shine.

A girl stared at her, wide-eyed.

"Help," Thom gasped, out of breath.

"What's wrong?" The girl wore white robes with an embroidered collar, too fancy to be a servant.

"Someone's chasing me," Thom said. For once, she was grateful for her small size, which made her look weak and helpless, a magnet for people who wanted to be heroes.

The girl took one look at her and pulled Thom quickly from the door. "I know where you can hide."

"Thank you." Thom didn't look back as they ran.

"Who's chasing you?" the girl asked as they moved through the labyrinthine halls. "And why?"

Beneath the white marble surface of the walls, something shimmered, reflecting light from the glass ceiling.

"This dragon. I don't know why. He just—"

"Here." The girl opened a closet door and pushed Thom inside. "Let me see if I can get rid of him."

Thom didn't know what to think, but the girl was gone, and she was alone in the small space. It was a storage room for a bunch of wooden fighting staffs, cluttered in the corner. Something moved in her pocket. Was it her phone? Had Ma woken up to discover that Thom was missing?

Her screen was blank. She had no signal.

Thom put the phone away, then almost yelped as her hand brushed against something . . . furry. And that furry thing wrapped its arms—claws? tentacles? legs?—around her finger. She yanked her hand out, then slapped the other one over her mouth.

A tiny, tiny Monkey King was swinging from her pinky finger and grinning. He couldn't be much taller than her thumb.

"Hello, Thom-Thom!" he squeaked. He sounded like someone who had inhaled air from a helium balloon. He tried to fly but could only manage a tall leap before landing on his butt, groaning. "My powers are diminished," he wailed.

Thom was so relieved that he was there she leaned against the door. But it didn't make sense. "I thought you were banished from the heavens?"

"I am. However, I knew that a single hair could pass through the Veil. I just wasn't sure I would be able to manifest in my true form once we made it to the other side."

She lowered her voice. "I still don't get it."

"I can duplicate myself with my hair, remember? Each golden hair is a piece of me."

She'd forgotten about that. The skin on the back of Thom's hands itched, and she scratched it absentmindedly, wondering what to do next.

"Where are we?" he asked.

"I don't know. I was running from Kha."

"That gangly snake-noodle is here?" The tiny Monkey King punched and kicked the air. "Take him down, Thom-Thom. If he tells the gods you're here, they will send you to the hells!"

"The hells? What—why?"

"That's the punishment for breaking into the heavens."

For a second, she couldn't speak. Why hadn't he told her that before she'd agreed to the plan? She wanted to throttle the Monkey King, but he was so tiny right now it wouldn't be a fair fight. "You didn't tell me that!"

"I didn't know the snake would follow you!"

There was a knock at the door.

"Who's that?" the Monkey King squeaked.

"This girl," Thom whispered. "She helped me hide. I have to go."

"Put me behind your ear," he suggested.

She lifted him to her face. His hands tickled as he climbed over the ridge of her ear and tucked himself snugly against her head. "Can you hear me?" he shouted.

"Ouch, yes. Maybe a little quieter."

"Okay," he whispered. He tugged her hair around himself like a curtain.

"Better." She took a breath, still reeling from what he'd told her. If she took too much time, she'd be stuck here forever and never see Ma again. But if someone caught her, she would have even bigger problems. She didn't want to get sent to the hells. She needed to find that cudgel, and quickly.

She opened the door, but she must have pulled too hard, because the entire thing broke off, leaving gaping holes in the frame where the hinges had been.

"Thom," the Monkey King breathed in her ear, adding to her horror. If *he* was shocked, then she'd really messed up.

"No, oh no." Thom tried to put the door back, but it stayed upright for only a few seconds before it leaned over and fell with a *slam* that shook the whole building, the whole cloud maybe.

Thom winced, then looked up and found herself face-to-face with the girl. She must have been close to Thom's age, maybe twelve or thirteen. Her jet-black hair contrasted and framed her pale face; her eyes were round.

"How did you do that?" the girl asked.

"I'm sorry," Thom blurted. "I didn't mean to. I can't control it."

"Control what?"

Thom bit her lip. "I'm strong—really strong. And I . . ."

I'm so sorry." How had she done that? She'd barely touched the door.

"You must be stronger in the heavens," the Monkey King whispered. "My powers are diminished here, but your power has increased."

But what did that mean? She wished she could ask him, but the girl was looking at her.

"It's fine," the girl said. "The dragon chasing you is gone. I told him you left the Academy."

Did that mean this was the Lotus Academy, the one the Monkey King had talked about?

"He's dealing with the Jade Soldiers now, too," the girl said. "They're mad that he caused needless trouble when they're already so busy."

Thom exhaled, suppressing the guilt she felt that she'd gotten Kha in trouble. "Thank you."

"How do you know Kha?" the girl asked Thom.

"You know Kha?"

"He's my archnemesis," she said matter-of-factly.

"Oh." Thom wondered what Kha could have done to earn an archnemesis. And did that mean the girl would help her? "I'm Thom," she said. "Who are you?"

"I'm Jae." She held out a hand, a surprisingly grown-up thing to do. As Thom focused on not gripping too hard and hurting the girl, she noticed a green stone glinting off Jae's finger.

"How is Kha your archnemesis?" Thom asked.

"He's the bane of my existence, the most annoying person I've ever met. He's obnoxious and relentless."

"Wow." Thom didn't think Kha was that bad, despite the fact that she'd punched him earlier. That was out of self-defense. He was actually starting to grow on her, even though he kept getting in her way. She knew he meant well. He just didn't understand what she was going through.

"Why was he chasing you?" Jae asked.

Thom couldn't think of a lie fast enough, so she told the truth. "He wanted to take me to his father."

"The general?"

Wait—Kha's father was a general? Thom was starting to get a headache there were so many things she didn't know. Had his father sent him to the mortal world on some sort of military mission? He'd said that he'd been sent there to stop the Monkey King. And that meant she needed to keep as far from the general as possible.

"Why?" Jae asked. "Is it because of your strength? Is Kha trying to recruit you for the general's division?"

Something tickled Thom's ear. The Monkey King. Thom bit back a laugh. "I *am* strong," she blurted out as the Monkey King crawled down her neck.

"Her ring," he whispered. But she couldn't ask what he meant.

"How strong are you?" Jae asked.

"Like, really strong. I can lift up an eighteen-wheeler." At the girl's look of confusion, Thom added, "It's a really heavy, um, vehicle. It weighs tons."

Jae's expression cleared. "Are you as strong as the Boy Giant?"

"I don't know. I don't think so. He's a god, right? I'm just . . . I was," Thom said, "just a mortal."

"The Boy Giant was, too, before he became one of the Four. Have you talked to him? He could tell you more about yourself."

"Talk to him?"

"Come on, I can show you to his office."

"Oh. That's very nice of you, but you're probably busy . . ." She needed to get to the Jade Palace and to the armory. She didn't have time to talk to the Boy Giant, no matter how much she wanted to learn more about herself. There was no point— not unless he could take her power away. And even if Thom learned to control it, Kathy knew now and would tell every- one. Thom didn't have any choice but to steal the cudgel so the Monkey King could get rid of her strength.

But the girl insisted. "I was on my way to see him anyway. Besides, we need to tell someone about *that*." Jae nodded at the broken door.

Thom scratched the back of her hands, then stuffed them in her pockets, but she didn't see any way out of it.

"Yes, yes," the Monkey whispered from her hair. "Follow her. We need that ring."

"Okay," Thom said weakly. "Where is it?"

"It's here in the Lotus Academy," Jae said. "The Boy Giant hasn't been here too long. Just a decade or so."

Jae didn't think a decade was long? How old was this girl? Thom looked around, at the high ceilings, the white marble floors and walls. The place was plain and yet somehow opulent. Its minimal decor said more about how important it was than any glittering chandeliers or heavy furniture could. This was where the Lotus Students trained to become Jade Soldiers.

"After the Boy Giant came back from the mortal realm, he secluded himself for years and we all thought we'd never see him again, like the rest of the Four," Jae said as they walked. "But then the Lotus Master convinced him to use his experience to train the Jade Army."

Thom ogled everything they passed. Inside open doors, students gathered in white robes, some sparring and fighting, some meditating, some studying from heavy books. No one paid attention to Thom or Jae, too focused on their own activities.

They reached a suite of rooms. Jae knocked gently on the closed door at the back of the suite, as if she didn't want to startle whoever was inside. "Master? Are you in there?"

"Yes," a nervous-sounding voice answered through the door. "Who is it? We don't have an appointment. Do we?"

"It's Jae. Father asked me to give you something, and there's someone here who needs to talk to you."

A moment of silence before the door opened, and Thom came face-to-face with the Boy Giant.

25

HE WAS ABOUT MA'S AGE. But he was much taller than her, his bald head smooth and unadorned. And he was dressed in elaborate purple-and-gold robes. As he moved, his skin was illuminated by the light, a golden color that seemed to glow. Thom thought she was imagining it, but when he opened the door, his skin brightened even more. He really was a god.

"Jae, hi! And Jae's friend, hi." His second "hi" was not as excited. Thom sympathized—she hated to be surprised by new people, too. But as his gaze fell on Thom, something odd happened to his face: a freezing motion, an unhinging of his jaw before he snapped his mouth closed. "Hi," he said again, his voice softer when he spoke to her this time.

"I'm Thom."

"Yes, I . . . Hello," he sputtered. "Come in, come in." He opened the door wider and ushered them inside. The room was bare, though colorful mats were spread across the floor. "Excuse the mess," the Boy Giant said, leading them toward the back of the room through another door. "We had a meditation class earlier, and then I had the strongest craving for moon cake. I was preparing some tea—and cookies, of course. Would you like to join me?"

His gaze flickered to Thom, but when she smiled back, he looked away, busying himself by ushering them to a table.

"Sit, please, I'll . . . um . . ." He dashed off.

His nervous energy made Thom want to help, and it was weird to sit down while the Boy Giant—a god—served her. But Jae gestured for Thom to sit with such authority that Thom sat. She focused on her surroundings. The Boy Giant's office was filled with ancient books, scrolls, and throw pillows. Brightly colored cushions cluttered the floor, the couch, even the chairs where they sat. A scent filled the air, a delicious savory smell, followed by something sweet and comforting.

The Boy Giant returned with a plate of cookies still hot from the oven. Then he said, "Pork buns? Or spring rolls? Or maybe wontons?" He didn't wait for them to answer. "Never mind. I'll bring them all out."

"Oh, you don't have to," Thom said, unable to relax when she had been trained from birth to help in such a situation. "We're not that hungry, and we don't want to take too much of your time."

She regretted saying that when she saw the Boy Giant's crestfallen expression. Jae nudged her with an elbow.

The Monkey King giggled in her ear. "Just eat the cookies, Thom-Thom."

Thom inhaled deeply. "Actually, I was wrong," she said. "It smells delicious, and I'm starving."

The Boy Giant smiled and nodded vigorously, placing a plate in front of her and piling pork buns and wontons onto it. "Eat, eat, eat. You are so small. I had no idea…" His voice grew quieter, and she thought he mumbled, "I should send them more peaches," but she couldn't be sure, because why would he say *that*?

He added the last wonton to Thom's plate, not noticing that Jae had been reaching for it. Thom slipped it to Jae when the Boy Giant wasn't watching, and the girl smiled and winked a bit too hard, like she had never actually done it before but had always wanted to.

The Boy Giant sat down. He looked at Thom, and she looked back. He seemed so nervous, which made her even more nervous, but there was also a familiarity about him, like they'd met before but she couldn't remember when. She was sure she wouldn't have forgotten an encounter with one of the Four Immortals, though.

No one spoke. Jae had her mouth full, Thom wasn't sure what to say, and the Boy Giant took up his teacup.

"Oh, sugar!" he said. "I forgot the sugar. Would you like

some, Thom? How do you take your tea? Creamer? Milk? Condensed milk is my favorite." He must have realized he was babbling, and he pressed his lips together as if to force himself to stop.

"Sure, I'll have whatever you have," Thom said politely.

"But what do you like?"

"I don't know. I don't really drink tea. I mean, I've never had it like this." She gestured at the elaborate table.

He set his cup down. "You don't drink tea? But . . . your mom must . . . Doesn't she?"

"I'm sure she does, but I don't. I mean, I like boba. Does that count?"

"Boba?" He seemed unsure, then got up abruptly and returned with even more ceramic cups, full of milk and sugar. "Try the condensed milk." He fixed a cup with a frown on his face. "It's quite difficult to believe you've never had tea like this. Your mother loves tea," he said. "Doesn't she?" he added quickly.

"I think so," Thom said.

"But she must!"

Thom gave him a weird look. How would *he* know what Ma liked?

He cleared his throat. "It's just . . . tea is so important! Here, try this."

She grasped the cup as carefully as she could manage and took a sip. Her eyes widened. "Okay, I know why Ma wouldn't want me to drink this. It's delicious." Deliciously sweet. Ma was okay with microwaved meals but not with too much sugar, though probably because she didn't want Thom jumping off the walls.

"Yes, condensed milk is the best." He made an okay sign with his thumb and index finger. "And how is your mother?" he asked, his eyes innocently wide. "Are the two of you close?"

"Yeah, we are." Thom and Ma had always only had each other.

"And does she still like—I mean, does she like . . . cookies?"

"Yeah, but she doesn't let me eat too much."

"Mm-hmm, mm-hmm," he murmured. "What about peaches?"

"We never have peaches at home." Why was the Boy Giant asking her all this? Thom hid her face behind her teacup.

"Ah," he muttered to himself, nodding.

They fell quiet as they drank their tea and wolfed down

the food, setting into a comfortable silence. Eventually, the Boy Giant spoke again. "Now . . . what was it you wanted to ask me?"

"Oh." She glanced at Jae, who gave a reassuring nod. "I have this ability, a superstrength," Thom said. "And . . . it's kind of a nightmare living with it. I'm always breaking things. I hurt my soccer teammates all the time—by accident. I broke a door earlier, here, at the Academy. And . . . so . . . I want to get rid of it. My strength."

The Boy Giant's face went very still. He didn't say anything for a second, making Thom afraid she'd said the wrong thing. What if she'd offended him? He had a superpower, too, and he didn't want to get rid of it.

But then he nodded, and she let out a breath.

"Why not try to control it instead?" he asked. "Rather than get rid of it? You might be able to do good with your power."

"See, I told you," the Monkey King whispered.

She ignored him. "I've tried," she told the Boy Giant. With the Monkey King's help, Thom had won a soccer match. But that hadn't helped. She'd almost killed Kathy when she knocked over the lamppost, and now everyone would know and her life was doomed.

"Why do you think I'm like this?" Thom asked. "One day, I noticed I was stronger than before, but ever since then, it's gotten worse and worse. Was it like that for you?"

"It was a long time ago," he said, "but when my family was

in danger and no one else had the strength to save them, it was almost as if my power had been in hiding and then emerged because we simply didn't have any other choice."

"But how? I mean, I know you're a god now, but weren't you mortal before? How did you gain that strength? Did another god give it to you?"

"I'd had no encounter with any gods before I became strong."

"So we're alike then? You just became strong out of nowhere also."

"In that sense, yes."

"Okay, but if your strength came when you needed to save your family, does that mean mine's the same? Am I supposed to do something . . . epic?"

The Boy Giant considered this. "Perhaps."

"Then what is it? Will my strength go away if I do the thing? Can't I just get it out of the way and go back to being normal?"

"My strength didn't go away after I fought the invaders."

"That's because you ascended to the heavens and became one of the Four Immortals, though, right?" She looked down at her half-drunk tea. "Will that happen to me? I don't want to ascend. I don't want to leave Ma."

The Boy Giant surprised her by patting her shoulder. "Perhaps you wouldn't have so much trouble with your power if you learned to control it."

"But I told you, I've tried. The—" She'd almost blurted out that the Monkey King had been helping her. "I'm afraid I'll hurt someone. There are these girls at school . . . and I . . ."

"You're different," Jae said, speaking for the first time in a long time, understanding what Thom couldn't bring herself to say.

"They make fun of me," Thom said. "They think I'm weird, and this superstrength only makes it worse."

Jae looked down at her plate but didn't respond.

"You could stand up to them," the Boy Giant suggested.

"I can't," Thom said automatically. "I don't want to hurt them."

"They seem to have hurt you much worse."

When Thom slumped in her seat, the Boy Giant went on.

"You don't have to use your strength. You can stand up to them in other ways. You may be stronger than most beings, but your strength is not the best part of you, Thom. You are mighty in other ways, too."

"Mighty?" She couldn't help snorting. That was definitely not a word she'd ever use to describe herself.

"Yes, mighty."

The idea was too ridiculous, and she giggled.

"You must believe me," he said, even though he couldn't help smiling. "It helps to practice saying it to yourself."

She shook her head. "I'm not mighty."

"Yes, you are. Say it. Say, 'I am mighty.'"

She laughed and looked at Jae, but the girl didn't seem to

think it was so silly. At the Boy Giant's stern but encouraging expression, Thom sat up straighter. "I am . . . mighty?"

"I am mighty," the Monkey King sang in her ears, sounding awed, as if he had only just realized it himself.

The Boy Giant smiled and held his fists on his hips. "I am mighty." He flexed his biceps. For the first time since she'd met him, he didn't look nervous or jumpy. He was smiling, comfortable, looking at her like he'd found something he'd been searching for, for a long time.

"I am mighty," Thom said, still hesitant.

"I am mighty." He thrust his chest out.

"I," the Monkey King sang. "Am." He tugged on the top of Thom's ear. "Mighty," he whispered into it.

Thom laughed and turned to Jae, who held up her own fists and exclaimed, "I am. Mighty!" Thom and the Boy Giant clapped.

"I never felt like I was part of the mortal world," he said, "even when I was a little boy. All my cousins were so loud and boisterous. No one understood why I chose to remain silent. They all thought something was wrong with me, and treated me . . . different. Until my strength was revealed, of course, when the world needed me to be strong. Everyone thinks having great power is . . ."

"Cool?" Thom suggested.

"Yes," he said. "But in truth, it simply means you must use it responsibly."

She had never thought about her power that way. Her superstrength had been a burden, not a responsibility. "Like Spider-Man," she said.

He gave her a quizzical look.

"He's also really strong, and he can climb walls and stuff," she said. "He's a superhero," she added.

"Are there lots of humans who have abilities like this?"

"Um, yes? They're not real, though. They're just stories."

"Are you sure they're not real? That they're not immortals?"

"Some of them are part god, like Wonder Woman. But sometimes there's an accident or something and they end up with powers. Or they're just really rich and can buy *things* with lots of power, like Batman. Or they're from outer space, like Superman."

The Boy Giant looked amused. "And you like these characters who have special powers."

"They don't just have powers. They use them to save people."

"Ah." His face brightened. "Like giants."

Thom laughed, then realized he wasn't joking. "They're normal-sized, though."

"Giants can be normal-sized, too. Look at me." He spread his arms. "And you."

"But I'm not a giant."

"Aren't you?"

"What do you mean?"

"Think about your strength, Thom. No mere mortal has this gift. You're different."

"But that doesn't make me a giant, does it?"

"Being a giant has less to do with size and more with using your powers to help others—like you said. Like this Bug Man."

"Spider-Man."

He smiled. "Is that something that would interest you?"

She didn't understand what he was asking.

"I could train you to be like me," he went on. "To help others. Defend those who are weaker than you."

"You want me to be the next Boy Giant?"

"Hmm. Something like that."

"But I'm not a boy."

"You would be the *Girl* Giant." He paused for effect, but Thom was too shocked to speak. "You would learn how to fight, do some good with your gift. How does that sound?"

It sounded ... impossible. Thom wasn't an immortal—she shouldn't be in the heavens at all. She was only here because she wanted her power taken away, not to use it. She remembered the look on Kathy's face in the parking lot, the way Bethany and Sarah look at her every day.

Something clinked, and they all looked down at the teacup in Thom's hand. She'd crushed it, and tea was dripping all over her fingers.

"Oh, I'm sorry." She held out the broken pieces, and a

wave of frustration, raw and bitter, rose up inside her. She had barely moved. She'd been holding the cup lightly.

"I think I see your problem," the Boy Giant said. "This is something I can help you with." He took the pieces from her and placed them on the table. "Think about it," he said.

But Thom wasn't really listening. She knew there was nothing to think about. The Boy Giant was a god! How could she take his place? She was nobody. Just a mortal girl with abnormal strength. A power that did more harm than good.

She had hoped talking to the Boy Giant would give her a better idea of who she was and where her strength had come from, but now she knew that it didn't matter.

Before they left, Jae handed the Boy Giant an envelope. "This is for the garden banquet later tonight. Father asked if you can see him later."

"Oh, I almost forgot," the Boy Giant said. "You should come, Thom!"

"Oh, please, Thom!" Jae lowered her voice. "I don't ever have anyone to talk to at these things. It would be so nice to have you with me."

"But I don't have anything to wear."

Jae grabbed her hand. "You can borrow one of my dresses."

Thom caught the Boy Giant's eye, and he smiled.

"It would be great to have you there," he said softly.

"Yes, let's go," the Monkey King whispered, tugging on her ear. "I want that girl's ring!"

"I can't stay long," Thom said.

"Oh, we won't," Jae said excitedly, pulling Thom to the door as if afraid Thom would change her mind. "Come on, let's get ready."

Thom tried to bow goodbye to the Boy Giant, but it was awkward since Jae was practically running.

"I'll see you later, Thom!" he called after them.

26

AS THEY LEFT THE ACADEMY, the Monkey King chattered excitedly, bouncing around against Thom's neck. "This is wonderful. The ring is the key to the armory. And she'll take us right to the palace and to the cudgel. We're almost out of here, my little thief."

It was difficult to pay attention to him when Jae was also talking and they were passing so many beautiful clouds with extravagant buildings on them. Temples with sharp points arching upward, each more elaborate than the last. Buildings that twinkled and glowed with their own ethereal light. A cloud filled with trees and flowers in every color imaginable, and the sweet scent of peaches.

"What is that?" Thom asked.

"That's the Forbidden Garden of the Peaches of Immortality, where the banquet will be held," Jae explained. "The fairies tend them. Kha's mother is the head of the order."

"Kha's mother is a fairy?" Thom exclaimed. No wonder he was always so well-dressed and knew exactly what to say and how to act.

"Yes, a fairy mother and a general father. He'll never let you forget it." Jae rolled her eyes.

"Why don't you like him?" Poor Kha. Thom felt even worse now about always pushing him away.

"I guess it's because our parents have always pitted us against each other." Jae looked like she was realizing this for the first time. "Father's always comparing me to him. 'You should be more like Kha. He always respects his elders.' Or 'Kha volunteers his time to tend the gardens and still has time to train. Why can't you do more with your time?' We've always been rivals."

"You've known each other for a long time?"

"Yeah. We're cousins."

Thom stumbled on the landing in front of the Jade Palace. Cousins? Thom turned to Jae, and saw her in a whole new light. Kha was more important than she had thought—his mother was a fairy, and his father was a general. If Jae was his cousin, then she was someone important also. But why else would she have a key to the armory? And live at the Jade Palace?

"Come on," Jae said, leading her inside.

And face-to-face with Kha.

"You lied to me!" His face was red and a bit shiny, like he had been running, and he was directing all his rage at Jae. "I was in so much trouble with the Jade Soldiers. They scolded me for an hour! And then I went all the way to Guanyin's temple—you said Thom went up there. Do you know how far that is?"

Jae crossed her arms. "Well, you shouldn't have been picking on a helpless girl."

"She's not helpless at all. Thom, show her how strong you are."

Thom looked between the two of them. "How? You want me to punch something?"

"Yes," Jae said. "Him."

"No," Kha said, holding up his hands.

"I'm not actually going to," Thom said.

"You did earlier."

"That was self-defense. You attacked me first."

Kha sighed. "Let's go see my father now."

"No." Jae held her hand out in front of Thom. "She doesn't want to go with you."

"Jae, stay out of this," Kha said.

"She's coming with me."

"She's not who you think she is—"

"I'm standing right here," Thom said, hoping Kha wouldn't tell Jae that she didn't belong in the heavens.

Jae stepped in between them, shielding Thom from Kha's narrowed eyes. Kha tried to bypass her, but Jae was too fast. "Leave her alone. She's my friend."

Thom felt oddly touched, but also like she was witnessing something private. As the two continued to bicker, the Monkey King's tiny hands grabbed ahold of the edge of her ear.

"These are the people who grow up to be gods and goddesses?" he whispered. "No wonder things never get done."

"What does the general want with her anyway?" Jae asked.

"I can't tell you," Kha said. "Father forbade it."

"Fine then," Jae snapped at Kha, grabbing Thom's hand. "Come on, Thom."

But Kha grabbed her other hand and pulled her away from Jae. "Thom," Kha whispered in her ear. The Monkey King darted behind her neck. "You can't stay long—you don't have much time. Look." He flipped her hand over and held up her knuckles.

Thom gasped. Her hand had turned a strange gray color where she hadn't been able to stop scratching earlier, her skin thin and flaking like a shedding snake. She had been itchy earlier, but now she was decaying.

"What's happening?" she asked, panicked.

"You're dying. The longer you stay, the worse it will get."

She hid her hands behind her back.

"Stop it," Jae snapped, pulling Thom away. She couldn't have heard what Kha said, but she had watched Thom's face with growing concern. "You're upsetting her. Go away."

Before Kha could say anything else, Jae pulled Thom into a room and slammed the door.

♦ ♦ ♦

Thom tried not to think about her hands as she and Jae got ready, Jae bustling around and talking about everyone who would be at the garden banquet. She tried not to scratch at her skin, tried not to think about the fact that the decay was spreading, tried to tell herself it wasn't permanent, that if she got out of here before it was too bad, maybe her skin would return to normal. She was so distracted she hardly noticed the decadent, rich details of Jae's room, and the servants who rushed in and out to help them. It was all a blur, and then suddenly they were leaving again, floating over to the cloud Thom had been so curious about earlier.

The first thing that struck her as they stepped into the Forbidden Garden was the overwhelmingly sweet smell of peaches. Beneath her feet, the mist dissolved to reveal the soft mossy ground. At first, she thought string lights hung from the trees, casting a bright and starry glow across the leaves, but when she looked closer, she saw that they were actually peaches, glowing from within.

People gathered in groups, talking and sipping from little teacups, their outfits as colorful as the flowers that bloomed in winding paths leading up to a long banquet table. Thom stared at a group of ladies, realizing that they must be fairies—goddesses of the heavens. They wore traditional silky áo dài and chiffon robes that streamed like gossamer behind them when they walked. Even the matching pants beneath their áo dài, usually a simple white, were intricately detailed with floral prints or gold trim. There were also men in áo dài, but some wore official black robes. Some of the immortals had that glowing quality to their skin, like the Boy Giant. They must have been the higher immortals, because everyone else bowed to them or stepped out of their way, showing particular deference.

Thom tugged on the collar of her own áo dài, still not knowing how she'd let Jae talk her into wearing one. Her hands were hidden in lace gloves she'd borrowed to hide her decaying skin. Was she really dying? Would she be stuck in the heavens or get sent to the hells? She needed to leave, but she had to time it right. The Monkey King still needed Jae's ring, and Thom didn't want to cause suspicion by disappearing abruptly.

The stiff collar of the áo dài bit into her neck, and the bright yellow fabric made her feel like a spotlight shone on her wherever she walked, especially when a group of three fairies glanced at her and Jae, then whispered to one another.

"Oh," the Monkey King sighed in her ear, sniffing at the air, taking in the sweet, fruity smell and another fresh, crisp scent, which reminded Thom of morning dew. "Oh, that's heavenly." His voice was soft, almost frail.

"Are you okay?" she whispered to him when Jae was distracted by an old man in a white robe.

"This small body grows weaker. It takes lots of strength to manifest beyond the Gate of the Heavens when my true self is in a different realm."

"Do you need to rest?"

"There's no time. Once the girl is having too much fun to notice, I will steal her ring so that we can leave."

He stopped talking when Jae tugged on Thom's sleeve.

"I want you to meet someone, Thom." Jae turned to the older man. "This is the Lotus Master."

Thom looked up at the old man, who almost glowed. Everything about him was blindingly white: his hair, his beard, his clothes, even his shoes. "Hi," she said, then remembered to bow.

"He's the sư fụ of the Lotus Students and master of the Seventy-Two Transformations," Jae explained.

"Lies," the Monkey King hissed. "This ancient fart may know about the Seventy-Two, but he has never mastered them. Everything he taught me was from *books*. I am the only one who has ever mastered the Transformations."

"You are the very strong one the Boy Giant spoke about," the Lotus Master said. "The one who wants to get rid of her powers."

"Y-yes, I . . ." Thom glanced at Jae, who gave a reassuring smile. "Did he speak to you? Do you know how I would be able to?"

"Even if I did, why would I assist you with such a foolish task?" the Lotus Master snapped, his white beard quivering.

Thom flushed. She wasn't used to grown-ups being so . . . mean. Not when she hadn't done anything wrong. But then the heat in her cheeks sparked into anger. Who did he think he was, anyway? He didn't know anything about her.

"I'm surprised you haven't talked some sense into her, Jae," the Lotus Master said. "You, of all people, should know better." He made an exasperated noise, flicked his sleeves, and walked away to a group of Lotus Students, wearing simpler versions of his white robe. They bowed and followed him, walking with stooped backs even when he barely acknowledged them.

"He hasn't changed at all," the Monkey King commented dryly.

"What did he mean?" Thom asked as Jae looped her arm through Thom's and pulled her deeper into the garden. The trees were luscious and green, and peaches glowed above their heads like lanterns. "That you, of all people, should know better?"

Jae smiled brightly at a group of ladies walking past them. They were also dressed in áo dài, with matching round head-dresses, creating colorful halos around their heads. Even though they bowed politely to Jae, they didn't stop to talk to her, and when they'd walked away, Thom noticed that they leaned their heads together to whisper and laugh. They reminded her of the dynamic trio. Thom was relieved when she glanced at Jae and saw her new friend briefly give the ladies a sour look.

"You can tell me," Thom said when Jae still didn't speak.

"It's just . . ." Jae looked down, blinking rapidly. "I'm not as strong as you."

"But that's good. I told you how much of a curse my strength is."

"No, it's not just that. I'm not as strong as *anyone*." Jae wiped at her cheeks. "It's not something people talk about really. At least not openly."

"What?"

"When a god falls in love with a mortal, their children come out . . . odd. Unpredictable. You never know what ability they'll be born with . . . Sometimes they have really amazing powers, and sometimes they turn out just like me." Jae held up her palms. "Weak."

Thom wanted to reach out to her. "You're not weak."

"Everyone here values strength and power," Jae said, looking around. Thom followed her gaze. Men in black robes and uniforms strutted around, and to Thom's shock, several Jade Soldiers were there. They towered over the other guests, attracting attention no matter where they walked.

"The Jade Soldiers are some of the most respected people here," Jae said. "All the Lotus Students study for years to join the army. The immortals are ranked according to their abilities. Even the fairies have gifts. But me . . ." Jae looked at her hands. Her jade ring glinted in the bright peach-colored light of the party. "I'm weak."

"You're not." Thom's defense of her was automatic. "I would give anything not to be this strong."

"But why, Thom? You could do so much with your power. You could belong here. You belong here more than I ever have."

"But you're part god, aren't you?" Thom pointed out. "Can't your father or mother help you? Can't they give you power?"

"It doesn't work like that, and Father wouldn't want people to think he abuses his position. And there's no one I can ask, because no one likes to talk about it. No one wants to acknowledge that I'm part mortal. It's a reminder that Father broke the rule." She took a shuddering breath. "I'm a walking sin."

"No, you're not." Jae was kind and sweet—how could anyone call her that?

"I am. I'm a warning sign, a cautionary tale for any god tempted to fall in love with a mortal, because then their children could turn out like me, or worse."

Or worse? Like Thom?

Was Thom part immortal? Was that why she'd turned out so weird? Was that why she was superstrong, maybe even as strong as an immortal like the Boy Giant?

"Jae," Thom said hesitantly. She didn't want to make this

about her, not when Jae was confiding something so emotional. But she was too curious to stop herself. "Did the Boy Giant fall in love with a mortal? Didn't you say he lived in the mortal world for a long time? Why did he come back?"

"Thom! There you are!"

They both startled at the voice of the Boy Giant himself. Thom went red—had he heard her talking about him?

But he wasn't alone. Approaching with him was a tall man who towered over the Boy Giant, with a black beard, in golden robes that trailed on the floor. Perched on top of his head was a glittering, jade crown. His skin had the same golden shine that the Boy Giant's had, and together, the two men lit up the path leading to Thom and Jae. His eyes studied Thom intently, his thick brows drawn together.

"Father!" Jae exclaimed, rushing to him. He spread his arms, lifting his robes, and the fabric was so heavy and immense that when he hugged Jae, she almost drowned beneath the golden folds of his wide sleeves.

Everyone at the party dipped into a curtsy, arms folded, heads bowed. Silence settled over the garden. Thom started to lower her body, but the man waved an arm at her.

"Enough of that," he said, turning to the crowd. "This is a party, isn't it?" He clapped, and music started, someone picking a happy tune on a đàn bầu, as conversation erupted.

"Thom, this is the Jade Emperor," the Boy Giant said.

Thom dropped into a bow. She couldn't help herself.

The Jade Emperor chuckled. "Enough, I said." He kept one arm around Jae, who beamed at Thom. That was when it clicked—if the Jade Emperor was Jae's father, then she was a princess. A princess! And Thom had been talking to her as if she were just a normal girl, as if she and Thom were on the same level.

Jae had continued to smile at Thom like they were best friends, but now her face was starting to tighten, like she was waiting for Thom's reaction. Thom gave a reassuring smile, and Jae's face relaxed.

"This is your new friend, Jae?" the Jade Emperor asked, keeping his eye on Thom.

Jae nodded, looking up at her father with pure adoration and love. Thom felt a pang in her chest, and she suddenly missed her mom so much it hurt.

"Then we must all sit together," the Jade Emperor said.

Jae and her father walked arm in arm, while Thom fell into step beside the Boy Giant, her mind still racing from the idea that they might be more similar than she'd thought.

They walked in silence for a while, and then he smiled down at her, something twinkling in his eye. "I have something that might be useful to you," he said, reaching into his pocket. He handed her a piece of string. It was golden and so thin it felt like it would snap if she pulled on it. "It's magical. It can't break, and will always be as long as you need it to be. Once bound, it can only be loosened by the person who tied it."

"Oh, wow." She wrapped it around her wrist twice, and the end adhered to the other coils, creating a bracelet. "Thank you! But are you sure you won't need it?"

"I think you might find more use for it."

She reflexively started to tuck her hair behind her ear, then remembered the Monkey King was hiding there.

"Why are you giving this to me, though?" she asked. "Wouldn't your other students like it, too?" Not that she was ready to give it back so quickly.

"It's my job, you see. To protect people."

"Like a superhero."

"Like a giant," he said with a smile. "I try, but sometimes . . ." He shrugged.

"You can't protect everyone."

He held his hands together, tucking them in the folds of his sleeves. "Thom."

She looked up expectantly. His mouth opened and closed a few times.

"I hope you know," he said finally, stumbling a little over his words, "if you need anything . . . I can . . . you can . . . always . . . I would help you."

Why did that bring a lump to her throat? He was just being nice, doing his duty as an immortal and a hero.

He nudged her, held up a fist. "Remember, Thom. You are mighty."

She ducked her head, her cheeks heating up.

When they reached the banquet table, the Boy Giant pulled out her chair, then took the seat next to her. Jae sat on her other side, the Jade Emperor at the head of the table. And directly across the table from Thom . . . was Kha. He wore a black-and-gold áo dài, with a headdress that made him look taller and older, more sophisticated.

He leaned toward Thom when no one else was paying attention. "What are you up to?" he hissed.

"Nothing," she whispered back.

"We need to talk."

"That's what we're doing right now."

"No, *in private*."

Then Jae noticed him and gasped, and both Thom and Kha straightened in their seats.

"Father," Jae said to the Jade Emperor. "Why would you seat him here?"

"I am not in charge of the seating arrangements," the Jade Emperor said cheerfully as servants brought out heaping platters of food. The smell of salted pork, steamed dumplings, fried rice, and oxtail soup flooded Thom's nostrils.

"I'm here in place of the general," Kha said, bowing his head at the Jade Emperor with such grace and sophistication that Thom hardly recognized him. Then when the Jade Emperor wasn't looking, he stuck his tongue out at Jae.

Servants set more food in front of them, on plates of gold that gleamed in the warm peachy lighting, each so full they threatened to spill over.

"Now is my chance to steal the ring," the Monkey King said to Thom. His fingers and toes tickled her as he crawled down the back of her neck.

"Did you say something?" the Boy Giant asked.

"What? No, uh . . . This is so much," Thom said, looking at all the food.

"Save room for dessert," the Boy Giant said. "I designed it myself."

"Eat!" the Jade Emperor commanded, and everyone at the table dove into the food, filling their plates, clicking their chopsticks, slurping their soup. Thom was too distracted to eat at first, as she watched the immortals stuff their faces and talk between bites. Light reflected off the jewelry on the fairies' necks and ears, the metallic details of the gods' hats and the soldiers' helmets. Conversations came from all directions, drowning one another out until it combined into a dull roar. She shut her eyes, resisting the urge to clap her hands over her ears.

"Thom," someone called out to her.

When she looked up, Kha was inclining his head toward the Jade Emperor.

The emperor smiled at her. "I hear you're incredibly strong."

"Um, yes, Your Highness."

"As strong as my friend the Boy Giant?"

Thom glanced at the immortal next to her. He smiled. "I don't know," she said.

"We should have a battle!" the Jade Emperor said, laughing.

"Now, now." The Boy Giant chuckled. "That wouldn't be a fair fight."

"To whom—you or the girl?"

Everyone laughed.

"My daughter would do anything to have your strength," the Jade Emperor said, clapping a hand on Jae's shoulder. Jae winced, but Thom couldn't tell if it was because of her father's hand or his words. The laughter died, cut off abruptly, leaving the Jade Emperor to chuckle alone at his joke.

An awkward silence ensued. The tension stretched across the table until Jae broke it.

"If only you could *give* me some of your strength," Jae said to Thom. She was trying to sound casual and happy, but Thom heard the hitch in her voice.

"We can't choose who we are," the Jade Emperor said. "And we can't choose our gifts, so we must make do with what we have."

Thom didn't know how to respond to that. He looked so confident and authoritative, a grown-up who knew things. Still, his words didn't sound quite right.

"But what about the people who don't have gifts?" Thom asked. *Or don't want them.*

The Jade Emperor spread his arms and shrugged. "They must make do with what they have."

"So you don't think people can change?" Thom asked.

The emperor looked surprised, as if he wasn't used to being questioned at all. "They can grow, definitely. Improve. But at the end of the day, you must accept who you are." His expression was kind, if a bit condescending. He spoke carefully, as if making sure she understood each word. "You can't avoid your true nature. In fact, you should be grateful for your place in life."

That was easy for him to say when he was an immortal and a royal in the heavens. But what if he had been born a demon instead? Demons never had a choice. Were they just supposed to accept their fates and live the rest of their lives in exile while the gods and fairies got to enjoy banquets and cookies and peaches of immortality?

Then again, some demons could change. She'd seen it. The monkey brothers in their peaceful sanctuary. The Monkey King, who had never been anything but a friend to her.

"But . . ." Thom said. "But I don't think that's true."

Whispers hissed down the table. The Jade Emperor leaned toward her.

"You . . . don't," he said slowly. His laughter was gone, and his fingers were curled into fists on the table.

Thom gulped. Everyone was watching her. She wished she hadn't said anything, but the Jade Emperor kept looking at her, and she felt like she had to go on.

"Some people do change their fates," she said. "Some demons can be good."

Faces twisted in disgust. "Demons?" one fairy blurted, dropping her spoon.

"Oh?" The Jade Emperor sat back in his chair. "Enlighten us."

Thom wanted to slink away instead. "Well . . ." she said slowly. "The Monkey King did."

Everyone reacted at once. The fairies gasped; some men thumped their fists on the table. The Jade Soldiers reached for their swords. The Boy Giant touched her hand, as if to quiet her. Kha held her gaze across the table and shook his head slightly.

Thom touched the spot behind her ear, but the Monkey King was still gone. She wished she could turn herself invisible.

The Jade Emperor held up a hand, and the crowd quieted. He never looked away from Thom.

"That demon certainly tried to change his fate, but he learned the hard way that he should have just accepted his position in life."

"The hard way?" Thom asked.

"He was defeated and captured," Jae explained, "sentenced to live for five hundred years under a mountain."

A mountain? No—Thom had found him in a temple.

They were wrong. They were wrong about the Monkey King; they were wrong about so many things. People could change. The Monkey King had changed. His brothers were good. Even the other demons on the island were kind and playful.

Thom understood now why the Monkey King wanted a better life for the demons. They didn't deserve the fairies' disdain, the way the gods sneered at any mention of them, this hatred from people who didn't know them. She looked at the immortals in their bright outfits with their stuffed faces and the piles of food, the glowing peaches, the golden plates on the table. All this decadence for people who made her feel as if she didn't belong. She thought of the demons, banished to a lonely island, the monkey brothers in their oasis, where she'd wanted to stay forever. The immortals in the heavens didn't understand, or didn't want to understand.

"But why?" Thom asked. "What did he do?"

"He tried to make himself a god," the Jade Emperor said. "Such a thing is impossible."

"But isn't he? Wasn't he born in the heavens?"

The crowd murmured. The Jade Emperor spoke loudly, drowning out all the whispers.

"He is a demon!" he boomed. Thom cowered at his voice. "And nothing will change that."

Under the table, Jae touched Thom's hand. Thom looked down at Jae's bare fingers, placed over her gloved ones. She gasped. Her forearm, just above where the gloves ended, was covered in that same ashy scab. Even while she watched, it was spreading, her skin cracking, turning into gray scales. It was getting worse. She was running out of time.

Thom jumped when something crawled up her arm. She stopped herself from swatting at her sleeve just in time when she realized that it was the Monkey King.

"I . . ." she said. She couldn't think of an excuse. "I need to, um . . ." She got up from the table.

"Go," the Jade Emperor said. He waved a hand dismissively.

The party guests looked at her with disgust. Pity. Embarrassment on her behalf.

The Jade Emperor was kicking her out of the party. She'd said the wrong thing, disgraced herself. What would Ma think?

Kha gave her an apologetic look, while Jae seemed like she might cry. The Boy Giant was simultaneously sad and yet reassuring. Sympathetic.

"Leave," the Jade Emperor ordered.

Behind her, she heard stomping. Jade Soldiers were standing at attention, ready to take her away if she disobeyed.

Thom took a few steps back. Then she spun around and walked as fast as she could away from the party.

27

WHEN SHE WAS SURE SHE was alone among the peach trees, Thom tugged up her sleeve and held the Monkey King in her palm.

"I have it!" He lifted the ring to show her, but remained lying down. "The key. We can go."

"Are you sick?" she asked. He looked terrible, his face sunken, his movements slow and heavy.

"I am weak," he said, closing his eyes. "I just need to rest."

Thom had been hoping he would tell her what to do, but he went completely still and began shrinking.

"Wukong! Wukong, what's wrong? What's happening?"

But he was just a hair again. She bounced her hand up and down as if that would revive him, but nothing happened. The jade ring he'd stolen rolled over in her palm.

What was she supposed to do now? She inspected the

scabs on her arms, pulled off her gloves, and bit back a gasp as flakes of dried skin fell off. Her fingers tingled as she turned them over, scrutinizing the damage, which had moved up past her elbows. She needed to decide now, on her own, before time ran out and she wouldn't have the chance.

Thom looked in the direction of the party. Even from the trees, she could hear people laughing and talking. She imagined how much fun everyone was having, already forgetting about her, the girl who had been kicked out. She should have been embarrassed, but she was too disgusted to care. Why would she want to sit with people who treated her friends with disdain? What did they know, anyway? The Jade Emperor was wrong—they all were. If the Monkey King could go from being a monkey demon into a god of his own making, if he could master the Seventy-Two Transformations and became undefeatable, then she could certainly get rid of her strength and make herself normal.

It didn't matter what Jae said, or what Thom might suspect about who the Boy Giant really was. Even if her suspicions were true, she had nothing in common with them. She didn't belong here, and it was only a matter of time before they discovered that. The only way out of the mess was to find the cudgel and bring it back to the Monkey King.

She put the Monkey King's hair in her pocket, took the ring, and slipped it onto her own finger before leaving the Forbidden Garden.

• • •

The Jade Palace was dim and quiet, servants and immortals all at the banquet. She still stepped slowly, cautious of the empty corners, jumping when the hallways infused with light as if sensing her movements. Jade plants grew along the walls, their leaves a beautiful mint green, which lit up the same way the peaches had.

The walls were made of a translucent stone, like emerald, and light shifted beneath the surface, following her as if guiding her path. Or making sure she didn't do anything wrong. She couldn't help feeling like she was being watched, and now that the Monkey King was gone and she was truly alone, she was unable to escape a sense of danger.

Every time she looked down at her hands, the decaying skin that was starting to crumple off in flakes, she walked faster. The skirt of her áo dài whipped around her legs as she rushed through the hall, breathing hard and trying not to scratch at the scabs on her arms.

She didn't know where the armory was exactly, but the Monkey King had said it was in the basement, so she headed down several sets of stairs until she reached the very bottom of the palace. The jade green walls lit up, and her footsteps echoed.

Something stirred in her pocket—the Monkey King's hair. As she took it out, one end of it grew bulbous, and his head appeared. He looked like a lollipop.

"Whoa," Thom said, not expecting that.

"Where are we?" he asked.

"The basement. I have the key. Where do I go?"

He sputtered, shrinking. "Red door! Glowing—" His head disappeared, and he was a hair again.

Heart thumping, she found a door with a reddish glow. Her fingers shook, stiff now, and tingling even more as another scab broke off and disintegrated like ash. She took Jae's ring from her finger, not sure what to do with it. She looked at it closely for the first time. The ring was made of jade, green and translucent, and carved in the shape of a teardrop. No, a jade-plant leaf. Like the one under the doorknob in front of her.

At first, the jewel didn't fit in the keyhole, like a puzzle piece that was almost just right but turned out to have a slight imperfection in its ridges. But then she turned the ring and tried again. It slid into place, and the door shuddered and swayed open.

She pocketed the ring and stepped inside. The room brightened slowly, the walls glowing to wash light over weapons stored in glass cases. A sword in one case, a gourd in another. A dagger, a throwing star, an ax. She stopped at a large case twice her size. It held a suit of armor with red-and-gold plating and a helmet with long feathers sticking out of it.

"That was mine," the Monkey King's voice squeaked. He was his full tiny self again. "My strength grows. The cudgel is near."

"The armor," Thom said. "It's so cool."

"Do you think so? They gifted it to me when I was named Master of the Horses. It's modeled after the armor the soldiers of the Jade Army wear, a symbol that I belonged to the Jade Emperor. But it was nothing short of glorified shackles. I belong to no one but myself. Now let's go find my cudgel. Go that way."

Something else caught Thom's eye. Next to the suit of armor's case was a smaller one, displaying a silver tiara. It glowed with power, drawing her attention.

"No, don't stop." The Monkey King hopped up and down in her palm to get her attention. "Every item in this room is dangerous. All magical objects have a mind and spirit of their own. They want you to take them. They'll lure you in and tempt you with their power, but they will only betray you when they are free."

She shuddered and kept walking, eyes ahead. And then there it was. The iron cudgel. Neither of them said anything as they approached the staff. It rested on top of a metal platform like the other weapons, but no glass case protected it. A gravitational pull reeled her in.

"Why isn't there any glass around it?" she asked. This felt too easy, like anyone could just grab it and go.

"The glass cases are protective wards, but no spell or any magical being has ever overpowered the cudgel. Many have tried, but it will not listen to anyone but me. And no one is powerful enough to wield it except me. And you. Take it, Thom. Speak to it."

She felt silly, but so far everything the Monkey King had told her had been right. The trip to the heavens hadn't gone according to plan, but he hadn't lied about anything, not really. She cleared her throat.

"Um, hi. Mr. Bang? I'm here to take you back to the Monkey King." Thom waited, but the silence only made her feel sillier. "Um, the full version of him." She held the thumb-sized Monkey King up to the cudgel.

What had she expected? For the staff to light up like a Christmas tree? Start dancing in midair? Nothing happened, so she placed the Monkey King on her shoulder and reached for the cudgel.

It. Was. *Heavy*. Much heavier than anything she'd ever lifted. At least five times as heavy as the truck in the junkyard.

She managed to drag it off its pedestal, but then it slipped through her fingers.

She caught it just before it could crash to the marble, but her arms ached, her fingers strained. More ash fell from her skin, which was now starting to burn.

It had been a long time since Thom had had to strain to hold something, and the effort was unfamiliar and difficult. She was *strong*. That was her thing. But the staff was too heavy.

There was no way she could carry this out of the Jade Palace, much less the heavens. And she was supposed to do that without anyone noticing? No way.

"Wukong," she said. "This is impossible. I can't."

"You must!" the Monkey King hissed.

"Can't you . . . ?" she started, but he was sputtering again, his body shrinking back into a hair.

"Something is happening—they know. Get it out of the armory," he managed to squeak. "The wards—" He was gone, his hair sticking to her shoulder.

Thom squeezed her eyes shut.

"Please, Ruyi Jingu Bang," she said, but only because she was desperate. "I'm going to take you back to Wukong. But I can't if you're this heavy."

Nothing changed. She remembered the Monkey King saying the staff would weigh the same no matter what size it was. She lifted the staff, her face heating with exertion, the muscles in her arms bunching. Somehow, she got it up and over her shoulder, though she knew its weight must be bruising her flesh. The cudgel was maybe three feet long—no longer than a yardstick—but it might as well have been as big as a temple. As she turned toward the door, her steps were labored and extremely slow.

She made it through the door. How long had it been? An hour? Her face was hot. Something slid down her forehead, and she swatted at it. A mosquito? In the heavens?

No, it was sweat. She was sweating. Which was weird. She hadn't broken a sweat like this since her powers had appeared.

"Come on, Mr. Bang," she groaned. "At least make yourself smaller." She didn't think it would work, but the weight concentrated into a sharp spot on her shoulder. The staff hadn't grown lighter, but it had shrunk to the size of a ruler.

She still had to use both hands to hold it and her muscles ached and strained, but it was easier than carrying the three-foot cudgel.

How the Monkey King was able to shrink the staff into a needle and tuck it behind his ear like a pencil, she had no clue. Maybe it liked him better.

And then somehow, she was outside. Stars lit up the heavens. The temples and clouds glowed even in nighttime. Flying in the heavens had always been weightless, freeing, like gliding in water. But with the cudgel, it was like swimming with your clothes and coat and shoes on.

Her dress was soaked with sweat, her hair matted to her face, but she was so close. The Judgment Veil was just a cloud away, just a hop, and the Monkey King, the real Monkey King, would be waiting for her on the other side. They would go home. Home to Ma. Home, where he would take her power, and she could go back to her life, her *real* life.

Her legs burned. Her arms ached. Even her teeth were numb, from clenching so hard against the strain.

She bent her knees, eyes on the Gate.

"Thom."

She almost fell sideways, but she caught herself, clutching the ruler-sized cudgel in her grip.

The Boy Giant stood next to her.

"Please grow small, Mr. Bang," she whispered to the staff. "Shrink, or he'll see you." She hid it behind her, her arm bent stiffly as she turned to face him.

"What are you doing?" he asked.

She considered lying, but that felt wrong, and even if she wanted to, her brain had stopped working, all of her attention focused on not dropping the cudgel. To her surprise, it had listened, and shrunk to the size of a thimble. She closed a fist around it, but it was still just as heavy and her palms were so slick she was afraid it would slip between her fingers.

His gaze flickered to the Veil, then back to her. "You're leaving us?"

"I miss my mom." It wasn't a lie. "I want to go home."

"But you only just got here."

How did he know that? Had he known the truth all along?

"I have to go." She turned toward the Veil, ready to fall if she had to and let the staff's weight carry her home.

"Thom." This time, his voice was deeper, as if he'd dropped his pretense. "I know what you're doing."

He couldn't know, not really. Maybe he knew she shouldn't be in the heavens, but—

"I know who you're doing it for."

She gazed ahead. She'd been caught. They would send her to the hells now. For some reason, the truth of that didn't scare her, not yet, like how a paper cut didn't sting until later. The stars twinkled; the moon cast the clouds in a silvery glow, bright cotton-candy tufts against the black sky.

The Boy Giant reached out a hand. "Give it to me. Before it's too late."

She shook her head. "It's already too late." If she gave herself up now, she would never get the chance at a normal life, never know what she could have done without her power.

"We can put it back. Before the guards come for you."

Her fingers tightened on the tiny cudgel.

"We don't have much time. Once you took the staff from the pedestal, the guards were alerted. But I'll help you. I'll tell them I took it, that I needed it—hurry, Thom."

She hesitated. But if she put the staff back, nothing would change. She was still in the heavens, where she didn't belong, and the Boy Giant would have to tell the emperor who she was.

"I can't."

"He's not your friend." The Boy Giant's voice climbed, almost desperate.

He was lying. He only wanted Thom to stay.

"He's betrayed everyone who trusted him," he said.

No, he would say anything to get her to give back the cudgel now. She had met the Monkey King's friends: the demons on the Mountain, Concao and Shing-Rhe, and all his monkey brothers. They wouldn't have stayed friends with him all this time if what the Boy Giant said was true.

"I'm sorry," she said. "But I have to do this."

"Thom, please. I can only help you if you stop now. There will be no going back from this." Something caught in his throat, and she looked at him in disbelief. Back from what? From what she'd always wanted?

"I know what the Monkey King promised you," he said. "But he'll betray you."

Sweat rolled down her temples. "You don't know him. He's been helping me."

"Helping you. Or using you?"

"He taught me to control my strength."

"Only so you would trust him. I can show you—*really* show you."

"How do I know you're not only saying that so *I* will trust *you*?"

"Because I don't need you to do anything for me. The Monkey King does. He's using you to steal his cudgel for him. But all I want is to teach you. I can help you. I can show you what it's like to be who you are and how to live with your strength. I know it's hard. I *know*. You and I are alike, remember? Small"—he smiled—"but mighty." He reached out a hand. "You can stay here with me. Train to be who you're meant to be."

Was it true? Or just another trick? Who was lying, and who was telling the truth?

"The Monkey King can't change you," he said. "Because you're not a demon—you're part immortal. Your strength is a part of you. You're good."

She knew it. Ever since Jae had told her about the children of gods and mortals turning out unpredictably, she'd suspected that that was what had happened. She was abnormal. She was a freak. "But I've done bad things. I stole the cudgel. I snuck into the heavens," she said. "They'll punish me, send me to the hells."

Only the Monkey King could help her. It was too late to turn back now.

"I won't let them," he said.

"What can you do?"

"I'm the Boy Giant. One of the Four Immortals. I can speak on your behalf."

"But why would you do that?"

"Because you're my daughter."

She choked. Of course she was. She had started to suspect as much, had maybe known the moment they'd met. It explained why he had shown her so much attention, why he had wanted to teach her to use her power, why he had offered to train her to become the Girl Giant. They even looked like each other, both small with the same careful, shy smile.

She didn't feel like a giant. Not now, barely managing to hang on to the massively heavy yet thimble-sized cudgel.

"Why did you leave Ma and me?" she asked. Heat boiled inside her, a tightening in her chest. He had been up here all along, hadn't given one thought to her, hadn't helped her at all, even though he must have known how hard it was for her to grow up so different, to develop a strength no one could explain.

"I didn't want to, Thom. Never. But immortals aren't supposed to fall in love with mortals, and once your mother and I had you, we knew you wouldn't be safe if I'd stayed. The heavens would suspect. They would have taken you away. They have never been tolerant of things they don't understand," he said quietly. "I might have taken you with me, protected you myself, but your mother wanted you to have a normal life."

Sweat dripped into Thom's eyes, stinging them and making them water. Her hands burned from clutching the cudgel, and from something else, from the decay that was now up to her shoulders. She needed to decide. "You wanted to bring me here?"

"Always." He took a step closer. "I never wanted to leave you. I wanted to bring you both, but a life for you in the mortal world meant so much to your mother. I regretted that decision every day that went by. And when I couldn't watch over you myself, I sent a guardian instead."

"Kha," Thom said, wiping the sweat out of her eyes.

"I wanted someone to keep you safe."

"*You* should have kept me safe! You're my father! You knew all along what I was, but you didn't tell me. You let me believe I was a freak." The cudgel suddenly hummed with strength. It was starting to grow bigger, as if feeding on her anger. Her palms were slick, but the weapon stayed put, like it was glued to her skin.

"I wanted to," her father said. "But your mother decided it was safer if I stayed away forever."

"Ma?" Why would Ma do that? Why hadn't Ma told Thom anything?

"She said it was too dangerous," he continued, as if reading her thoughts.

The staff grew back to its full length. The Boy Giant took a step forward, but the cudgel hummed violently in response. He stopped.

"Thom, please."

She shook her head. "You don't know what I've been through."

"I'm sorry." His voice cracked. "I can't undo it, but I will try to make it up to you. I'll explain everything. I'll fix everything."

A tear rolled from her right eye. If she had known about her father, the truth about her strength, would she have made a different choice? She looked at the staff. She couldn't go through with this. What was she thinking? She was about to steal a forbidden weapon from the heavens and give it to a demon-god who had tricked her.

"Come back, Thom. Give me the cudgel. We can return it to the armory. I'll explain to the Jade Emperor, before it's too late."

Thom's knees threatened to buckle. She started to move toward the Boy Giant.

"Don't do it, Thom!" the Monkey King squeaked in her ear. He was back, jumping on her shoulder, like someone was tapping her with a finger. "He's lying to you."

She stopped.

"Thom?" The Boy Giant held out a hand.

"He abandoned you." The Monkey King's voice was weak as he whispered. "He could have helped you all this time, but he left you to think you were a freak."

The Monkey King was right. Where had the Boy Giant been when her power started? What was he doing when her life was falling apart?

"Give me the cudgel, Thom," the Boy Giant said, his voice no longer soft or kind, but demanding. "You don't know what you're doing."

"And whose fault is that?" the Monkey King asked, even though the Boy Giant couldn't hear him.

"That was your fault," Thom said to her father. "If you had just . . . If *anyone* had just." She thought of Ma and stumbled.

"There's only one person who has ever been there for me. And it wasn't you."

Something changed in the way the Boy Giant looked at her, a realization that maybe he had underestimated her, that he couldn't manipulate her into trusting him, as if he could make up for eleven years of abandonment with one afternoon tea and a golden string bracelet. He lunged forward.

Thom reacted out of instinct and swung the cudgel. It smacked the Boy Giant's head.

A dazed expression blanketed his eyes, and he trembled from head to toe. Then he dropped to the cloud.

Thom gasped. She hadn't meant to hit so hard, hadn't gauged the combined weight of the cudgel with her super-strength, hadn't factored in that she was much stronger in the heavens. "No, no, no—"

Shapes appeared behind them, flying—no, *charging*—toward them. Toward *her*.

The Jade Army. At least twenty soldiers.

Turning away from her unconscious father, her gut churning, Thom jumped off the cloud. The staff's weight pulled her down toward the Veil.

Behind her, the soldiers shouted. Blood roared in her ears. She was close to the Veil, just a few feet away. She could see the shimmering magic.

The Monkey King giggled on her shoulder, sounding weak but exhilarated. She fell onto softness. A cloud. Her head throbbed, temples pulsing with each heartbeat. To her left, the Veil glistened with an inviting shimmer. Ahead, the Jade Army soldiers blocked off the light of the moon, their shapes blackened by the bright glow behind them.

A dark shadow loomed and made her duck instinctively. A soldier hovered above her, sword in one hand. Swords always looked so fake and harmless on TV, but when one was in your face, it was real, sharp, and dangerous.

"You are wanted at the Jade Palace," the soldier declared. "Surrender the item you stole from the Forbidden Armory and come with us."

Forbidden? The Monkey King hadn't said anything about that.

"Fight back, Thom-Thom," the Monkey King said. "Fight, or they will capture you and send you to the hells."

The soldiers descended upon her.

She swung the staff. It crashed into a soldier's arm, ricocheted, and swiped another off his feet. Each blow was followed by the terrible crunch of bones breaking, with surprising and horrifying ease, like cracking a piece of celery in half.

Heat surged through her veins, and she couldn't stop. She took them down, all of them, until her way was cleared. Her arms burned, her breath short, she stepped past their fallen bodies.

What had she done?

"You had no choice, Thom-Thom," the Monkey King said. "They would have sent you to the hells."

"Thom!" someone called behind her. Kha, as a dragon, slithered through the air, turning into his human form before landing next to her. They were both still dressed in their elegant áo dài from the garden banquet. "Thom, don't do this, please."

"I've already done it," she said, exhausted, numb.

"We can still go back."

"No." She shook her head, looking frantically away, toward escape. Just a few more steps, and she would be free of this place. Just a few more steps, and she would be closer to getting what she wanted more than anything. "I can't go back."

Kha's face fell. She was glad when he didn't try to stop her. She didn't want to hurt Kha, too.

The Monkey King *ooh*ed softly in her ear, sounding fainter than before. "It's time to go," he said, his voice fading as he became a hair again. The golden pin in one hand, the cudgel in the other, she walked into the Judgment Veil.

28

THOM FELL TO HER KNEES. She almost dropped the cudgel. Her arms were shaking violently now, as if it had grown even heavier. Or maybe she was weaker. Maybe it hadn't been her imagination—she *had* been stronger in the heavens.

Gone were the soldiers' screaming and moaning. A roar filled her ears, followed by a high-pitched ringing.

Fog swirled around her as she heaved the staff over her shoulder, looking around.

The Monkey King, the real one, would be waiting. She tried to take a step, but her feet wouldn't move.

She turned back to the Veil.

"You!" Xuan-Ling the Gatekeeper rushed at her. "You traitor!" He reached for a dagger at his belt, but he was no match for the cudgel. Thom swung it without thinking.

As the Gatekeeper crumpled to the floor, so did Thom. Her body trembled uncontrollably. She let go of the staff, and it rolled across the marble while she curled her knees close to her chest and hugged herself.

It wasn't supposed to have gone like this. Get in, steal the cudgel, get out—that was the plan. No one had said she would meet her father. No one had said she would have to hit him or hurt anyone else. Ash was falling in small mounds around her. She looked at her hands and gasped. The scabs had peeled away, revealing a baby-smooth layer of skin that was golden tan. And glowing.

She was *glowing*. The same way the Boy Giant had, and the Jade Emperor, too. But as she dusted off the rest of the ash, the glow faded until her skin was normal again, smooth and slightly raw, as if she'd scrubbed it too hard.

She didn't have time to contemplate what that meant. Footsteps echoed across the floor.

"Thom!" Kha was out of breath. He'd followed her through the Veil. "More soldiers are coming."

"What?" She panicked and grabbed the cudgel. "They'll send me to the hells."

Kha looked worried, then planted his feet firmly. "I won't let them take you."

She could have cried. "Why are you helping me?"

He didn't seem to know the answer at first. "Because," he said, "you're not the bad guy."

"But I stole the cudgel. I hit those soldiers—and the Boy Giant. I think . . . I really hurt him. What if I killed him?"

"You didn't," Kha said. "I saw him getting up. He was trying to stop the soldiers, but they wouldn't listen to him."

"Then what makes you think they'll listen to us? They won't understand no matter what you say. They won't believe us."

Why would they? Look how they had treated the Monkey King, and he had been one of them.

"Then what are you going to do?" Kha asked.

"I can't go back," she said. "You should, though," she added. "Before they think you've been helping me."

He shook his head.

"If you stay with me, they'll think you're my friend," she said.

"I *am* your friend."

Thom shook her head, not because she disagreed but because she didn't understand why.

"Thom, I'm here to help you."

"You'll be in lots of trouble."

"Yeah." His jaw clenched. "Yeah, I will. But it doesn't matter. We'll be in trouble together."

Thom looked at him, and she knew he was telling the truth. He really was on her side. Maybe he had been sent to her as an assignment, but he had proven time and again that he *wanted* to help her.

"What do we do?" she asked. "The soldiers will follow us."

"Not if they can't get through the Veil."

They turned to the arch. "You mean . . ." Thom couldn't bring herself to say it.

Kha looked down at the cudgel in her hands. "It won't stop them, but it will slow them down."

She couldn't do it—how could she destroy the sacred Judgment Veil?

But what choice did she have if she wanted to escape? She'd already stolen the cudgel. Was this much worse?

"Okay." Before she could change her mind, she hoisted the cudgel up and swung. It collided with the arch with a thunderous noise. The Veil flickered. The columns cracked, then crumpled, and the Veil disappeared.

Kha stared, mouth opening and closing, as if just realizing the enormity of what he'd suggested.

"Is there another way out of the heavens?" Thom asked. He didn't answer. "Kha?"

"The Bridge of Souls." His voice was flat.

"How long will it take?"

"A few days from here."

"Then we'll have some time before the soldiers catch up." She knew they would eventually, but she'd be with the Monkey King by then, and he would protect her, once he had the cudgel and all of his powers back.

But he wasn't outside the Gate. "Wukong?" she called. She picked up his hair. "Wukong?" Nothing but the wind blowing in her ear.

She stood at the edge of the cloud, white mist swirling around her. As the sun started to rise, warm yellow light moved across the sky, casting it in a pinkish tinge. "Where is he?"

Did her abandon her? Didn't he realize that she couldn't go anywhere without him? That she needed him?

Kha didn't have an answer. "It's morning. Your mom's going to wake up soon."

Thom didn't want to ask him, not after what she'd done, not after the way she'd treated him. But she didn't have to.

"I can take you home," he said. "And we can figure out what to do." At her look of despair, he added, "Together."

◆ ◆ ◆

It was difficult maneuvering onto the dragon's back. She couldn't hold on to Kha and the cudgel at the same time, though she was relieved to see that her hands had returned to normal—plump and full of life. Then she saw the golden coil wrapped around her wrist, the magical string the Boy Giant had given her. A twinge of guilt shot through her as she thought back to earlier that afternoon, and what she'd given up to help the Monkey King. To help herself. But along with that guilt came the anger she'd felt at her father, at how he'd abandoned her. No. She was going to go through with this. She'd come too far.

As she wrapped the string around the cudgel and then pulled it up over her shoulder, she never reached the end of it.

It was so thin it felt like it would snap, but it remained solid and strong. The Boy Giant had been right.

"Hang on!" Kha stepped into the air, and they plummeted off the clouds. Someone screamed—Thom thought it was just her at first, her mouth stretched and frozen. But then she realized Kha was screaming, too.

"Fly! Why aren't you flying?" she shouted.

"I'm trying! The staff is too heavy!"

"We're going to die, we're going to die—"

"Stop that! You're not helping!"

This was so much worse than flying with the Monkey King. That had been unpleasant. But this—hurtling through the air, unable to do anything to stop—made Thom realize how fragile her life was, how quickly it could be taken away.

Kha jerked, fell again, skittered. Their descent slowed. Thom looked around. Kha's tail and head were slightly raised, the middle of his body, where she sat, sagging with the added weight. He looked like a pool noodle, struggling to stay afloat, but at least they were no longer plunging to their doom.

By the time they made it back to her house, the sun was up, casting her bedroom in bright light. Kha hovered outside her window while she untied the string from her shoulders and gently lowered the staff to the floor. It slipped from her fingers and fell with a *thump* that shook the whole house.

She cringed. Ma would hear that. Hopefully, she was still

asleep—a quick glance at the clock told her she had an hour before Ma would wake her to get ready for school.

"What are you doing?" she asked as Kha transformed into his human form and followed her through the window. "You can't be in here. My mom's going to freak out if she thinks you snuck in."

Kha gestured at the staff. "Really? That's what you're worried about?"

Thom felt a powerful hum from the staff. She was reaching for it, to remove the golden coil, when the bedroom door burst open. She kicked the cudgel, sending it rolling under her bed.

"Cưng, you ready for—Oh!" Ma stopped, eyes widening at the sight of Kha.

Thom looked from her mom to Kha and back to Ma, then startled when she saw what was in her mom's hand. A yellow áo dài, still in the plastic wrap from the dry cleaner's. Thom looked down at the áo dài she was still wearing, the one Jae had let her borrow for the garden banquet.

"You're already dressed," Ma said, then frowned as she took in the áo dài Kha had worn.

Thom tried to think of an excuse as to why Kha was there that wouldn't get her grounded for a year, but nothing came out. Ma scowled and opened her mouth.

"Culture Day!" Kha announced, cutting her off before she could say anything. "Culture Day . . . is today! I was so excited I couldn't wait. Right, Thom?"

Thom stared at him. "I don't want to go to Culture Day," she hissed. They had other things to worry about, like finding the Monkey King.

But he gave her a look, then gestured at her mom.

"What going on?" Ma asked, crossing her arms. Parallel lines formed between her eyebrows. "Thom?"

Thom stayed silent. If Kha had been standing close enough, he would have probably kicked her.

"I was so excited I came over early," he said.

"I didn't hear you come in," Ma said. "And where you get that áo dài, cưng?" she said to Thom. "I don't remember buying it."

Thom tugged on the front skirt panel. "Um."

"My grandparents bought it," Kha said. "They thought . . . it might . . . match mine."

Ma looked at the one in her hands, which was almost the same color as the one Thom had on.

"Can you give me a ride to school, Mrs. Ngho?" Kha asked quickly.

"Of course, cưng." Ma touched Kha on the head affectionately.

Cưng? Only Thom was Ma's cưng.

"Just wait downstairs, hah?"

Kha gave Thom another meaningful look before disappearing down the hall.

When they were alone, Thom took in the sight of her mom—really stopped to look at her. She was dressed in the tank top and shorts she wore to sleep, her hair mussed in a way she'd never have allowed in public. Heavy crescents shadowed her eyes. She must have been exhausted, and she'd still gotten out of bed early to check on Thom.

Thom wanted to be angry, after what she'd found out about her father—how her mom had known about her strength all along but had never explained. But she also knew her mom had only wanted her to have a safe life, as normal as possible. Her parents had both lied to her, let her think she was a freak, but at least Ma had always been there. She had never left Thom like her father had. It must not have been easy for her, either, raising Thom on her own, keeping secrets. Thom knew how hard *that* was.

"That dress is nice," Ma said, holding Thom's shoulders at arm's length to inspect her outfit. "I think your father would really like to see you in it."

Thom stared at her. Ma didn't like to talk about Ba—why was she bringing him up now? Did she know somehow where Thom had been? That she'd met the Boy Giant?

The thought of her father brought on a pang of guilt. The image of him fallen, unconscious, flashed in her mind, but she pushed it away. She couldn't worry about that right now. There were too many other things she needed to do, and if she thought about her father, then she would end up crying and unable to face any of it.

Her mother blinked rapidly, tilting her head back. "Wait a

minute. Let me get my camera." She hurried across the room.

"Ma, I can't go to Culture Day."

Her mother stopped halfway out the door. She turned, and Thom knew she was in trouble from the look on her face. "What you mean you can't go?"

"There's something I have to tell you. I have to go back . . . The Monkey King . . . His cudgel . . ."

"What you talking about? You not making sense."

Thom knew what she had to do. She reached under her bed.

"You are going to Culture Day," Ma declared in that tone that meant there was nothing Thom could do or say.

"But I have to show you something." Her fingers brushed the golden coil.

"I mean it, Thom." Ma crossed her arms.

"Ma—"

"Stand up. *Right. Now.*"

Thom froze.

"Did you hear me?"

She let go of the coil. Stood up straight.

"I'm tired of this. We already talk about it. You can't be ashamed of your culture. It's who you are."

That wasn't what this was about. Not anymore. Thom knew being Asian was part of who she was, like her strength was part of who she was, and there was nothing she could do to change it. Not that she even wanted to at this point. But

Ma was giving her *that* look, the drawn brows, the sharpened pupils.

"Okay," Thom whispered.

Ma's features softened, just slightly. "You go to Culture Day, and after that, we'll talk. Okay?"

Thom nodded, trying to calm her rapid heartbeat. *It's okay*, she told herself, even though part of her was still freaking out. She would get through the day, and afterward, she and Kha would find the Monkey King and figure out what to do. She didn't have any other choice.

29

COLORS FILLED THE SCHOOL, LIKE at Halloween, only instead of monster and princess costumes, kids walked around in kilts and cowboy hats. Even the teachers were dressed up. Banners and decorations hung from the ceiling, announcing the first annual Culture Day, and each hallway had been transformed into a different country. Thom's locker was strung with red lanterns, and as she walked with Kha to turn in their art project before the presentation, they passed a classroom decorated with colorful cutouts like ones hung up for the Day of the Dead.

Thom didn't have much time to feel nervous, because Ma still wanted a hug, a kiss, just a couple more pictures in front of the school, in front of that flower bush, and that fountain, standing up, sitting down, how about with Thom's hand in the shape of a heart, under her chin, at her sides, now next to Kha, arms around each other, one more in front of that tree, maybe another in the shade—

"*Ma.* We're going to be late," Thom said.

Click. Whir. "Okay, one last one."

Thom sighed while Kha struck a different pose.

"Perfect!" Ma's face disappeared behind her Instax. "So cute. Just one more, okay? Get closer."

Thom looked at Kha, who shrugged. They draped their arms around each other's shoulders.

"Smile! Bigger!"

Thom grinned, cheeks sore from so many pictures. And just as Ma pressed the button, Bethany, Sarah, and Kathy walked by and her smile dropped. They weren't dressed up at all: Bethany and Sarah were wearing their regular clothes. Kathy looked nicer in a white dress and cardigan, but she always wore a dress or skirt; her outfit had nothing to do with Culture Day.

Thom suddenly felt ridiculous. An antsy feeling crawled over her skin. She wanted to be anywhere else but here.

She remembered Kathy, who knew the truth about her and must have told her friends what she'd seen.

But Kathy wasn't looking at Thom differently. She wasn't looking at Thom at all.

Ma frowned at the last picture. "Thom, why your face so weird?"

Bethany and Sarah nudged each another and laughed.

Only this time, it wasn't just Thom they were ridiculing, but Ma as well.

Heat boiled in Thom's veins. It was one thing to make fun of her, but her mom had nothing to do with them.

Ma turned to the girls and smiled. "Are you Thom classmates?" she asked kindly.

All her life, Thom had never thought anything of the way Ma talked. Sure, she didn't sound like other parents, but there was nothing wrong with it. But now, as Bethany and Sarah looked at each other, she heard how different Ma sounded, the slow, careful pronunciations bracketing her words, the accent difficult to understand for someone who wasn't used to it.

And then when the girls didn't say anything, didn't even say hello or nod, Ma's face reddened. Was she embarrassed or angry? Thom couldn't tell, but watching her mom's face fill with color, her own ears grew hot.

Bethany, Sarah, and Kathy turned away and disappeared down the hall.

"You know them?" Ma asked Thom.

"They're my soccer teammates." Thom's eyes followed them. If she had the cudgel on her—

No. Of course she wouldn't hurt them. She had never wanted to use her strength that way, but she thought of the Girl Giant she could have been if she had chosen differently.

The Boy Giant's words came back to her. She couldn't stand by helplessly anymore. She would stand up to those girls, if not for herself, then for those who couldn't. It was time she used her strength.

"I'll be back," she said to her mom and Kha. "Bathroom."

• • •

They didn't hear her follow them down the hallway. Normally, the girls looked so . . . cool, especially when they were together, dressed so fashionably. But today, in their casual clothes, surrounded by the festive cultural decorations, they looked out of place, and Thom saw them for who they really were. Pretenders, struggling to fit in just like everyone else. Just like her.

"Did you hear what her mom said?" Sarah whispered to Bethany.

Bethany snorted. "Yeah, but I didn't understand a word."

"Aah yoo Thom clatmayt?" Sarah mimicked. They both convulsed into giggles.

Kathy didn't join in, but she didn't stop them, either.

Thom's hands balled into fists. "Hey!"

They whipped around.

She marched up to them. "Don't talk about my mom like that."

They were stunned for a second, and then Bethany snickered. "Nice dress," she said. But of course, she didn't mean it.

"Yeah? Thanks," Thom said anyway. "It's much prettier than the basic outfit you're wearing."

Kathy cracked a smile, standing behind her friends, but

caught herself and tugged on Bethany's sleeve. "Come on, let's go. It's not worth it."

"And at least I'm not ashamed of my culture," Thom continued, looking directly at Kathy. She held her gaze, and after a few seconds, Kathy was the one who looked away. "You guys can laugh all you want, but you should be careful who you're messing with. You saw what I did on the soccer field."

Their mouths went slack, and they all took a step back. Thom hadn't meant to admit to anything, but she was tired of hiding who and what she really was. A silky panel of the áo dài whipped around her legs. Her father's words came back to her.

"I may be small," she said, "but I am"—she gulped— "mighty." And even though the words felt silly, had felt silly even when she was with the Boy Giant, they made her stand taller, filled her with something she couldn't name.

Bethany and Sarah took a few more steps back, looking at each other in confusion.

"Yeah, well, whatever," Bethany said finally. "Let's go."

Thom's heart pounded as she watched them walk away. Her knees wobbled, and she felt like she was going to collapse.

"Wait, Thom."

Thom was surprised to see Kathy jogging back to her. She stopped and interlaced her fingers in front of her stomach like she wasn't sure what to do with her hands.

"Look, I . . . I'm sorry."

Thom didn't believe her at first. It didn't sound like Kathy, whose voice was always clear and confident, not hesitant and soft.

"I shouldn't have, like, stood by and watched . . . you know. With Bethany and Sarah. When they bullied you." Kathy's hands now swung to her sides, and she clasped them behind her back.

"Why did you?" Thom asked.

"I don't know. All this time, I didn't realize that it was a culture thing—I mean, they've never made fun of *me* like that. But they really shouldn't have mocked your mom. It wasn't cool." She exhaled, sounding frustrated, but more with herself than with Thom. "I thought they just didn't like you. But I just . . . I guess I just didn't like you."

"Why? I haven't done anything to you."

"Yeah, I know, okay? You're, like, a really nice girl and everything, and my mom's always telling me to be like you and study and be obedient, and then you joined soccer and you're actually pretty good when you feel like kicking the ball."

"Wait." Thom scratched her ear. "You're saying all this time, you were jealous of *me*?"

Kathy crossed her arms and looked up at the ceiling.

"You're kidding, right?" Thom said. "Kathy, look at you."

Kathy flicked her hair over her shoulder. "No, I wasn't *jealous*, obviously. I thought you were a little pathetic, wanting to be Bethany and Sarah's friend when they hated you and bullied you. And you kept putting up with it." She paused, finally looking at Thom. "But then I saw you. Practicing by yourself almost every night. That time you kicked the ball so hard . . ."

Thom closed her eyes. She'd known this day would come.

"And you're not weak at all," Kathy continued. "You're . . ."

"Inhumanly strong," Thom said.

"Well, yeah."

Thom waited for the freak-out, but Kathy looked like they might have been discussing different hairstyles.

"And I think it's kind of cool, you know," Kathy said.

"What is?"

"That you *could* really hurt Bethany and Sarah—all of us— but you don't, even though we probably deserve it. It must be hard . . . to hold back the way you do. And . . . well, yesterday with the lamppost. You saved me. I never thanked you."

Thom didn't know what to say. Of all the things she'd expected, it wasn't this. An apology had been hard to believe, but an admission from Kathy that Thom was cool? It almost sounded like she respected her.

"Are you going to tell anyone?" Thom asked.

Kathy thought about it. "Not unless you want me to."

Her heart almost exploded. "Why?"

"Who knows." Kathy shrugged, and half turned to walk away. "I might need a really strong friend one day."

◆ ◆ ◆

She walked back to her mom and Kha with shaky knees.

"You okay, cưng?" Ma asked. "Who were those girls?"

"No one," Thom said. "But they won't bother me anymore." And she knew it was true.

"Oh yeah? You beat them up good, hah?" She laughed hard at her own joke.

Thom frowned at her mom.

"Okay, one more picture, and then I'm done," Ma said. "Promise."

"What happened?" Kha asked as they posed in front of the camera.

"I think I may have just ruined my life," Thom muttered through her grin. But it didn't feel ruined, not any more than it already was. Actually, admitting the truth felt like the best decision she'd ever made.

The rest of Culture Day passed uneventfully. Kha and Thom presented their art project along with the rest of the class, and it went so well that the teacher asked to keep their poster as an example. The only hitch had been when they got to the part about the Boy Giant, and Thom found herself unable to speak at all. Luckily, Kha took over until she was ready to pick up the presentation again.

Bethany and Sarah left Thom alone, and even though Kathy wasn't exactly friendly with Thom, she didn't avoid or ignore her, either. Thom and Kha stuck together as much as possible, and between classes, she told him about everything that had happened in the heavens while he had been gone, including what the Boy Giant—her father—had said. A part of her wanted to make it up to Kha for how she'd acted toward him, and another part was just grateful to have a friend who knew what was going on.

"Is it true?" she asked. "He sent you here?"

Kha nodded as they walked to Mrs. Abbot's class. "My

dad, the Dragon-King of the Jade Army's Seventh Legion, owed him a favor. When the Boy Giant came back to the heavens, he asked my dad to send you a guardian, someone to keep an eye on you and your mom. He couldn't send one of his soldiers, not without the Jade Emperor finding out. They suspected something was up with your mom and dad at first, but your mom hid you pretty well, eventually moving you all the way out here. They couldn't prove anything, couldn't find you. Your dad could, though, so he sent me."

"The Jade Emperor doesn't know about me?"

Kha coughed. "I mean, he didn't. Your father didn't want anyone to know. He wanted to keep you safe. He's always missed you, and he tries to keep a close eye on you since he can't actually be here. That's how he found out you released the Monkey King. He kept it a secret from everyone else in the heavens, so you wouldn't get in trouble. It's not like you set the Monkey King free on purpose, you know?" He adjusted his headdress. "But the Jade Emperor probably knows about you now, with everything that happened last night."

Kids glanced at them as they passed, but Kha's headdress was attracting more attention than Thom's yellow áo dài. And instead of laughing, kids complimented and high-fived them as they walked by, especially the ones who'd also dressed up. Thom had thought she would feel weird in her long dress, and she did at first, but as the day went on, she started to appreciate the beauty of the print, the smooth flow of the silk over her skin.

"My father will think I've failed," Kha said quietly.

"But you haven't."

"I did, though. The cudgel is out, isn't it?"

"That's my fault."

"I was sent to stop you."

"Kha." She didn't continue until he looked directly at her. "No offense, but even if you tried, you couldn't beat me."

He held back a smile.

"I'm really sorry," she whispered, as if speaking quietly would make her feel better.

"Are you still going to give the cudgel to the Monkey King?"

She wrung her hands. "I don't know."

"Do you want him to take your strength away that bad?"

She thought about everything that had happened, about her talk with the Boy Giant. Guilt laced through her, shame so heavy that she sagged with the burden of it.

"No," she admitted. "I don't think I do."

Kha was silent now, as if afraid to push her too hard.

"I hated my strength before," she said, "but now I know I can use it for good, the same way the Boy Giant does."

Even though she was still angry at her father for abandoning her and leaving Ma, she had to respect him for doing what she'd never considered. Maybe she could do the same—use her strength to stand up for others who weren't as strong.

"How come your dad sent you to stop me?" she asked

Kha. "Isn't it too dangerous for his own son? This is the Monkey King, after all—not just any weak demon."

"Excuse me, but I'm a *dragon*." He grinned, but at her serious expression, he became more somber, too. "My father . . . like everyone else in the heavens, he values strength over everything else. He doesn't like that I'm closer with my mom. He wants me to be more dragon than fairy, even though technically, I'm half of each." Kha sighed heavily. "So he insisted that I go, to prove how strong I really am. Even though you didn't exactly make it easy," he added pointedly.

"I'm sorry." She looked at her hands, which had picked up trucks, fought with the Monkey King's cudgel, and broken bones. "I thought I could fix everything by myself."

Kha smiled. Was he already accepting her apology?

"Partners?" he said.

She shook her head. "Friends."

◆ ◆ ◆

"How did it go?" Ma asked after school, grinning from ear to ear and making that face she made when she saw a puppy or some other adorable thing. "So cute. You should wear áo dài every day." She reached out to pretend to pinch Thom's cheek, and Thom was surprised that she didn't hate the attention. "Where's Kha?" Ma said.

"His grandparents picked him up." She couldn't take her eyes off Ma. This morning had gone by too fast, a blur of movement and rushing to get out of the house on time, but it hit her that if things had gone worse in the heavens, she might have never seen Ma again. She smelled wonderful, the subtle vanilla scent of her lotion filling the car.

"What? Do I have something on my face?" Ma touched her cheek and looked at her hand.

"No. It's just nice to see you."

Ma ruffled Thom's hair. "See? I told you, áo dài is like magic. Put it on, and everything feel better. So how was it? Did anyone laugh, like you say?"

"No. They liked the dress."

"I knew it. Even if they laugh, you stronger than them, remember. You can stand up for yourself."

It wasn't the first time Ma had made a comment like that; it wasn't even the first time today. But she always joked about it.

And it *wasn't* a joke. Not to Thom. Not after what the Boy Giant had told her, especially not now that she knew that Ma had known everything all along.

"I'm stronger than them," Thom said.

"Yes. Much stronger." Ma chuckled, flexed a bicep.

"Ma," Thom said slowly.

Ma looked surprised at Thom's harsh tone. "What is it? Why you mad now? You were so happy earlier."

"You know, don't you?" Memories came back to her like punches to the gut. How Ma had brushed off each accident, saying it wasn't a big deal when everything else was a big deal to her. Thom couldn't leave a jacket on the couch without receiving a lecture, but breaking five bottles and spilling water on the new rug was fine.

"You know," Thom whispered, "about my strength, about the Boy Giant, about my dad."

Ma tightened her grip on the steering wheel. "What do you mean, your dad?"

"My dad is the Boy Giant."

Ma pinched the bridge of her nose. "You giving me a headache."

"He told me himself."

"He what?" She braked hard, stopping just in time at the red light.

"I met him. Thánh Gióng. The Boy Giant. Whatever he calls himself, he's my father." Thom hated how Ma's sunglasses blocked most of her face, how it hid her expression, but she could tell that she had struck a nerve, because Ma's jaw was tense. "Did you know that I'm like him?"

They pulled down the street of their house. Kha wasn't home yet, his driveway empty.

"What you mean?" Ma spoke softly, with a slight waver in her voice.

"That I'm just as strong?" Thom watched her mother, and the longer the silence stretched, the deeper her heart sank, until it sat at the pit of her stomach like an anvil.

"You knew," Thom said, the lump in her throat so painful she could barely squeeze the words out. Ma had known all along, but instead of telling Thom, she had just let Thom think she was a freak. She had kept Thom in the dark and pretended everything was normal when nothing was normal. It never had been—her father was the Boy Giant! Thom was part immortal.

Thom had always thought Ma was different from other parents, that even though Ma could be tough and strict, she was always honest. She never lied, even when it hurt. But now, it hurt more than anything because she *had* lied. She was just like everyone else, manipulating the truth to get what she wanted.

Ma parked the car and turned to her. "I wanted to keep you safe."

"But not telling me the truth wouldn't have kept me safe."

"I was going to tell you, but you weren't always so strong... You were normal for so long, there was no reason to ... and I thought maybe ... you wouldn't be so strong after all. But then there was never time."

"We live in Troy," Thom pointed out. "The most boring city in the world. The nearest boba place is thirty minutes away."

Ma sighed. "I was going to tell you when we moved, but you were so upset you didn't want to listen to anything I say."

"You still should have said something."

"I was scared, cưng. I thought if you find out who you really are . . . you might want to leave."

"Where would I go?"

"To your father."

"What?" Thom breathed faster. She would have had a choice?

"Your father always wanted to take care of you. He loved you—he never wanted to leave, but he wanted to protect us. I wish . . . I wish we could have all stayed together, but . . . he would have taken you with him, and I wanted you to have a normal life."

Thom's heart pounded. "Why couldn't we have all been together?" Thom asked. "Why did you make him leave?"

"It's not allowed. I wanted him to stay, but it's against the rules, and if the heavens knew, they would have taken both of you away. Part mortal, part god—they think you're dangerous. But you're not. I know you're not."

Thom looked straight ahead. Why did everyone think that they knew what was right for her? How did they decide if she was dangerous or not? She was sick of having other people keep things from her, sick of being lied to and unable to decide for herself, when she was the one who was stuck with her abnormal strength.

Ma sighed. "Before we move, a warrior came to the house. He wore armor, big." Ma held a hand over her head.

"He didn't know you were the Boy Giant's daughter, but he remembered me and suspected that you were part immortal. It was right after you broke the windows in the house, remember?"

Thom would never forget. That was when her strength had first gotten really bad.

"I was scared. I told him it's not true, that an earthquake shook the house and shattered the windows. You were normal girl. But I don't know if he believed me. I was afraid he might come back and take you away."

"But why would that be bad? I would have gone to the heavens. I could have stayed with Ba. He would have trained me. Why didn't you give me the choice?"

"Because you're *my* daughter. You belong with me."

"I'm the Boy Giant's daughter, too," Thom said softly. Her life could have been so different. She could have lived in the heavens, like Jae. She would have fit in, wouldn't have had to prove herself to people who were so completely unlike her. She would have been respected for her strength. She wouldn't have just been normal up there; she would have been popular. People would have looked up to her.

Ma didn't say anything. Her bug-eyed sunglasses stared back at Thom.

"You should have let me choose," Thom said. "I could have learned more about my strength. The Boy Giant . . . Ba . . . He said that giants are supposed to help people and protect those who are weaker than them. But I've only been hiding."

"I won't let you go. You would never be normal like that."

Thom grabbed the door handle, turning her face away. "Maybe I don't want to be normal anymore."

30

THOM RAN TO HER ROOM, ignoring Ma's calls for her to stop. She slammed the door and locked it, pressing her forehead against the cold surface.

"You're back!"

Thom whirled around. The Monkey King bounded to her, throwing his arms around her shoulders and spinning her in the air. Despite what everyone had told her, and the possibility that maybe he'd betrayed her, used her, tricked her, it was still a relief to see him. He was the only one who had understood her, accepted her, had never wanted to change her. Maybe it wasn't true, what they said. They'd been wrong about so many things. Maybe he had a good reason for saying what he'd said.

"Where were you?" she asked, pulling back from the hug.

"I had to leave." He smiled, but Thom remained hardened, thinking of all the trouble he'd put her through. "My friends needed me. I had to help them."

344 • VAN HOANG

"*I* needed you! You sent me into the heavens! And you weren't there when I got out. How was I supposed to get home?"

His face formed into an expression of sympathetic concern, as quick as putting on a mask. "I went back to the Gate as soon as I could, but you weren't there. I waited, but when you still didn't come back, I figured your dragon servant fetched you."

She scowled, trying to decide what else to yell at him about. "You lied about the heavens. You didn't tell me . . ." *Everything. About the Boy Giant and Jae.* "You didn't tell me it was a mortal crime to intrude."

He cocked his head. "Well? What did you think? That you could enter freely and not face consequences?"

Fury laced through her. "Yes! You made it seem like it was okay. You tricked me!"

He leaned back on his haunches and held out his hands. Despite her anger, Thom almost took them, but she clenched her fists instead.

"I might have failed," he said, "to disclose that inf—"

"*And* that I'll be sent to the hells once they catch me."

"I will keep you safe from them."

Her chest heaved. This was true; it was what she had told herself. She had followed through with the plan only because she knew the Monkey King would fix everything. But it didn't mean she wasn't angry at him.

"Do you have it?" His thick lashes fanned over innocent large brown eyes. "The staff?"

"I . . ." She hesitated, stepping back. "I'm not giving it to you. I changed my mind."

Only, there was no point. As if the cudgel knew they were talking about it, a hum came from beneath the bed. The Monkey King's eyes widened. He didn't need Thom. He ducked down, and the moment he found the staff, the humming took on a different tune, like a cat's purr. Thom felt it more than heard it, the sheer bliss emanating from the cudgel as it reunited with its master.

The Monkey King's eyes misted over, a look of pure joy on his face. He held his staff in both hands, studying it from one end to the other, turning it over, inspecting it for damage. The golden coil was still wrapped around it, but he didn't seem to care. He tossed it from one hand to the other. Thom's mouth opened. She'd barely been able to drag the thing using all her supernatural strength, and the Monkey King wielded it like it was a toy.

He spun it, twirled, practiced a few moves. He floated off the floor, giving a few good whacks at the air, giggling with glee.

And then, without another word, he held the staff in one hand and bounded for the window.

"Wait!" She ran after him. He hung from the sill, looking back at her curiously. "Where are you going?" And even though she knew now that it was impossible for him to get rid of what she had been born with, even though she didn't *want* her strength taken away anymore, she couldn't help but ask. "What about my power? You said you would make me normal after I got you your staff."

"Oh." He stepped back into her room. There was something in his voice that she didn't like. "About that. I . . . lied."

Even though the Boy Giant had warned her the Monkey King had told her a lie, a part of her was hoping he was wrong, was hoping that there had been a misunderstanding, an explanation. Hearing the Monkey King admit that it *had* been a lie was worse than what she'd imagined. Something twisted deep inside. A fist squeezing her intestines.

"I can't take your power away, Thom. No one can do that. Your power is a part of you."

"He was right," she whispered, more to herself than to the Monkey King.

"I thought you would learn," he said. "Find out in the heavens who you really are."

Tears clouded her vision. "Then give me back the staff," she demanded.

His face hardened. "What?"

"A deal is a deal. You won't take my power away, so you can't have the cudgel."

The doorknob rattled. "Thom!" Ma shouted. "I told you not to lock the door. Open it right now!"

The Monkey King tightened his grip on the staff. His upper lip curled over his sharp teeth. She'd seen him direct this look at others, but now that it was turned on her, fear made her limbs feel weak. But she meant what she'd said. A deal was a deal.

"Give it back," she said.

He flipped the staff over his shoulder. "Aren't you forgetting something, Thom? The heavens are against you now. The soldiers will come after you. I'm the only one who can help you, who can stop them. I have something that will save you from the wrath of the heavens, keep you safe forever."

"Stop lying. You don't have anything."

He leaned toward her, their noses almost touching. "I have myself."

Thom scowled, stepping back. "What?"

"I'm going back to the Mountain to free myself."

She shook her head, not understanding.

"Someone in the heavens should have told you. They love to tell the story of how Buddha imprisoned the Monkey King under the Mountain for five hundred years."

"But you . . . you're here. You're . . ." And then she understood, her gaze landing on the fur at his shoulder, the same color as the golden pin she'd found in the temple. Like the hair she still had in her pocket, which she'd taken into the heavens. For luck. "You're not really you. The real you is still under the Mountain."

The Monkey King had the power to clone each of his hairs, and this, the one she was talking to, was just a replica. It wasn't the real one. Jae had said the Monkey King was trapped under the Mountain, imprisoned for five hundred years, and Thom had thought she was wrong, that she didn't know the truth. But Thom was the wrong one.

"Once I am free, truly free," he said, stepping close again so that her nostrils filled with the earthy smell of him, "I will be the most powerful being in the world. Unstoppable. I have defeated the heavens before. I will do it again. And this time, even Buddha will not be able to stop me."

What had she done? She needed to take it back, undo everything. She needed . . .

The cudgel. Without it, the Monkey King wouldn't be able to free his true self. She could still stop him.

The door flew open. Ma burst in, keys jingling. "Thom, I told you—" She stopped short. Her eyes widened on the Monkey King, who'd raised his staff, ready for a fight. Her mouth opened in a shriek. "Thom! Get back!" She lunged for Thom and grabbed her in a wrenching hug.

The Monkey King regarded Ma with disinterest before turning to Thom. "I can still help you."

"Help her?" Ma stood between them. "You go away! She don't need you."

"Ma, stop."

The Monkey King bared his teeth, and Ma screamed and swatted at him. Her hand smacked his face, and he stepped back, his mouth open, hand raised to his cheek, shock making his features ridiculously innocent.

And then the mask of anger was back.

"No, don't," Thom said. "She didn't mean to—"

The Monkey King's staff whirred so fast it blurred. Its hum grew louder, filling Thom's ears and lungs and the blood in her veins. She couldn't see straight. The air was thick and fast, and when she tried to move, it was like walking against a heavy gust of wind.

When she reached for her mother, her fingers found nothing. Ma was gone.

The hum died. The staff stopped moving. The Monkey King held it at his side, his chest puffed, his jaw tight.

"Ma?" Thom looked around, but Ma was nowhere. "What did you do to her?"

"She slapped me." As if that answered the question.

"Where is she?"

He pointed the cudgel at the floor. At first, Thom didn't see what he was indicating. But then she dropped to her knees.

"No," she whispered. She held out her hands, and the cricket—the *cricket*—hopped onto her palm. "No. No . . .

no . . . you couldn't . . . She can't . . . This isn't . . ." She looked up at him. "You turned her into a cricket!"

The cricket chirped.

The Monkey King lifted his chin. "She smacked me! Like I was a bad dog!"

"Turn her back."

"No."

"Wukong!"

He bared his teeth. "Only my friends call me that."

"I helped you. I got your cudgel back from the heavens."

He batted his eyelashes and bowed dramatically low, his forehead skimming the floor. "And in return, I will keep the heavens from punishing you."

"Turn her back," she demanded again, holding the cricket up.

He laughed, and it was like spikes were being driven into her ears. "No."

Thom didn't think about what she did next. She dropped the cricket to the floor and lunged at the Monkey King. His face registered surprise right before she crashed into him.

They fell through the window.

He wrapped an arm around her. Tears blinding her, she swung her fists anywhere she could reach. She hit him hard, with punches that should have hurt, but he only giggled like she'd tickled him. It made her angrier.

"Thom!"

She looked up, relief making her cry out. Kha. In his dragon form, circling them.

"Let her go!" His tail whipped at the Monkey King, and to her shock, he did let her go. She reached for something to hold on to and found the magical string still wrapped around the cudgel. But as she tried to pull herself up with it, she accidentally unraveled the knot around the cudgel, and she dropped again, the coil winding itself around her hand.

The Monkey King's arms stretched toward her as if on reflex, like he hadn't meant to drop her.

But Kha was the one who caught her, diving to grab her with his short, clawlike arms. Still, Thom lunged for the Monkey King. She wanted to hurt him, drag him back to her mom, make him undo the transformation.

The Monkey King hovered above them, giggling.

"Turn her back," Thom choked out.

"I'm sorry, Thom," he said. "But I have other things to do. Someone I need to free."

"No," she gasped as he turned to fly away. "Don't leave."

"I promise not to let the heavens punish you," he said over his shoulder. And there, that honesty was back in his gaze. The genuine concern. For her. "I promise to keep you safe."

"Liar!"

Then he zipped off faster than she'd ever seen him go, the staff glinting in the setting sunlight.

"Follow him, Kha."

"Thom, I can't. It's pointless. He's too fast."

She cried in frustration. But she knew he was right. Kha hadn't been able to keep up when they'd flown to the heavens. She could only watch as the Monkey King became a dot in the sky and disappeared completely.

31

THOM FOUND THE CRICKET HOPPING near her bed, and placed her—Ma—safely in a glass mason jar. Kha poked small holes through the lid, and Thom dropped some carrot shavings into the jar before closing it. They did everything methodically, until they couldn't think of anything else to do for the cricket.

Nothing except change her back to a human.

"You can't stay here by yourself," Kha said.

"I'm not going to." Thom's voice was flat. Her skin tingled, her body numb. "I have to finish what I started."

Kha was quiet. Then he said, "You're going after him."

"I don't think I have any other choice." She met his eyes. "Will you still help me? I don't . . . I can't do it without you." She meant this literally, of course, because even though she had a special power, it didn't involve flying, and she didn't know how else she would be able to follow the Monkey King to the Mountain.

But she knew it was true on a deeper level, too. She needed Kha, and she was sorry she hadn't realized it earlier. Sorry she hadn't listened to him, sorry she'd chosen the Monkey King over him.

"I'm . . . I've been so stupid. You were right about him. You tried to warn me."

He touched her arm. "You're not the first person he's fooled. He's the trickster god, remember? This is what he does."

Yes, he was the trickster god, but it hadn't felt like that to her, even though some part of her had always known. He had been her friend, a real friend, one who understood exactly how she felt and knew what she wanted and was willing to help her get rid of her power.

His face flashed in her memory again: the puckered brow, the brown eyes wide and shining against the furry face. *Your power is a part of you.* His voice echoed, the words solidifying something she hadn't grasped before, a truth she hadn't seen, blinded by her desire to get rid of her strength, to be someone different.

He was right, wasn't he? Despite what he'd done, despite what he'd planned all along, he had always known something, what had taken her a trip to the heavens and a close encounter with the hells to figure out.

Her superstrength was a part of her. She couldn't get rid of it. That would be like getting rid of her soul—replacing it with something that didn't belong to her. Sure, it was difficult, being so ridiculously strong, but if she weren't, she wouldn't be the same person she was now.

"I can stop him," she said. "I'm stronger than him." She hadn't been so sure before, but when she'd wielded the cudgel, she had felt the true extent of her power, had felt the strength surge in her veins, had known what she was capable of. She hadn't wanted to hurt anyone, especially her father or the soldiers, but now she knew she could fix everything. She would stop the Monkey King. And to stop him, she would need her power.

How else would she stop the Monkey King? Who would she even be? With the knowledge that she'd never be able to get rid of her strength came the relief that she could learn how to control it and simply move on.

She looked at her hands, holding the mason jar gently so she wouldn't accidentally break it, her fingers too short to wrap completely around the glass. She thought of her father's offer to train her. She thought of the heavens, of Jae and the immortals, of the different life that had been offered to her there, one where she didn't have to hide her power but was instead respected for it. Valued for it. Where she maybe could master her strength.

Staying in the heavens hadn't been an option back then,

but now she knew it wasn't because she'd needed to get rid of her power. It was because of what she had chosen to do with it.

She still had a choice.

Maybe she had lost her chance to be the Girl Giant, but she could still use her power to do something good. She was going to stop the Monkey King.

"We have to go after him," she said to Kha. "With the cudgel, he's even more powerful. And he . . ." She held the jar up. This was the worst thing he could have done to Ma. She hated crickets. "He's going to set his true self free."

"And once he does," Kha said, "once the real Monkey King has the cudgel, he'll be just like before. So powerful no one could stop him. No immortals, fairies, gods, dragon-kings. He'll be undefeatable."

Thom looked again at her mother the cricket in the mason jar. Her fingers wrapped around the glass so tight it threatened to crack. "Then we'll have to stop him first."

Mochi barked, his nails clicking on the tiled floors as he ran up to Thom and Kha. They stopped to look down at the dog, then at each other. Thom's dog had been so quiet, they hadn't even noticed him following them around.

"What are we going to do with Mochi?" Thom asked.

Kha knelt down and held out his hand for Mochi to sniff. "You can't just, like, leave out a bowl of food or something?"

"What? No—he's not a cat. He needs to be walked and stuff, and we don't know how long we'll be gone." She looked out the kitchen window where a tall green hedge blocked her view of the house next door. "What about your grandparents?"

Kha stood when Mochi didn't look like he was going to allow himself to be petted. "No way, they can't take care of a dog. They'll just want to keep him outside."

Thom reached down for Mochi, who shied away from her at first, but then came closer as she coaxed him. "We can't bring him with us." She remembered the hungry looks on the demons' faces, their brute strength and rough manners. Mochi wouldn't stand a chance, not all five pounds of him.

"So what are we going to do?" Kha asked.

Mochi nudged Thom's hand with a wet nose, then rubbed his forehead under her palm when he was sure she wouldn't hurt him. She scratched the back of his ears gently, reveling in the fact that he was no longer terrified of her anymore. But then again, she was better at controlling her strength now. She didn't have to be afraid of it anymore.

Then it came to her. "We can ask Kathy." Thom rushed to Ma's home office, a sparsely decorated room with bare walls, a black desk, and neatly alphabetized books.

"What?" Kha followed her. "Kathy? Why should she help you?"

Thom dug through Ma's filing cabinet and found the one clearly labeled "Cứng's Soccer." She'd never been more grateful that her mom was so meticulously organized.

"She loves dogs," Thom said. She had once caught Kathy

scrolling through video after video of cute puppies sleeping. "And. I don't know. We have a thing now."

"A thing," Kha repeated, holding Mochi in his arms and standing in the doorway.

"Shh." Thom punched the number listed beside Kathy's name on their soccer team's player packet into her phone, hesitating as she thought of what to say. But she didn't have much time, and the longer she hesitated, the further the Monkey King got. He could be at the Mountain of a Hundred Giants now. He could be breaking his true self free while she was too scared to send a text.

Her thumbs flew over her screen. *Hey, it's Thom. This is weird and random but I need a favor.* She sent it before she could change her mind, then looked up at Kha with her fingers shaking.

"What kind of a thing?" he asked, petting Mochi's fluffy fur. Thom's dog licked Kha's chin, and then grinned like it was the best thing that had happened to him.

"An understanding," Thom said, just as her phone buzzed with a reply.

Sure, Kathy had written. *What is it?*

◆ ◆ ◆

Kathy's house wasn't far, and with Kha flying them, they made it in a matter of minutes. He stopped in a park nearby, transforming back to his human form behind a copse of trees.

Thom pulled Mochi out of his carrier bag before clipping on his leash and leading both of them down the street.

Kathy opened the door just as the bell stopped ringing. Her face went from its usual mask of indifference to open delight as she dropped down to pet Mochi.

"Oh my gosh, he's adorable!" she squealed. Mochi wagged his tail, his body wiggling as he launched into Kathy's lap and began licking her face.

Thom breathed a sigh of relief. Mochi liked Kathy. He'd be happy here, for now.

"Thanks for doing this, Kathy," Thom said, setting Mochi's dog carrier down on the porch and taking a small bag of dog food and treats out of her backpack.

Kathy finally looked up, her grin fading as she took in the sight of their packed bags, sneakers, jeans, and hoodies. "Where are you guys going, again?" she asked.

"There's . . . something we need to take care of," Thom said.

"Okay." Kathy rose to her feet, holding Mochi to her chest. "Is your mom going?"

Thom thought of the cricket chirping from the mason jar in her backpack. "Yup, she's coming."

"Oh. All right." Kathy petted Mochi's back, still looking unsure. "Is everything okay? Does this have anything to do with your . . . you know . . . secret?" She whispered the last word.

Thom's first instinct was to lie, but she was tired of keeping everything a secret. "Yeah, it does."

Kathy's eyes widened. "Will you be okay?"

Thom's throat tightened. She couldn't remember the last time someone asked that question. "Yeah." She nodded, trying to convince herself more than anyone else. "I think I can handle it."

Kathy looked between her and Kha. Then she nodded. "Okay. Good luck."

"Thanks again." Thom gave Mochi one last scratch behind his ears.

Kha waved, and together, they turned and walked away.

"Are you ready?" Kha asked as they went back to the park so he could transform.

Thom opened her backpack to make sure the cricket was okay. Her eyes blinked up at Thom, her whiskers twitching as if in a wave.

She turned to Kha. "Yes, I'm ready." She pictured the Monkey King's face when she caught up to him, pictured all the things she would say. All the ways she would make him pay for tricking her. "Let's go get him."

ACKNOWLEDGMENTS

I legitimately could not have done this without the encouragement, guidance, and resilience of my half-blood unicorn witch agent Mary C. Moore. Thank you, thank you for literally making my dreams come true, and for all the support texts and emails and phone calls, for pushing me to be a better writer, for championing this book, for finding it a home, and for giving Thom and me our strength.

Thank you to Mekisha Telfer and the team at Roaring Brook for believing in me and for all the hard work, care, and attention you put into making Thom's adventures the best they can be; to Aurora Parlagreco, Taylor Pitts, Allyson Floridia, Celeste Cass, Connie Hsu, and Jennifer Besser, and to everyone who made this book what it is and went way above everything I ever dreamed—thank you! Thank you also to Phung Nguyen Quang and Huynh Kim Lien for the beautiful illustrations, the magical cover, and that expression on Thom's face.

To my sister Vy Hoang, who made sure I practiced just enough Vietnamese to binge-watch all the Asian dramas (but thank God also for English subtitles), for instilling in toddler-me such a deep love of books that she probably regrets it to this day. To my other siblings, Cat-Anh, Mackhai, and Martin, for keeping my ego in check. And to my parents, Ms. Tan Nguyen and Mr. Lon Hoang, who remind me every day who I am, where I come from, and why I should still study to get good grades.

Thank you to Brandi Zeigler, Rachelle E. Morrison, Kylie Lee Baker, and Darren Watson for reading the early stages of this book and for vastly improving it. Special shout-out to our other agent-sisters for creating such a safe and supportive online space. Incredible heartfelt thanks to Diane Landolf for your insightful thoughts and for making this story so much stronger—I owe you so much.

Thank you to my soul mate, Susie Tae, for the encouragement, the hikes, and the self-care challenge, for going on adventures no one else is crazy enough to agree to, for supporting me every step of the way in every way possible, and for being the kind, compassionate, generous person who makes the world a better place. Thank you to the other members of Books and Tea for talking nerdy with me, especially Adrian Garza for our shared love of weird fantasy; Asia Evans for making us a cool book club, not a regular book club; Christar Wan for my favorite hanbok bookmark; and everyone else for keeping our reading interests . . . interesting.

Thank you to my closest friends for listening to me talk way too much about this book, especially Alex Lee for being the Kha in my life. To Christine Nguyen Truong for always asking when you can buy the book already. To Maribeth Arriola and Beverly Borromeo Silvas for virtually holding my hand that day I turned in the first draft—and for all the other days, too.

Thank you to all my work wives, especially Abby Tapia and Jessica Castro for the giggles; Laura Jenkins for the Monday-night talks; and Justin Pham, Marisa Mascorro, Sharon Watkins, Michele Guitierrez, Richard Crosthwaite, Cynthia Flores, Jessica Framson, Melissa Ronning, Steven Park, Christine Moore, Christany Edwards, April Lammers, and the many other librarians, clerks, pages, security guards, maintenance crew, and staff at Huntington Beach Public Library who make the world a more well-read, kinder, and better-researched place.

Most important, thank you, thank you to my bestest friend, alpha reader, creative partner, master of mischief, and supportive husband. For going with me to research that staff fighting class where we earned more bruises than we were emotionally or physically prepared for, for reading the cringey stage of this story, for watching a million movies on the Monkey King, for loving Thom almost as much as I do, and for all that you do. There are not enough words to express my gratitude. So I'll just end with this. Kissy-winky face, kissy-winky face, heart, heart, kissy-winky face.